T0354459

THE
SPY

THE
SPY

JOHN CHARLES GIFFORD

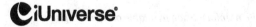

THE SPY

iUniverse books may be ordered through booksellers or by contacting:

iUniverse
1663 Liberty Drive
Bloomington, IN 47403
www.iuniverse.com
1-800-Authors (1-800-288-4677)

Because of the dynamic nature of the Internet, any web addresses or
links contained in this book may have changed since publication and
may no longer be valid. The views expressed in this work are solely those
of the author and do not necessarily reflect the views of the publisher,
and the publisher hereby disclaims any responsibility for them.

Any people depicted in stock imagery provided by Getty Images are
models, and such images are being used for illustrative purposes only.
Certain stock imagery © Getty Images.

ISBN: 978-1-5320-4346-8 (sc)
ISBN: 978-1-5320-4345-1 (e)

Library of Congress Control Number: 2018903633

Print information available on the last page.

iUniverse rev. date: 04/18/2018

A murderer is less loathsome to us than a spy. The murderer may have acted on a sudden mad impulse; he may be penitent and amend; but a spy is always a spy, night and day, in bed, at table, as he walks abroad; his vileness pervades every moment of his life.
—Honoré de Balzac

I became insane, with long intervals of horrible sanity.
—Edgar Allan Poe

Chapter 1
UP SHIT CREEK
WITHOUT A PADDLE

Georgetown, Washington, DC
Wednesday, July 18
11:00 p.m.

ALEX LOGAN WALKED OUT OF THE THEATER humming the melody of "Que Sera, Sera—Whatever Will Be, Will Be." He strode to the curb, turned around, and stood under the edge of the overhead chasing marquee lights with his arms akimbo. In front of him was a poster in a glass frame, advertising the movie he'd just seen: *The Man Who Knew Too Much.* He studied the faces of James Stewart and Doris Day— panic, with eyes wide, fixed in the stare of arrant terror. They were convincing, the pair of them. Logan wondered whether they'd recalled dreadful moments in their own personal lives and then transferred those experiences to the characters they played. Maybe they merely faked it. He supposed it didn't matter. They were convincing. That was what mattered.

The poster proclaimed that the movie was being shown in VistaVision, a higher-resolution and wider-screen format than what Paramount had previously used. Logan had liked that just fine. He'd been thrilled to see his favorite Hollywood actress on the big screen again. Doris Day looked even better than she had when he'd watched her films on his small black-and-white TV set in his apartment by himself in the dark. Furthermore, he knew she was going to have a hit song on her hands—this "Que Sera, Sera." Its melody was catchy, the kind that would stay with you for days because you couldn't shake it. *Yes*, he thought, *it is going to be a jim-dandy song.* What Alex Logan didn't know at the time—how could he?—was that he'd never be able to shake it.

Although he'd enjoyed the entire movie, he'd been particularly engrossed by the scenes filmed in Morocco. He was certain that those scenes had indeed been filmed there and not on some Paramount lot or soundstage in London. While he'd sat with his eyes fixed on the screen, he could feel the heat of the sun on his face and the hot sand between his toes; he could smell the fetid sweat off the clothes of the main characters and extras; he could smell the cumin, cinnamon, and ginger and a thousand other aromas of spices in the marketplace. But the film hadn't transported him back to North Africa at all. It was his own mind that had done that.

He hadn't thought much in the last eleven years about his time there, but while watching the movie, he had caught his mind wandering back to Casablanca during the war, where he'd first met a beautiful French woman named Simone. As if it were all a dream, she had walked into a café one evening on rue Attabari, sat down at his small round table for two, no bigger than a manhole cover, and warmly spoken her name. Logan had ordered two espressos, followed by brandy, and they'd talked for hours, until the barman walked over to them and said he would be closing soon. That was how his relationship with her had begun—with little fuss.

After that, they had seen each other nearly every day, except when he was away on urgent duties. On those days away, his thoughts were filled with her, and he could hardly wait to return. He might have married her had things turned out differently—that was how intense it had been with them. The relationship certainly had been moving in that direction. But there was a war going on, and they were part of it. It changed everything that was whole and beautiful and left it wasted and deformed, and it did so with such amazing speed. But then again, if it hadn't been for the war, they never would have met, and he would have been denied one of those rare experiences in life that came all too infrequently. All he had of Simone now was an image of her in his mind that was still strong and vivid: her dimples on the sides of her cheeks as they danced when she smiled, her silky, blonde hair that flowed over her shoulders, her narrow waist, her long shapely legs. But whenever he thought of her, it was always with great sadness and heartache. And terrible guilt.

The theater hadn't been crowded, because it was midweek. He'd left his sports jacket on during the movie because of the air-conditioning, but he took it off now and draped it over a shoulder. Earlier, it had been horribly hot, and although it was somewhat less so now, it was still muggy and sticky. He started to sweat under the marquee lights, and his shirt clung to his skin. He pulled on the shirt slightly to let the air circulate, but it didn't help much. It was days like this that he wished he'd bought that air conditioner he'd been looking at last month. It was a one-day sale, but he'd passed on it. There were always consequences for actions. Tonight, he'd be returning to a veritable furnace of an apartment. *Whatever will be, will be*, he thought.

Alex Logan continued to hum the two blocks to where he'd parked his car, and the tune helped him transform his sudden mood change, for his thoughts were still on Simone. For the first time, he was truly happy with his life. As an associate professor of history, he had the job he wanted. He was expecting to be granted tenure soon from Georgetown University, which would give him the stability he now sought in his life. He'd lived in too many countries and been to too many places before and during the war—enough to last him a lifetime. If he never left Georgetown again, that would be fine with him.

Although he'd considered (but never seriously) settling down with one woman a number of times since the war, he greatly enjoyed the flexibility that the single life had given him. There were sufficient numbers of single women around campus to keep his interest from flagging, and of course, there was a smattering of married women here and there who were bored with their lives just enough to seek him out when the odd occasion presented itself. Alex Logan, young, handsome, and unattached, was ethically and morally upright in his conduct and concerns in life, but he did have his weaknesses. He enjoyed his life now so much that he might even say it was perfect. At thirty-nine, he could look forward to many more years of doing the same thing he'd been doing for the last eight years—and right here in Georgetown.

He unlocked the door to his tan Austin-Healey and put the top down even though the three-mile drive to his apartment wouldn't take that long. He was looking forward to the breeze cooling him off as he drove. He put the key into the ignition and turned it. The car purred nicely. This gem was quite capable of reaching a hundred miles per hour in a matter of seconds. On weekends during the summer months when he wasn't working, he would often take her out on the country roads and let her rip on the open stretches. But Logan thought better of this on Georgetown's narrow roads. Instead, he just gently pressed his foot to the accelerator and eased off down the street. He turned the radio on and heard Jim Lowe singing "The Green Door," so he sang along with him. Perhaps that would help him get Doris's song out of his head. At the very least, maybe he'd figure out what that secret was that lay beyond the door.

But something wasn't quite right. He drove for about a mile before he decided to do something about it. The traffic was light, so it was easy for him to see that a car, a black one, had been following him, keeping a safe distance behind. Perhaps it was nothing more than his imagination getting the best of him. Perhaps whoever was driving the car was going home and happened to live in the same direction. Perhaps the driver drove home every night like this, turning left and then right, just as Logan had done minutes before, in order to reach his destination. Perhaps.

But there was still something of the old spy left in Logan that raised and fired his senses. It wasn't intuition, which most people had in varying degrees. It was something more deeply visceral, more primitive, than that; it was brooding inside of him now, alerting him to—what? He hadn't felt the presence of this sense since the war, since his time in Casablanca, but it was there now. He'd always listened to it because it had always kept him alive.

Logan reached a stretch of road that he knew would remain straight for at least another mile. The road was lined with red oaks and sugar maples, dotted here and there with wide snow goose cherry trees, their snowy white flowers gone with the previous spring. The houses were set back behind large emerald lawns. Only the occasional light was on inside of them. Tomorrow was a workday; most people were sleeping. He floored the car, and it took him little time to reach sixty miles per hour. He looked into his rearview mirror and saw the headlights of the car behind him fading, becoming smaller by the second. Luckily for him, there were no other cars in sight. He accelerated to sixty-five miles per hour. Again, he glanced at the rearview mirror, but this time he saw the highlights behind him gradually becoming brighter. He'd been right. Someone *was* following him.

When he saw that the road ahead was going to curve to the left, he stepped hard on the brake and made a sharp right turn. He drove another block and stopped at a corner in a residential area. In little time, he saw the other car make the same right turn. Logan accelerated again for a block and then turned right and floored it again. The car was handling beautifully, but he had to be careful in case someone shadowed between parked cars suddenly stepped out in front of him. His hotshot sports car could become a killing machine in the blink of an eye. He then made a left turn at the next intersection and drove on. Just before he turned again, he looked at the rearview mirror and caught a glimpse of two long headlight beams rounding the corner. Whoever it was had a powerful engine under that hood—that and determination. But why would anyone want to follow him?

They—Logan and the determined driver of the black car—played this little game for another ten minutes before Logan finally lost him. He was quite a distance from his apartment now, somewhere off of Connecticut Avenue in Chevy Chase, because he wanted to lose the car completely before driving home. He drove around for another thirty minutes—partly because he knew his apartment would be hot and stuffy and he was enjoying the breeze and partly because he wanted to be certain that he had really lost the car—and eventually ended up on Wisconsin Avenue, which took him close to home. Jim Lowe had stopped singing miles ago and had been replaced by Elvis Presley, Frankie Limon and the Teenagers ("Why Do Fools Fall in Love?"—one of his favorites), Gogi Grant, Gene Vincent, and Howlin' Wolf. By the time he got to his neighborhood, Little Richard was blasting away.

When he reached the street where he lived, he turned off the radio and drove slowly, looking on both sides for a black car. He really hadn't gotten a good look at it and could identify it only by its color, but just the same, it never hurt to be too careful. He was used to checking and double-checking things. That too had kept him alive during the war.

He spotted a black car parked about a block away on the opposite side of the street from his apartment building. He pulled the Austin next to it and got out, leaving the engine running. He gazed around him warily but saw no one. He placed a palm on the hood. *Cold as a witch's tit. Wrong black car.*

His street was located in the historic district of the city where row houses were common. Few had garages, so street parking was sometimes a nightmare, especially late at night when the other denizens had been home and tucked into their beds for hours. He found a small space between larger cars, two blocks away. He backed into it, squeezing the Austin between the two. Anything larger than his car never would have made it in. This seemingly insignificant act made him feel good because he frequently had to walk more than six blocks, since he often came home late at night. Doris Day's song returned with a vengeance as he walked back to his apartment. He couldn't stop himself from humming it. Too much of a good thing, as they say. The full moon gleamed down between the overhanging branches of large elm trees and landed on the parked cars as he passed them—dappled night creatures, bumper to bumper, at rest.

Who would want to tail him? He thought about it but had no answers.

He took every other step up a short flight of stairs to the redbrick house that had been converted to apartments a decade earlier. He took his keys out under the overhead nightlight and entered the building. The heavy door locked itself when he closed it. He walked slowly and lightly down the hallway so as to not wake up his neighbors in the adjacent apartments. He unlocked and opened his door and reached his left hand around the doorjamb to flip the light switch on. Instantly, before he could reach the switch, a hand reached out and grabbed his wrist, yanking him hard into the apartment. Behind him, he felt the hands of someone else on his shoulders, pushing him to the floor with speed and power, and then the person straddled him, pinning him hard to the wooden floor with his weight. *Jesus Christ*, Logan thought. But before he could have another thought, an arm wrapped around his throat. He felt a bicep on one side of his neck and a forearm on the other. Logan knew precisely what was happening to him because he had performed this same maneuver himself many times on others. He felt pressure on his neck that he knew would restrict the blood flow to his carotid artery. He was unable to move and now unable to even think. The attacker quickly applied more pressure, and soon Alex Logan was unconscious.

As the two men carried Logan toward their black sedan parked a block down, they passed an older gentleman with silver hair wearing a tweed jacket. They'd actually heard him whistling before they saw him, since he was hidden in the shadows of a large elm. One of the men looked at him and flashed a smile. "He had one too many."

"I've been down that road myself," the older gentleman said over his shoulder, never breaking stride as he passed them. "He'll wise up when he's older."

Once they reached the car, one of the men opened the back door, and they both hefted him in. As they were doing that, another black sedan, indistinguishable from the one in which Logan now lay comatose, pulled up alongside of them from the opposite direction. The driver leaned out and looked at them.

"We got him," one of the two men said to the driver as the other slammed the door shut.

"Did you have to hurt him?" The driver looked genuinely concerned.

"No. It went down just as we planned."

"Good. He spotted me. That Austin of his is damn fast, and he lost me. I don't know where he went, but I figured he'd show up here sooner or later."

"You go on ahead of us, and we'll meet you back at the Farm. Stop somewhere along the way and phone them to tell them we're coming."

The driver nodded and drove off.

For the first half of the drive to the Farm, the two men were silent. Then the one in the passenger seat spoke. "I hate this!" He paused a moment and shook his head. "The whole rotten goddamn thing."

"I know what you mean, but they didn't have a choice."

"I can't believe they couldn't get someone else for the job. The guy's a hero in my book. He doesn't deserve to be treated like this. Jesus, I put a stranglehold on him!" The passenger shook his head again. "What a pisser."

"Hero in my book too. But listen—Logan's a one-of-a-kind guy. He had everything they were looking for and then some. Besides, they didn't have time to look for anyone else. He was right there." The driver's eyes darted to his watch, then the speedometer, and then the rearview mirror and finally fixed on the road ahead of him again. "July 26 is coming up fast. They don't have to train him. All they have to do is brief him and then turn him loose."

"Yeah, but if he doesn't cooperate, they're going to have a big problem on their hands." The passenger scratched his chin and shook his head a third time, as if to shake the cobwebs out. "And believe me, the world's going to know about it."

"Don't worry. After he's briefed, he'll cooperate. He won't have a choice."

———«»———

From Georgetown, it had taken them three hours to reach the road from State Route 168 that cut to the east going toward Williamsburg, Virginia. They drove for a half mile, turned left, and proceeded for another fifteen minutes through the countryside before pulling up to the gate of the Farm. The driver was ready to show his credentials to the naval guard who was on duty, but the guard waved them through and explained that he had expected them. The car went down a dirt road that rose, dipped, and twisted with the terrain, the headlights throwing long beams ahead of them. The man in the passenger seat looked over his shoulder at Logan, who was lying on his side in the back seat. His arms and legs were tied securely with strong, narrow rope, and he had a gag in his mouth. His ears were plugged and taped over with strips of thick adhesive material. Two open eyes—eyes that could kill—looked back at the man.

The sun was coming up over the horizon as they pulled up to a small gray building with a dark green door, scattering a white-tailed deer, a fox squirrel, and a few rabbits that were hidden in the shadows of tall, loblolly pines. This door too, as in the song, had a secret behind it. As the driver got out of the car, a man came out of a much larger building a short distance away and started walking in the driver's direction.

"Is he okay?"

"Yes, sir, he's fine. We had no problems, but he's going to be a little sore. He's awake and in the back seat."

"Good work, Rankin. Carry him in and take the ropes and tape off, but leave his wrists bound behind his back. I'll be in shortly."

"Yes, sir."

They maneuvered Logan out of the car. Rankin, the larger of the two men, grabbed him from behind, slipping his hands under Logan's arms and balancing his weight on his chest and stomach. The other man picked him up by his ankles, and together they carried him inside the building. As they did so, they could both hear Logan humming an unfamiliar but not altogether unpleasant tune.

It had been a long night for associate professor Alexander Logan. It had begun with Doris Day and his memories of Casablanca and Simone and was ending in an isolated countryside 153 miles away in Virginia. But for Logan, it wasn't the end.

It was only the beginning.

Chapter 2

REVENGE IS A DISH
BEST SERVED COLD

Alexandria, Egypt
Thursday, July 19
5:58 a.m.

ADDISON DAVIES PICKED UP HIS DAGGER FROM the small desk and held it up before him. God, how he loved it! He was spellbound—thrilled, even—by its beauty, feel, and balance. The Fairbairn-Sykes was a masterpiece, and Addison considered it a piece of art as much as a deadly weapon. Holding it by its black ring grip in his right hand, he put his left index finger on the pointed tip of the tapered steel blade and then ran his finger and thumb along both razor-sharp edges, drawing blood. The blade was seven inches long and could slice through a man's neck with an angled sweep of an arm or plunge upward through the ribcage into his heart in an instant, if it were used by a skilled executioner. The dagger was the most effective and quietest way to kill a man that he knew. Death occurred immediately, without the fuss of an untidy struggle. He'd once known the number but had since forgotten how many times he'd used this very dagger against his enemies.

He was suddenly startled by his alarm clock. He'd set the clock the night before for six in the morning, but he had been up since four thirty and had forgotten to turn it off. He set the knife down on the desk, walked to his nightstand beside his bed, and turned off the alarm. He then picked up a rag and wiped the blood off his finger and thumb, keeping pressure on them. He'd had a restless night of sleep, waking up several times during the night. He'd tried to clear his mind of his thoughts because to Addison, restful sleep was of strategic importance. It allowed him to function the way he found necessary during the day. Lacking it, he was afraid of making a miscalculation. The last few months had been extraordinary, and the next week would be even more so. After tossing and turning in bed for hours, he'd been unable to purge his mind— of what? Of everything, as a Zen Buddhist would do in deep meditation. Having failed, he'd finally decided not to fight it and gotten up. Addison Davies was no Zen Buddhist.

He couldn't remember when he'd last gotten a good night's rest. His mind had been consumed with the coming week because there was much more planning yet to do and times and dates to confirm and reconfirm. And of course, he had the other two people to worry about. He preferred to work alone, holding only himself accountable for the planning and implementation of the strategy he so carefully worked on. Working with others was always risky business because he trusted no one other than himself. The few times he'd worked with others during the war, they'd always let him down.

But this time was different, and it was critical that he have help. He had no choice. He'd always said that every person, when tasked with a responsibility, had options before him. *Sort through the choices and decide! There's never only one.*

Look, goddamn it, and then choose. Choose ... and then act! Act ... and then take responsibility!

Now he was forced to consider that there were exceptions. It was impossible for him to accomplish what had to be done in the next week alone. He was compelled to trust someone other than himself. This too kept him awake at night. Worrying was for some slutty bint, not for him. He used to say that as well, but now his worrying kept him up at night and ate away at the clarity of his mind that he needed during his waking hours.

Addison hadn't had his morning tea yet, so he descended the creaky wooden stairs that led into the back room of his shop and entered a small cubby that he used as a kitchen. It certainly wasn't what he was used to, but over the last five years he'd grown accustomed to the cramped space. He kept a paraffin burner on the countertop near the small sink. Underneath the countertop were a few dishes and bowls, some cutlery, and an assortment of pots and pans. Directly in front of it, leaving enough space for him to squeeze by, was a wooden oval table on which he ate his meals. The walls were bare, and altogether, the space made him feel depressed. However, he'd done nothing to cheer the place up. He'd always seemed to have more important things to do with his time. After next week, though, that would no longer matter.

He lit the burner with a matchstick and filled a brass kettle with water from the spigot. While he waited for the water to boil, he folded his arms against his chest and crossed one ankle over the other, leaning his backside against the counter. He let his mind wander to his childhood in London's West End—something he'd inexplicably done all too frequently lately and the only luxury he allowed himself to have. What he wouldn't give now for some good old bangers and mash that his family's cook had made for him in his youth, maybe with a little gravy over them and some spring peas on the side. The mere thought of that sent his mind traveling farther back in time.

His parents had moved to Chelsea from the seaside town of Margate in East Kent when he was three years old. As freethinkers, they had found Margate a bit too provincial for their tastes. His father had discovered one day that he was a *bohemian*, so off they had gone to the part of London that would accommodate his unusual leanings. With that sudden knowledge, he couldn't very well stay in Margate. He found employment with the Chelsea School of Art soon after arrival and taught various aspects of painting, even though he himself was a mediocre artist. His influence as an artist and as a free spirit never captured the attention of his son, who remained quite indifferent to it. But as the years went by, his father's involvement with the Fabian Society did catch his attention.

As a socialist, Addison's father worked hard to create a just society for the British worker. He advocated for the welfare state, speaking out for cheap council housing; for free medical and dental treatment; for free spectacles; and for generous unemployment benefits. As a teen, Addison had thought this was all Edwardian socialist rubbish. No country could provide all that without impeding the individual rights of its citizens. That kind of thinking was not only impractical (the government would end up taxing workers to death) but also dangerous for a free people.

His father had been disappointed by Addison's lack of enthusiasm for art, and he'd been even more disappointed in his son when his only child joined the Tories.

Addison put three teaspoons of tea into a pot, poured the boiling water, gave it a good stir, and then took it upstairs. Thinking about how unlike his father he was, he remembered the plaque his father had proudly displayed above the fireplace, illuminating a Fabian ideal, engraved in beautiful

Edwardian script. It would have a profound influence on the son—one of only two things that ever did.

> For the right moment you must wait, as Fabius did
> most patiently when warring against Hannibal,
> though many censured his delays; but when the
> time comes you must strike hard, as Fabius did,
> or your waiting will be in vain, and fruitless.

I've waited long enough, he thought.

He placed the pot of tea on the desk, picked up his dagger again, and went to the closet. He slid his clothes aside on the pole and then stuck the point of the dagger into a narrow groove in a false wall, dislodging the wood slightly. Grabbing the panel with both hands, he lifted it out and set it aside, exposing a hidden compartment. On a flat wooden plank about three feet off the floor sat a Creed Model 7 page teleprinter, unplugged from an electrical outlet that he himself had installed. He would no longer have any use for that. He reached behind it for a black leather attaché case, solidly made and well worn. He picked it up and carried it to his desk. He set a mirror in front of himself and opened the case. Inside it was everything he needed to make a complete transformation. He was so used to this morning ritual that he could almost do it with his eyes closed. He looked at himself in the mirror and examined his face. "Damn it, you bloody gobshite," he said aloud to the person in the mirror. He'd been daydreaming in the kitchen when he should have been washing his face.

He went back downstairs and scrubbed his face in the sink with a bar of soap he'd gotten in his last shipment from his wholesale import supplier. It contained a special oil that was easy on his skin. Ordinary soap contained too much lye and left his face with a rash. He had to wash his face well in the morning because it was important that his skin be extremely clean before he applied his makeup, or as good as it was, it wouldn't stay on properly. He'd once gotten himself into a sticky wicket in the shop while waiting on a customer. Part of his disguise had begun to peel off, and he'd felt it. Luckily for him, the customer had only been a wog and hadn't noticed when Addison cleverly diverted the man's attention. On this present morning, he scrubbed and scrubbed, and when he thought his face was clean enough, he dried it and returned to his room upstairs.

He poured some tea into a cup and took a sip. *Good enough*, he thought. He sat down and examined his face in the mirror. His skin was smooth and clean. His beard was light, so he needed to shave only every other day. At forty-three, he looked much younger—but that didn't matter. He checked his hair. It was short, but a bit longer than what he preferred. He reminded himself to trim it tomorrow. He gulped a mouthful of tea, which had cooled down by now, and began his transformation.

His makeup wasn't the ordinary theatrical kind. It had been developed by brilliant chemists employed by Her Majesty's Secret Intelligence Service and could withstand virtually any climate, save the coldest, if the face was properly prepared. The makeup functioned particularly well in the hottest and muggiest of weather and was well suited for North African countries. Once on, it would stay on, even if the wearer swam in salt water. Only a specially designed remover, also developed by the chemists, could remove it. And that too was harsh on Addison's face. He'd ordered another supply of makeup earlier this year from headquarters, which had come to him from London via the British consulate office in Alexandria. It had been picked up and delivered to five secret locations within the city by five different Egyptian courier services to ensure that no one could trace the package to him. Finally, an Egyptian import wholesaler, whom he used infrequently and who was generously compensated for his trouble, had placed it inside a wooden crate containing Batchelors Marrowfat Peas and delivered to his shop along with an order. Addison felt his current supplies of makeup should last for at least another year.

First, he lightly brushed on some foundation cream. Over that, he applied two different creams that made his face appear older, drying into very slight wrinkles. He paid special attention to his neck just below his chin. If that area wasn't done right, it would be a sure giveaway, for necks aged faster than faces. The extra cream he put on at the Adam's apple made the skin appear to sag somewhat once it was dry. When finished with that, he dabbed a little more onto his chin to fill in a small scar. The creams had been specifically developed to blend with his coloration and skin type.

When he was satisfied with what he'd done, he put on the eyebrows and ran a finger over each one, using slight pressure to make certain the adhesive was in place. *Damn those buggers*, he thought. He'd been doing this same ritual for years now and was getting sick of it. He'd given his best years to the British Secret Intelligence Service, and they'd stuck him in this hellhole of a place as his reward. He'd supplied them with valuable intelligence over the last five years, and still they wouldn't pull him out and give him an assignment in a civilized country.

Well, that will all soon change now.

He placed a mustache above his upper lip, applying pressure with the tips of his fingers, and then pursed his lips, making sure it was in place. He hated both the eyebrows and the mustache because the adhesive was so good that removing the pieces caused him pain.

Next came the hairpiece. Made of human hair, it also had been developed by MI6; like the makeup, it was not available in the general marketplace. It was medium-brown, slightly lighter than the eyebrows and mustache, with streaks of gray throughout, especially at the temples. He pulled it over his own closely cut hair and adjusted it and then took a brush and flattened the hairs down. The elastic had thousands of small needlelike protrusions in it to hold the hairpiece to his head, and it had been designed in such a way that if someone pulled at the hairs, it would still hold firmly. Addison could do cartwheels (not that he was capable of that), and it still wouldn't come off; however, he'd never gotten used to its pressure, which formed a band around his head and sometimes gave him headaches.

"Jolly good show, old man," he said aloud to himself in the mirror—not as an attempt at self-deprecating humor but instead as an expression of solemn, poisonous cynicism. Thoughts of the Fabian Society flashed before him again, like a small explosion in the dead of night. What was the symbol in its coat of arms before they abandoned it, like dimwitted Philistines? He remembered: a wolf in sheep's clothing, appearing to stand upright on its hind legs. If he'd had his own personal crest, he thought he would have used just that.

Yes ... that will all change soon.

He thought about the cable he'd received from MI6 headquarters nearly three months earlier, which had sent him down the road on which he found himself today. Headquarters had quoted the British prime minister, Anthony Eden, during one of his closed cabinet meetings. What Eden had said was now seared into Addison's brain. Eden had told his ministers that he didn't want the Egyptian president, Gamal Abdel Nasser, neutralized; he wanted him destroyed. Addison had repeated that to himself many times that night after receiving it.

"Well, you'll bloody well get what you want, Mr. Eden," he said, looking directly into his own eyes. He leaned forward and put on his wire-rimmed glasses with nonprescription lenses. "Now," he said, twisting his head about slightly in the mirror to see better, "Bob's your uncle!"

He had this ritual down to under twelve minutes. Once again, he was a sixty-three-year-old proper English shopkeeper selling imported British goods.

He closed the case and placed it inside the false wall again and then took his clothes off hangers and spread them over his bed. He put on a white shirt and buttoned it all the way up, leaving the collar open. Next, he slipped his legs into the cream-colored trousers and zipped them up. He went back to his desk and picked up a leather scabbard that had been reinforced at the bottom. He strapped it around his left shoulder so that it hung down at his side and slid the dagger into it. Then he put on a matching lightweight suit jacket. Finally, he slipped into a pair of tan leather loafers and stood in front of a full-length mirror to admire himself.

"Yes, Mr. Eden, you will bloody well get what you want."

Chapter 3
A ROCK AND A HARD PLACE

The Farm
Thursday, July 19
5:30 a.m.

ALEX LOGAN SAT ON A GUNMETAL-GRAY PADDED armless chair with his wrists tied firmly behind him and his arms looped around the back, making it impossible for him to stand up without lifting the chair with him—if the chair hadn't been bolted to the cement floor. Three feet in front of him was a desk, and behind that, an empty chair.

He'd been unconscious for most of the trip, but now he felt exhausted, the sleep having done little to revive him. He was sore down to his bones, and it seemed to him that every muscle in his body throbbed. Logan took pride in keeping himself in good physical condition. He ran five days a week and watched what he ate. He was rarely ill. But now he felt similar to the way he had felt those few times during the war when he'd had malaria—not the fever that would come and go, not the resultant chills and sweats that left his body a hopeless mass of nothing, just the god-awful pain that racked his muscles and bones. The pain must have been the result of the awkward position in which he'd been transported in the back seat of the car. Everything had happened so fast—and as far as he could tell, with such expert precision—that he had no idea where he was. What he did know for certain was that he needed to get up and stretch badly.

His arms and legs had been tied and his ears stuffed with cotton and heavily taped over, preventing him from hearing. It was a common way to disorient someone. Logan knew all the tricks. The two men who'd made the snatch should have blindfolded him as well. But they hadn't, and Logan wondered why. He hadn't been able to do much else other than to think while he was awake during a part of the trip—though whether it'd been three hours or three days, he couldn't tell.

Logan had a sharp, analytical mind. It had served him well during the war and later when he attended graduate school. So it was natural for him to use his time since regaining consciousness to contemplate who these men were and what they wanted with him. He'd been kidnapped; that much was certain. But why? Ransom? He was well off by most standards; he didn't lack for anything. But he was far from being rich. Only idiots would risk a kidnapping charge (conviction meant the death penalty in Washington, DC) for the measly three thousand dollars in his savings account. Kidnappers seeking money would have gone after a bigger fish. He'd weighed the possibility of organized crime, but he excluded that too. They didn't look the type, the little that he had seen of them. And besides, he wasn't involved in criminal activity. Upon being taken out of the car, he'd gotten a better look at the two men, and he considered the possibility that they might be plainclothes law enforcement officers. Not city cops, but more like federal agents by their demeanor. But what would they want with him that required a kidnapping and a few hours or days of road time away from Georgetown?

When they'd taken him out of the car, he'd caught a few glimpses around the immediate surroundings. The building with the green door that the men had taken him into and a larger one off at a distance, as well as the general layout of the land, seemed familiar to him, but he couldn't quite place the location. Had he been here before? The certain order to the environment and the precision of things that had happened were beginning to gnaw at him.

The room he sat in was square and small, windowless and claustrophobic. The walls were constructed of cinder blocks that had been freshly painted an ugly grayish-green. It looked like a police interrogation room or a prison cell, neither of which he had firsthand knowledge of. The two men who'd brought him there were standing behind him, flanking him. They stood with their hands behind them and their feet apart. *A silly version of the military position of parade rest*, Logan thought. Both wore dark-colored wrinkled suits that looked as if the men had slept in them, and their ties were loosened at the collar. When Logan twisted his neck, looking over either shoulder at them, neither one would make eye contact with him. One looked at his fingernails and the other at his shoes, ignoring him.

"You want to tell me what this is all about?" Logan's voice was calm and low. He was in no position to demand anything from them. He had to maintain his cool and resist the futile and impossible urge to rip their hearts out. He waited for a response but didn't get one.

He decided to pursue a monologue, hoping that it eventually would turn into a dialogue, but twisting his neck every time he said something was too much effort. So he spoke to the wall in front of him, beyond the desk. "That sleeper maneuver you put on me was done well. You could kill a person with that, if it were done wrong. Someone very skilled taught you, right? You learned well." He paused a moment and then added, "Lucky for me, eh?"

No response.

"I bet you're federal agents, right? You must have learned it at the FBI academy."

Still no response.

Logan thought a moment. He decided to use a slightly different approach to encourage a bit more discourse on their part. After all, he didn't have anything to lose. If they intended to harm him, they would have done so long before now. He kept his voice measured as before, giving them the impression that he was fully in control of his faculties. "You know, you're just a pair of sniveling, cowardly twits," he said. "You're lackeys, doing someone else's bidding." He paused to see whether or not that would cheer them on to say something. When it didn't, he added, "When I get out of here, I'm going to hunt you bastards down and rip your heads off with my bare hands."

One of the men looked down and scratched the tip of his nose. The other one forced a cough into his fist. Both readjusted their positions somewhat. Neither said anything. Logan assumed that they were hoping their boss would come in soon. For all they knew, he was just getting started. He might even be planning another barrage any second now.

Ten minutes went by in silence.

Logan really did need to get up and stretch now. The thing he hated most was being in a situation that he couldn't control. He'd experienced that only one other time—in Casablanca. It had been momentary, but it had left him feeling emotionally sick and hopeless, as if his world had come crashing down on him. He'd been crushed to bits, and the experience had left scars that he still had today.

He looked at the clock above the door. It was one of those round, nondescript brown clocks that looked government-issued, bought in bulk at a huge discount from a civilian wholesaler. It was five fifty-two, probably in the morning, but he wouldn't bet on that; he was still disoriented. If it was indeed morning, then he had just exited the theater in

Georgetown six hours and fifty-two minutes ago, and all he wanted to do now was to go back to his apartment and go to bed.

As he was thinking about that, the door suddenly swung open, startling all three of them, and a man carrying a thin manila folder in his hand entered. He started to speak before he was even fully in the room. "I'm sorry to keep you waiting, Mr. Logan," he said deferentially.

The man was taller than Logan by a few inches and broad at the shoulders, and his posture was erect. His beige seersucker suit hung loosely on him, but Logan could tell he was muscular under it. He wore a crew cut that made his face—which was pleasant enough—look fuller than it was. He walked toward the gray metal desk in front of Logan with a strong and purposeful gait and sat down. The heavy door slammed shut by itself. Logan noticed a bulge under his left arm.

"Cut the niceties," Logan said. "Who the hell are you, and why did you have your thugs kidnap me?" He felt that if you asked a direct question, the majority of times, you would get a direct answer. He didn't believe this was going to be the case now, but it was worth a try.

"My name is Morgan Stance, and I'm a CIA officer," the man behind the desk said. He reached up to his neck and undid the top button of his shirt, and then he spread the collar with his fingers, pulling down on his tie slightly. "You're at our training facilities at Camp Peary, Virginia. I want to apologize to you for the manner in which we brought you here and for your inconvenience, sir." His expression was neutral.

Logan was taken off guard. However, the way Stance had spoken to him put him at ease somewhat. He didn't believe that he'd undergo intense interrogation or be held very long. Killing him was out of the question. They must want something very important from him to have gone to such lengths. But what the hell was it?

He now realized why this compound had looked familiar to him. He'd been here five years earlier when it was used primarily by the Navy. He'd been asked by the CIA to give a lecture to new recruits about his covert experiences during the war. His movements had been restricted, so he hadn't seen much of the installation, but he'd seen enough to remember it.

There was a moment of silence in the room while Stance opened the manila folder containing several sheets of paper.

"So are you going to tell me what this is all about?" Logan asked. Guessing it was the morning, he added, "I've got an appointment with my barber at ten. I need to keep it."

"Yes, sir," Stance said, looking up at him. "I understand." He looked down at his desk for a moment and then up again at Logan. "I'll explain in detail why we brought you to our facilities, but first, sir, I want to read a few things from this file concerning you."

All business and no sense of humor, Logan thought. Typical of spooks.

Stance cleared his throat and then read from one of the sheets he'd taken from the file, looking up every so often. "Your name is Alexander Rashidi Logan. You were born on May 10, 1917, in Alexandria, Egypt. Your father's name was Patrick Logan, and your mother was Layla El Mahdeya, an Egyptian national. For the first five years of your life, you lived in Alexandria. Then you moved to Paris, where your American father became the consul general. You remained in Paris until you were eighteen, at which time you moved to America. You attended Harvard from 1935 to 1939 with a double major in history and languages. In 1945, you returned there for graduate school. During your studies, your parents were killed—"

"Why in the hell do you have all this information about

me? I know how you got it, but I want to know why before you go any further." Logan tried to stand. He couldn't, but the two men behind him nevertheless placed a hand on his shoulders.

"I'll get to that, sir, but first I'd like you to just listen," Stance said, unperturbed. He cleared his throat again and continued. "Your parents were killed in a car accident in the Adirondack mountains when a truck collided with their car. In 1948, you began teaching at Georgetown University, where you remain today as an associate professor of history. Besides English, you speak fluent French, Italian, and Arabic. The only relatives you have are on your mother's side. Your uncle's name is Abubakar El Mahdeya. Your aunt's name is Akila. You have a male cousin named Shakir El Mahdeya, who is the chief of criminal investigations of the Alexandria police department, and one female cousin whose name is Aria. They are Coptic Christians, and they all reside in Alexandria, Egypt. You travel there frequently, and I can give you the dates if you like." Stance looked up at Logan. "But those are not the most important things in your life that interest us, sir. What you did between 1940 and 1945 is." He paused a moment and then added, "During the war, sir."

Jesus Christ, Logan thought. *I wonder whether he knows what pipe tobacco I smoke.*

Chapter 4
THE DOOMSDAY THREAT

Alexandria, Egypt
Thursday, July 19
8:30 a.m.

ADDISON LOCKED THE DOOR TO HIS BEDROOM, tugged on the knob to make sure it was secured, and then descended the steps into his shop below. He put some water into the kettle and lit the burner. He couldn't possibly think about starting his day without a few more cups of tea. He decided to skip his usual breakfast today and settled, instead, for a couple of digestive biscuits.

While he waited for the water to boil for his second cup of the morning, he went into the main room of his shop. It was small by British standards, but in Egypt, it was considered average size for a retail business. The shop had done extremely well over the last five years and had become indispensable for Addison.

Because his job as an intelligence officer was to spy on the Egyptian government, most of what concerned him was in Cairo. However, he'd decided early on, while considering which cover to employ, that his own presence in the capital wouldn't be necessary because he'd be using a local spy to acquire

28

the intelligence for him. Should something go wrong and compromise the situation, he would be safely in Alexandria. So this shop had indeed provided him with an excellent cover, and the spy, Donatella, brought the intelligence right to his doorstep. Furthermore, if circumstances ever required him to go to Cairo for any reason, it was only a two-hour drive there.

The front counter was located near the entrance. Three of the walls were lined with unpainted wooden shelves. Four shorter, freestanding shelves were located in the middle of the room, with enough space between them for customers to walk. Reaching under the front counter, Addison picked up a clipboard with an order form attached to it and went to the first shelf along the west wall to rearrange some of the jars and cans. He'd noticed yesterday that he was getting low on some of the more popular canned goods, so he would have to place an order with the local wholesale importer before he ran out completely. He used a British wholesaler as his main supplier rather than one of the no-good shaggin' wogs. His wholesaler would get him his supplies within a few days, unlike the Egyptians who would take weeks, sometimes even as long as a month, to fill his order.

He was beginning to think that the British government itself was becoming much like the wogs here: inefficient, lazy, and cowardly. Anthony Eden had been quite prepared to move forward with having President Nasser assassinated, and he'd been right—after all, Nasser was planning to nationalize the Suez Canal! The future of Britain as a world power was being directly challenged by a ratty, two-bit, third-world dictator. A well-thought-out plan devised by Whitehall had been painstakingly put into place, and it directly involved MI6 agents, Addison included. Nasser had to be eliminated once and for all.

So how had Eden responded when the Soviet premier, Nikita Khrushchev, threatened out of the blue to launch nuclear warheads against London if Egypt were invaded or anything happened to Nasser? He had backed down like the coward he was and sent a cable to the embassy in Cairo, pulling all of his MI6 agents out of Egypt. He feared that miscommunication with and among the agents could lead to a war with the Soviets. Unconscionable!

All of MI6 was back in London now, except for Addison, who had refused to go. Whitehall had him sent cable after cable, demanding that he pack his bags and return. Although his superiors could, until recently, communicate with him (Addison had simply unplugged his Creed Model 7 page teleprinter so it couldn't be traced), they had no idea what his cover was or where he was, so they could hardly send the cavalry after him and yank him out of Egypt.

Eden was a right arse for having caved to Khrushchev's idle threats. Khrushchev would never start a nuclear war that would inevitably involve England's greatest ally, the United States, especially over a third-rate country like Egypt. Addison found Eden's response totally unacceptable. Imagine, sending every MI6 agent back to London because some overweight, bald Soviet nutter who looked more like a longshoreman than a world leader threatened him! Brilliant, just brilliant! Jolly good show, Mr. Eden. Yes, Addison would return to London—indeed he would!—just as soon as he completed a little job he had going here next week. Then he would say goodbye to this shop and to these dreadful wogs. From London, who would know where he'd end up?

He took a Biro from his jacket pocket and began writing down his order while sifting through the shelves: Bisto gravy, Batchelors Marrowfat Peas, Branston Pickle. He stopped to wipe the sweat from his forehead. It was still early and already hot. It would be another scorcher today. As much as he hated being in Egypt, this shop did provide a good living for him. The few British who still lived in Alexandria couldn't possibly do without their pickle or spotted dick pudding. And there were enough wealthy wogs who enjoyed emulating the British and sent their servants to the shop to ensure that his business venture would keep operating. But far more than that, the business provided the necessary cover that allowed him to engage in endeavors that the world would soon learn about.

He went from shelf to shelf, adding to his order: McVitie & Price's Digestive Biscuits; Ambrosia Creamed Rice Pudding (he couldn't forget that—it was a good seller); Bird's Custard Powder; Dundee Orange Marmalade; Tetley and Twinning's teas; John West Kippers & Salmon. The kettle began to whistle, so he set the clipboard on top of the shelf and returned to the cubby to make his tea.

He sat down at the table and grabbed a tea towel. His finger and thumb were still bleeding slightly, so he patted them a little. Nothing too bad, though. He made his tea and then allowed it to cool. He was sure he'd thrown No. 54 Broadway for a loop when there was no response from him to their cables. He wasn't about to leave until his job was done. After all, that was what Mr. Eden wanted—Nasser dead as a doornail.

Addison had joined MI6 before the war started, landing in section D. His section's specialties were covert and paramilitary operations. Shortly after the war began, however, Winston Churchill had merged section D with other similar units to form the Special Operations Executive. As part of that unit, Addison had helped organize resistance, gathered intelligence, and performed sabotage operations. It was then that the British government had begun issuing the Fairbairn-Sykes dagger. And it was in Germany that he had become an expert with it, so much so that one of his superiors enlisted him to instruct other agents in its use.

At the end of the war, he had returned to MI6 and was sent

to its headquarters in London to sit behind a desk. Everyone simply referred to the headquarters as No. 54 Broadway. A sign outside the building proclaimed, "Minimax Fire Extinguisher Company." It was supposed to be a secret that the SIS worked from there, but every taxi driver and tourist knew what it was. The organization needed experienced men with a certain expertise to oversee their field agents. MI6 had considered it a promotion, and most agents had considered it as such, but not Addison, who had seen it as a punishment. Every day, the ritual had been the same: Get up at seven, shower, shave, brush his teeth, have breakfast, take the underground, be behind his desk at nine. Type a few memos, determine which agent is in what location, send messages to the embassies. Take lunch at his desk at one. Then more memos, more messages. Leave the office at five—sharp! Back on the underground and back home at five thirty to an empty flat. A promotion indeed!

In the early 1950s, when the Secret Intelligence Service started to rotate its agents in North Africa, they had sent Addison to Egypt—*temporarily*, they said. Another punishment, especially for a man of his skills and talents. But he'd made the best out of what he considered a bad situation. At least he was away from that bloody desk. In a short time, he'd recruited a local to spy against the Egyptian government. The spy had turned out to be so effective that Addison had been able to provide MI6 with a stream of valuable intelligence. Perhaps that was why they'd left him here in Egypt; he'd become too important for them to change his assignment.

Now they wanted him back. *Feck all*, he thought. *Those wankers can all go to hell.* He knew exactly how SIS would work it—what they'd do to get him back. He dipped a biscuit into his tea and took a bite. They'd send someone after him, perhaps a few agents, sure enough. He wondered which idiots it would be. He knew most of them. It really didn't matter, however, because they'd never find him. From the beginning, he'd kept headquarters in the dark about his cover, and as long as he'd continued to feed them intelligence, they really hadn't been interested in finding out. But soon, they would be. When his job was finished, he would simply disappear—permanently. Things would really get interesting then because those bloody blokes *would* send the cavalry after him. Perhaps he would indeed return to London after all and live right under their noses in a suitable disguise (developed and paid for by Her Majesty's Secret Intelligence Service, of course). He knew of a flat across the street and down a half block from No. 54 Broadway. He imagined himself drinking a pint in the pub two doors down where all the top brass hung out after work. It would be good crack—something to look forward to!

There was only one crease in his plan that he had yet to iron out. He needed more money. Although he did have a great deal stashed away already, after next week he'd be an international fugitive. That required even more funds for a man on the run. He also had his standard of living to consider. Scrimping for the rest of his life was out of the question. Economizing wasn't one of his strong suits. As luck would have it, he had come across—quite by chance—his pot of gold in the form of an American double eagle twenty-dollar gold coin. Unfortunately, it was in the possession of the Egyptian agent who had been and was still spying for him.

Donatella Marinetti was the mistress of Kamal Naguib, President Nasser's minister of the interior and also his director of intelligence and internal security. She covertly acquired intelligence from him and passed it on to Addison. It was Naguib, her obscenely fat lover, from whom she had stolen the coin, figuring that it was worth far more than twenty dollars because it was gold. What she hadn't known and still didn't, however, was that it was worth a fortune on the black market and that the American Secret Service was actively looking for it.

The 1930s had seen a devastating banking crisis, and President Roosevelt had taken action to end it by issuing an executive order. It made most gold in the form of coins, certificates, and bullion owned by private citizens illegal. A subsequent order had declared that gold coins were no longer legal tender; citizens who held such coins had to exchange them for legal currency.

During that same period, 445,500 twenty-dollar gold double eagles were inadvertently minted and then subsequently melted down because they were no longer legal tender. Two of those coins were retained by the government for historical reasons. They should have been the only two in existence. But they weren't.

Unknown to the Mint, twenty coins had been stolen by the person responsible for melting them down and sold to collectors. The Secret Service eventually discovered their existence and went after them. They confiscated all but one and melted them down as well. They had no idea where that last one was.

During this time, King Farouk of Egypt was known as a consummate collector of anything that could be collected: paperweights, fountain pens, postage stamps, ornate bottles, Fabergé eggs, and of course, coins. His coin collection, it was rumored, exceeded ten thousand. So on a trip to the United States, when he was offered the 1933 double eagle, he couldn't refuse it. He applied to the United States Treasury for an export license for the coin, and in a series of missteps, the license was granted.

The US government realized its "missteps" and requested through its embassy in Cairo that the coin be returned. But the war had just begun, and both countries eventually forgot about the coin. Furthermore, when the war ended and the United States became involved in rebuilding Europe's infrastructure, the coin slipped further from anyone's mind—that is, until 1952.

On July 23 of that year, Gamal Abdel Nasser and the Free Officers staged a military coup that launched the Egyptian revolution. Farouk was out the door and went into exile, leaving most of his personal belongings behind. Most ended up at a public auction run by Sotheby's in Cairo, including the coin. The Treasury Department discovered this, and the US government requested its return. The new Egyptian government, wanting to remain on good terms with the Americans, stated that it would comply with the request. To that end, one of Nasser's ministers and close friends, Kamal Naguib, personally kept the coin in his possession. However, the day before he was to take it to an American treasury agent at the US embassy, he discovered that it was missing. It had disappeared and was not seen again. Cairo had been so embroiled in both internal and external state affairs that the government never once seriously considered looking for the thief. It simply wasn't high on its list of things to do.

Donatella had kept it hidden for years until recently, when she had offered to sell it to Addison. She too needed money to secure her future after their job was done. He knew the coin's history, of course, so when she came to him and told him about it, he had offered her one thousand British sterling pounds for it, knowing she wouldn't settle for that. They had finally agreed to 2,500 pounds, which had pleased them both. If Donatella would have held out, Addison would have paid much more than that, for he knew that he could easily sell it anywhere in Europe for several hundred thousand pounds or more. The coin had a rich history, and there were enough millionaire coin collectors who wouldn't hesitate to fork over cold, hard cash for it.

That had been two weeks ago. After the agreement,

Donatella must have considered how easily the business deal had been concluded and become suspicious because a few days later, she had told him that she wanted more money for the coin. Perhaps she was just playing a game. If he'd told her no, he wouldn't pay a pound more for it, she might have been savvy enough to look for another buyer. He'd have to pay what she wanted, but that was fine with him since he had the money and would be getting much more after he sold it. He couldn't risk a refusal. Besides, she was too beautiful to kill her for it. Even if he wanted to, it would have to be done after their job was finished; she was too valuable to him now.

He took another sip of tea and looked at his watch. *Damn,* he thought. The time had gotten away from him. He'd planned to run an errand before opening the shop, and now it was too late. On Thursdays before he opened, he always took some cases of tinned foods to an orphanage two blocks away as a donation for the children. It had always given him great joy to do so. He'd begun doing this three years before, after passing the orphanage one day. He had stopped and looked through the steel gate and had seen ragged children, all undernourished, mostly nothing but skin and bones. His heart had been torn to shreds by the very sight of them. He was used to seeing poverty in Egypt, but this was something entirely different. Those children also had to endure the hardship of not having parents to comfort them. In the early morning hours, while it was still dark, he would take cases of food to the orphanage and leave them in a secure place for the administrator to find. He also special-ordered canned goods for the children that he wouldn't normally stock in his shop—food that was more suitable for their diet than Branston Pickle. Furthermore, once a month, Addison would send the administrator cash anonymously for the upkeep of the orphanage. Now it was too late for him to go today, so he decided to make his delivery tomorrow morning instead. He must also remember to send the five thousand pounds (far more than usual) to them as his final donation before he left the country next week. Those children would be the only thing he'd miss in Egypt.

His thoughts were interrupted by a knock on the door. He dipped another biscuit into his tea, ate it, and wiped his mouth on the tea towel. He wasn't set to open for another forty-five minutes, and no shipments were scheduled. He wondered who it might be. He went to the door and pulled back the curtain that covered the glass. "Christ," he said. "What's she doing here?"

Donatella Marinetti looked at him through the security gate in front of the door, her penetrating emerald eyes staring at him.

Chapter 5
BETWEEN YOU, ME, AND THE BEDPOST

Camp Peary, Virginia
Thursday, July 19
6:15 a.m.

LOGAN TOOK A LONG, HARD LOOK AT MORGAN Stance. He wondered what Stance had done before joining the Agency. The crew cut, the broad shoulders, the way he carried himself—Logan pictured him as an intelligence officer or maybe an infantry platoon leader in the Army or Marine Corps. He had probably served in the war as Logan himself had done and was most assuredly at least a captain, perhaps even having risen to the rank of major before leaving the military. He had a pleasant but determined face, and Logan was beginning to like him. Under other circumstances, they might have become good friends. But what the hell did he know? Stance could have been a cook in the Navy. Maybe he'd been insubordinate and gotten bounced out on his ear.

"You served in the war?" Logan asked him.

"Yes, sir. I was a company commander in a line outfit with the 101st Airborne Division."

Logan had nailed it. The Screaming Eagles—a no-nonsense unit. Maybe he'd been in the Normandy landings. Stance seemed like a no-nonsense guy.

Stance ran his tongue over his upper lip and looked at him. Logan was twisting in his chair, trying to get more comfortable. His muscles were still sore, and his shoulders were beginning to ache even more. Stance motioned with his head to one of the men standing behind Logan. The man walked to the door, locked it with a key, and returned.

"Sir, I'm going to have one of my officers untie your wrists," Stance said. "Please feel free to get up and stretch. You must be pretty sore from the ride down here."

Once his wrists were free, Logan rubbed them and looked again at Stance. Stance was bigger and more powerful than Logan, but not by much. He glanced at the other two men. They were roughly his size and weight. He calculated his chances of getting out of the room in one piece, should he decide to leave. This was more of an automatic response to the situation than a viable option. He'd have to disable the three men and then get the key—a superhuman feat. And once out of the room, how would he get out of a building full of armed spooks? Moreover, the compound would be swarming with military personnel. He'd gotten himself out of other dicey situations before, but he didn't give himself much of a chance with this one. He stood up and shook his arms and then stretched them above his head to get the circulation moving again. He bent over at the waist, touching the floor with the tips of his fingers like a boxer waiting for a fight to begin, and then he sat down again.

"I hope you have a good reason," Logan said to Stance.

"I beg your pardon, sir."

"You kidnapped me, which is a federal offense. I hope you have a good reason."

"Please allow me to continue. I think what I'm about to say will be of interest to you."

"I doubt it, but it looks as if I really don't have a choice in the matter, do I?"

"Sir, with all due respect, no, you don't."

A no-nonsense response, Logan thought. Logan leaned back in the chair and put his hands behind his neck, stretching his elbows outward and then inward toward each other. The movement felt good and relaxed his muscles. "I'm all ears," he said.

Stance glanced at the clock above the door and then looked down at the file. After a few seconds, he looked back up at Logan, making eye contact. "Sir, on April 23, 1940, at 0100 hours, you met a State Department official named Griffith Maxfield Oberon at the Roosevelt Hotel in New York City in room 611 who offered you a job as a vice consul in Casablanca, Morocco. Our records indicate that you accepted this position enthusiastically. With Hitler on the horizon, you were eager to serve your country before the US became militarily involved in the war.

"However, the position of vice consul was a diplomatic cover. Your real job, along with eleven other men who would also become vice consuls in Morocco, Algeria, and Tunisia"—Stance stopped for a moment to read the file again and then looked up—"involved propaganda, espionage, sabotage, clandestine communications, and arms running for the US government. You were the youngest member of this group, and your targets were French Vichy officials, military and naval establishments, the expatriate community, German officials, the Gestapo, and Italian espionage agents. Your mission was to collect political, economic, and military intelligence while working with French colonials, Arabs, and Berbers to defeat Vichy and Axis agents in Casablanca. Your actions as a spy were crucial in paving the way for the successful invasion of

North Africa through Operation Torch, which opened French North and West Africa to Atlantic Mediterranean routes and the Suez Canal and which ultimately led to the liberation of Sicily, Sardinia, and Corsica." He paused briefly to look at the clock and then continued. "Sir, you were part of the first organized US spy team in World War II to operate under diplomatic cover. President Roosevelt referred to you and the eleven other men as his Twelve Apostles. You taught the CIA much about operating under diplomatic cover. I attended your lecture on the subject here at the Farm several years ago."

Logan now realized why this place looked so familiar. He *had* been here before. The lecture had taken place in another building, and he had been here only that one time and had never gotten a good look around the compound, so it was a vague memory.

"After you successfully completed your mission with the State Department, you served out your time during the war as an officer with the OSS. Where you were is not important, but what you did is. You functioned as an assassin." The Office of Strategic Services was the precursor to the CIA. Most of the first officers in the Agency had been with the OSS previously. What Stance had just said was highly classified information.

"It's ad-Dār al-Bayḍa'."

"Sir?"

"Casablanca. That's its name."

"Yes, sir."

"What's this all about? What do you want with me that required kidnapping?"

"I apologize for that, sir."

"You already did. And stop calling me sir."

"Yes, sir. We hoped that you would be as eager now to help your country out of a situation that is even more significant than North Africa was."

"What?"

"You could help us prevent a nuclear war with the Soviet Union. Let me explain."

"Listen, Stance, you seem like a nice guy and all that, but I don't want to hear your explanation. What I want is a ride back to Georgetown, where your thugs broke into my apartment and put a goddamn sleeper hold on me." He stopped to rub his neck. "Better yet, I'll hitchhike to Williamsburg and take a bus back."

There was a moment of silence in the small room that weighed heavily on both men. Stance glanced at the clock again, and Logan could see that he was trying to formulate something in his head. He deduced that time was a factor.

"Just hear me out. Remember, you have no choice in that matter. And if you still want to return to Georgetown after what I have to say, we'll provide you with the transportation." For the first time, Stance seemed annoyed. It was sudden and subtle, but Logan picked up on it immediately.

He would listen to what Stance had to say, yes, but he knew they couldn't force him to do anything he didn't want to do. "Go ahead. Like I said, I'm all ears."

"As you know, we work closely with the British Secret Intelligence Service. They have an agent known by code name Lucky Break who is deeply embedded in a cover in Alexandria, Egypt. Lucky Break had recruited an Egyptian spy who is either in or closely associated with President Nasser's close inner circle. He's been feeding Lucky Break intelligence, which Lucky Break then passes on to MI6 in London. In the last four months, they've been receiving some significant information concerning the course Egypt is on. Basically, it's this: one, one of the aims of the Nasser regime is nothing less than the total destruction of Israel; two, Egypt is gearing up for complete domination of all Arab governments, including those of our allies, ultimately for the Soviets, who are seeking to control the oil reserves; and three, Nasser has become a willing instrument of the Kremlin." Stance paused to wipe his lips and then continued. "All of our own sources in the area believe this intelligence to be completely false. We believe Nasser hates communist ideology and considers the atheistic Soviets to be a threat to Islam."

"Some of that's true," Logan said. "The Soviets have been selling weapons to Nasser for the last year to use against Israel, and when we pulled out of our commitment to fund the Aswan Dam, the Soviets jumped right in."

"Yes, but the Egyptian government came to us first for weapons, and we refused to sell them any. The Soviets became their last resort. And it was Czechoslovakia, not the Soviets, who made a deal to trade them arms for cotton. We believe that those weapons are being used for defensive purposes only. We also believe that Nasser is using the Soviets to help develop his country, nothing more. But let me finish. MI6 has been using anti-Nasser Egyptians for years now to undermine the government. They've been behind numerous assassination attempts."

"And your fellas lent a helping hand."

Stance ignored that and continued. "In fact, until very recently, Britain was moving forward with a viable plan to assassinate Nasser because of his plan to nationalize the Suez Canal. Soviet intelligence caught wind of it. Nikita Khrushchev made it known to both Anthony Eden and René Coty that if Britain and France did anything to undermine the Nasser regime—and we firmly believe he meant that if they tried to assassinate Nasser—then they should not be too surprised if nuclear missiles were launched against London and Paris. If he did that, of course, the United States would have to support our allies, which means that we would be forced to engage in a nuclear war with the Soviet Union. I want you to know that our government has taken the Soviet threat seriously. Whitehall's response was to back down. To ensure against the risk that miscommunication could lead to war, the British pulled all their MI6 agents back to London temporarily, until the whole thing blows over. Remember, it was those same agents who hired Egyptians to assassinate Nasser in the past."

"Eden's response was pretty extreme, don't you think?" Logan said. "So what's the problem?"

"No, I don't think so. But the problem is this. They have all their agents back in London now except one—Lucky Break. They've sent numerous cables ordering him to return to London immediately, and all have gone unanswered."

"Jesus, how difficult could it be for an intelligence agency to find one its own?"

"By now, it's become apparent that Lucky Break doesn't want to be found. MI6 has every reason to believe that this agent is going to assassinate Nasser himself. From what they've told us, he's savvy, intelligent, and vehemently anti-Soviet, and he has the skills to pull it off."

Logan thought for a long minute about this. He didn't like where it was leading. He wondered how much longer Stance was going to wait until he asked him. "Why don't they send one of their own agents to find him?" Logan asked.

"I suspect they have already. They probably sent more than one. But there's another problem. They know he's in Alexandria, or at least that's where he's been for the last five years, but he's deeply embedded in his cover. And—"

"Let me guess. They have no idea what that cover is."

"That's affirmative. And it seems that he's skilled at using disguises and changing identities that can fool even the best of their own agents. MI6 had been in frequent communications with him until recently, but no one has actually seen him. They left him alone because they were getting what they thought was valuable intelligence from him. But as I said, we believe that the intelligence has been incorrect. He's a chameleon, and now he's dangerous."

"And you want me to find him for the Brits?" Logan felt he had been reeled in by Stance, little by little, in the last hour. He had to admit to himself that he was now interested, but he couldn't determine when exactly Stance had set the hook.

"Yes, and kill him. This doesn't involve just the British government any longer. It also involves the French, who have basically stayed out of it, and us as well. We don't want a third world war on our hands because of this one maniac."

"How do you know for certain Lucky Break is planning an assassination? Maybe he hasn't answered the cables because he's dead. Maybe he's off somewhere in the South Pacific sunning himself with a couple beautiful women on either side of him."

"If either were the case, we'd be extremely happy about it. But there's too much at stake for us to assume that. The tone of his cables to MI6 headquarters over the last months strongly suggested that the organization should consider assassinating Nasser, even though he didn't come right out and say that. Those cables were sent after Whitehall pulled the plug on their operation. His subsequent nonresponses to MI6 headquarters indicate that he's going to take matters into his own hands. We have to proceed on the assumption that he's going to do just that."

"And just how do you expect me to find him if the Brits can't?"

"We don't know for certain when the assassination is planned for. But all of our North Africa analysts agree with MI6 that the most likely day is July 26. On that day, Nasser will be traveling to Alexandria to give a speech in Mansheya Square in celebration of the fourth anniversary of the coup. Our man in Cairo believes he's also going to announce to the world that he's planning to nationalize the Suez Canal on behalf of the Egyptian people. That would be a devastating blow to many countries, especially Great Britain. It seems reasonable to conclude that Lucky Break will make his move on that day."

"Jesus Christ," Logan said. "That's all we need."

"We believe he's going to use this opportunity to assassinate Nasser, either somewhere along the route from the Alexandria airport to Mansheya Square or during the speech."

"That's a lot of territory to cover. And you expect me to find one man in Alexandria who uses disguises and kill him—in what, seven days? My God, there's four million people in that city!"

"Yes. You should be back in Georgetown in eight days, nine max. Maybe sooner."

"You're crazier than a loon. You're asking me to do the impossible."

"At this juncture, Mr. Logan, we have no other option. You're the only man who we're sure can do this job in that time frame, if it can be done at all. You know the city well, you speak the language, and you have the skills and knowledge required to hunt Lucky Break down and kill him."

There was another long, cold silence in the room. All Logan wanted to do now was return to Georgetown and to his life there and forget this had ever happened. He was trying to absorb the barrage of information that Stance had just thrown at him when his thoughts inexplicably went to Simone again. It had all happened so fast and with little fuss. He'd been sitting in a café when she came in. She noticed him and smiled. They ordered espresso and then a brandy and talked as if they'd known each other for years. It was so natural, so easy.

She'd taken an immediate interest in him that he thought was flattering. She wanted to know everything about him, his job, where he had been. Logan was intoxicated by her beauty, by her smell, and by the sight of her smooth tanned skin. He told her everything about himself. She swooned over every little detail. And it hadn't stopped with his personal life. After only a few days, he'd explained his job, which she found utterly fascinating for she'd never known a vice consul before, someone of his rank and stature. She wanted more and more of him.

In a matter of days, he'd fallen in love with her. He hadn't been surprised by this sudden revelation. Back home in the States, people would have said it was a whirlwind romance. But in Casablanca during the war, things happened with such amazing speed that such a romance was considered commonplace. Their relationship had continued to flourish for months. When they were apart because his duties required it, they couldn't wait to be together again. When they were together, they couldn't keep their hands off each other. That last week, they had made love to one another passionately and frequently. They were both very happy. He was quite prepared to ask her to marry him.

After it ended and he had time to reflect, he realized that he had known next to nothing about her. Oh, she'd told him that she was from a suburb of Paris and that she had been a hairdresser before the war, but she hadn't volunteered much more. Logan had guessed that she must be a little shy about herself or that her reticence might be the result of something that she didn't want to share with him at that stage in the relationship. At the right time, Logan had believed, she'd open up, and he would know her better. Some people were like that; they needed time. He'd just have to give her that. But time ran out. Later, it all made sense to him.

On that last night, he sneaked into her villa and quietly went to her bedroom. He stared at her for what seemed to be an eternity. Her fine blonde hair was splayed out on the pillow, and her breathing told him that she was in a deep sleep.

After a while, she stirred somewhat but remained asleep. He wondered what she was dreaming about.

Then with about as little fuss as when they'd first met, he raised his gun with a silencer attached, put it to her head, and pulled the trigger.

He'd been devastated upon discovering that she was a spy working for the Germans. Some of the information that she'd supplied the Gestapo had come from him and led to American deaths. It was a mistake he'd never repeat.

He had to admit to himself later that it wasn't out of revenge that he'd killed her. He'd loved her too much for that. He simply hadn't wanted her to suffer. If the Free French Forces had discovered her first, they would have executed her. Most likely, they would have raped her beforehand too, cutting off her hair first. That was what happened to French females who spied for the Germans. Logan decided that a bullet in the head while she was sleeping was easier and certainly painless.

Logan looked up at Stance. His heart began to race, and in spite of the air-conditioning, he began to sweat. "When do you want me to go?" he said, barely above a whisper.

"Immediately," Stance said, relieved. He pulled several items from under the papers in the folder. "This is your ticket to Alexandria. And this is a key to a safe deposit box at Barclays Bank." He shoved both to the edge of his desk in front of Logan. "It contains money in US dollars and British and Egyptian pounds, as well as a gun, a silencer, and ammunition. You'll need your own passport. Travel on a tourist visa on the pretext of visiting your relatives like always."

"I'll need to fly to Montreal first."

"Sorry, no can do. We're pressed for time as it is. What's in Montreal?"

"I have to see an old friend. If you're willing to trust me with this mission, you'll have to trust me on this."

Stance stared at Logan intensely. "Okay, but we want you in Alexandria in twenty-six hours."

"Fair enough. What else can you tell me about Lucky Break?"

"Nothing besides what I already told you. We're trying to find out more about his identity from MI6, but we have to be careful that we don't tip them to what we're doing. We don't want them to know about you because it could compromise your movements there. Expect to run into MI6 agents because they've probably been sent to find Lucky Break as well. Don't break your cover. If we get any more information we think could be useful to you, we'll cable you at the US consulate office in Alexandria, and our people will get it to you. You have reservations at the Hotel Cecil. The view is good."

"I know. I've stayed there before."

"Mr. Logan, you need to know that you'll be on your own. We'll support you, of course, but only with new intelligence should we find any. You understand that this is a sensitive situation, and we've got to protect the government and the—"

"And the Agency. Yes, I know all about that. I'm fine with that. I prefer to work alone."

"Good. We have a pilot at our airstrip here, waiting to take you back to Georgetown. Good luck."

The two men stood and shook hands. One of the other men unlocked the door. Logan opened it and then heard Stance clear his throat. He looked back at him.

"And please, Mr. Logan, lay off the women in Alexandria while you're there. We know all about Simone Fontaine."

Chapter 6
THE BEAUTIFUL PARAMOUR

Alexandria, Egypt
Thursday, July 19
9:15 a.m.

ADDISON DAVIES UNLOCKED THE DOOR AND THEN the security gate in front of it and let Donatella slip past him. She walked through the shop toward the back room without acknowledging him. He didn't appreciate the snub, but it was nothing for Addison to be concerned about. In fact, he was only mildly irritated. He knew Donatella the way a psychiatrist knows a neurotic patient. Depending on the social setting and intent, she could be charming and gracious or devilish and impertinent. Or, as he himself had found out many times, she could be indifferent—to the point of arrogance, he would say—to those around her. When she got into this mood, it used to swallow him up, but he'd built up a fortification against it, so it no longer bothered him—mostly. He locked up and followed her through the shop to the kitchen area.

"I told you never to come here before business hours," he said to the back of her head as she continued to walk. She'd been working for him for five years, and she could be a very foolish woman at times, but he knew there were limits to his anger when it came to her. There was a line he would never cross.

Addison's gaze ran from the length of her long black hair to her ankles as he followed her. She'd broken his heart long ago and continued to do so each time he saw her. He'd recruited her in a suite at the Windsor Hotel in Cairo five years before. He'd ordered a fine Italian dinner for them along with an expensive wine. Gradually, over the course of the meal, he had explained his proposal and how she could earn more money than she ever could have imagined. Donatella, of course, had been interested in what he was telling her. Money had always been important to her. After explaining what she had to do, what was expected of her, he had sat back in his chair and waited for her reaction. He'd had his eyes on her for quite some time, spying on her daily and nightly movements throughout the city, so he'd gotten a taste of her character. But he really didn't know her well enough to anticipate how she would react to his offer, and of course, there was a potential problem. He'd exposed himself as a British intelligence officer. If she declined, he couldn't very well let her leave with that knowledge. He had expected her to think about it, to mull it over for some time, so he was surprised when she accepted his proposal immediately, with her arms crossed at the table and a matter-of-fact expression on her face. "So when do you want me to start?" she had said. Donatella would never know that had she not accepted his offer, Addison had been quite prepared to wrap a piano wire around her neck and choke the life out of her. He was ever so glad he hadn't had to do that.

To celebrate, Addison had opened a bottle of champagne and put on a record of an Italian opera he thought she might like. They then sat down on the divan and toasted their new arrangement. He went into more detail concerning what she had to do for him. She listened intently and asked a number of questions for clarification and contributed some insightful thoughts of her own. Addison thought they were particularly intelligent questions and perceptions and was impressed by her acumen. He refilled her glass—he'd selected a coupe-style glass for that night because he thought it evoked the grand, extravagant elegance of the 1920s—and after a while the discussion turned to small talk.

Throughout their conversation, something else had been on Addison's mind, and after an hour or so he'd worked up enough courage to invite her into his bedroom. He was ill-prepared for her response. In fact, he was shocked by it, and he wasn't easily shocked by much in this world. She'd told him no in the bristliest language he could imagine a woman ever using. A sexual relationship was out of the question, if he wanted her to work for him. Of course, he wanted her to work for him! That was why they were there in the first place. It was because of her beauty that he had recruited her. But he'd never thought he would become infatuated with her. But he was. And that was that.

She'd broken his heart, and he'd never mentioned it again. However, each time she came to him with intelligence she'd obtained, his heart was broken again by her mere presence and by the knowledge he would never know her the way he truly wanted.

On this morning of her unexpected visit, they sat down at the small table in the cubby.

"I need more money," she said flatly.

"Can I offer you tea instead? I could easily make some for you. Or do you prefer something cooler?"

"My expenses are increasing, and it's been months since I had anything from you," she said.

He saw disgust and defiance in her face. *What—for me?* he thought. "But our job is nearly finished, my dear. You have a big payday coming soon, in just a week. Certainly, you can wait until then."

Addison resented the power she had over him. Without her, he couldn't complete his job, and she knew it all too well. Other than explaining what he wanted her to do and checking up on her progress frequently, he had little control over the way she conducted herself. So he had made a point of not paying her when he said he would so she'd have to come to him. He enjoyed it when she begged him for money. It tortured him to see her each time and to know he couldn't have her; however, it did give him the illusion of having power over her. Even though it was little and fleeting, at least it was something.

"I have to *eat*, and I can't wait a week to do so. And if you forgot, I have a mother to care for," she said. She stared at him with those emerald eyes of hers, but there was no fire in them, at least not the kind he wanted to see.

What he longed for was for her to look at him with passion in her eyes while they made love. He would have to be content with that happening only in his fantasies. His eyes dropped to her arms. Her skin was smooth and, atypical for an Egyptian woman, white. He marveled at its contrast with her black hair, which had a permanent sheen. Like his dagger, she had the power to mesmerize him. But not this time. She worked for him, and every so often, she needed to be reminded of it.

"Don't you get enough money from that fat little boyfriend of yours?" he asked with an edge of sarcasm in his voice.

"It's none of your business how much I get from him. Whether I get a millieme or one hundred pounds, it makes no difference to our arrangement. You pay me to do a job, and I do it well. I've gotten intelligence you consider valuable so you can pass it on to whoever it is you send it to, yet you make me beg for what belongs to me. You're no different from the other English who were forced to leave Egypt." She wiped her forehead with her palm. "Get me a cool cloth. It's hotter in here than it is outside."

He got up and dipped a cloth in some cool water he kept in his small paraffin refrigerator and brought it to her. She folded it and placed it on the side of her face.

"There," he said. "Do you feel better now?"

Addison enjoyed it when her temper flared, but she was correct. She'd provided valuable intelligence he couldn't have gotten himself. Without it, he wouldn't have been able to do this job. He knew that her temper would diminish as fast as it flared, as was the case with all Italians. Her pregnant mother had come to Alexandria from Bologna after her husband abandoned her. Here she had given birth to Donatella and raised her alone. No doubt, Donatella had inherited her mother's temper as well as her strength and tenacity from having had to struggle in a new country with a new language by herself. Those qualities were exactly why he'd recruited her in the first place. But they came second to her beauty.

"Donatella, Donatella, why do you continue to make life so complicated for yourself? If you want a few bob, I will—"

"I want only what I have earned, nothing more. And from now on, I want it in British sterling." She had brains as well as beauty.

"You planning on going somewhere?" he asked, playing dumb.

"You know I am, but not until after next week."

He suddenly lowered his voice to just above a whisper, as if there were another person in the room. "You know it'll be difficult for anyone to get out of the country after the president is assassinated. The borders will be closed. You may have to stay longer than you had planned."

"I know that, but I want to be ready. Maybe I can bribe someone to take my mother and me across to Italy."

"Perhaps, but I wouldn't count on it." He got up and walked to the counter in front, where he pulled a cigar box from a lower shelf and opened it. He counted out five hundred-pound sterling notes and returned to her. "Here," he said. "I'm giving you a little more. I will give you the remaining amount next week where we planned to meet." There was another pressing matter that concerned him. "Now, have you decided how much you want for that gold coin of yours?" He didn't want to sound too eager. He'd decided not to argue about the amount. He couldn't take the chance of a refusal.

"Yes," she said with confidence. "But I've found another buyer who will pay me five thousand pounds sterling for it." She paused for a long moment.

Addison's brows raised and stayed in place.

"What will you give me?"

"That's an awful lot of money, my dear. Why didn't you take it?" He knew she was lying through her teeth.

"Because I told you that I would return with a price."

"How much more do you want?" he asked, playing her little game.

"Nothing less than seven thousand."

She has a good mind, he thought, *but she has much to learn.* "I'll give you ten thousand pounds for it, if you agree to that price now without going back to the other buyer."

"It's settled then," she said flatly.

He knew she was pleased with the price and wanted to scream with joy, but her face never changed expression. She still had that cold and indifferent look she had come in with.

Time was running out. He had to conclude this deal before next week. After that, it would be impossible because he would no longer be in Egypt. "It'll take me a few days to get that much money. In the meantime, please don't change your mind. It might bloody well go bad for you if you do," he said with a slight grin, nearly a smirk.

She looked at him closely when he said this. He could sense something strange in her eyes he'd never seen before. Perhaps she had taken him seriously this time.

"Don't worry. I won't change my mind."

"Good," he said. "Now is Naguib coming this weekend?"

"Yes, but earlier than usual. He'll be here tonight."

"You must confirm with your boyfriend where Nasser will give his speech and his route from the airport. That is vitally important. I need to use the remaining days to plan."

"That shouldn't be a problem. Naguib's talked with me freely in the past and will continue to do so this weekend. As soon as I know, I'll contact you."

"After the assassination, your boyfriend—"

"Stop calling him that. You're the one who said I must start a relationship with him."

"Yes, I did do that, didn't I? After the assassination, Naguib will have the borders sealed immediately. However, I anticipate that the people will be overwhelmingly joyful over Nasser's death and will support a more moderate government that will not play stooge for the Soviets. There will be a short period of chaos. The new government will purge Nasser's inner circle of the socialists. Your boyfrie—the minister," he said, correcting himself, "might even end up president himself because he's the strongest anticommunist within the cabinet. When that happens, the government will reopen the borders. At that time, you and your mother will be free to leave the country. It will not take long for that to happen, regardless of who's in power."

"Whatever time it takes, it will be too long," she said.

"In the meantime, to more immediate matters. Have you been going to the catacombs?"

"You treat me as a brainless child," she fired back at him, her temper getting the best of her. Then she relaxed again. "Yes, of course, I've been going to the catacombs."

"And the progress?"

"Yes, every day is better than the day before. You will see when the time comes."

"Good. Very good," he said with a pleasant smile.

He was pleased, for her role was vital to his plan to assassinate the president. *Seven bloody days left*, he thought. He had much to do yet.

Chapter 7
A WORD WITH THE
SPYMASTER

Westmount, Quebec
Thursday, July 19
11:25 a.m.

LOGAN'S PLANE LANDED AT THE DORVAL AIRPORT,
and he took a taxi for the forty-minute drive to Westmount,
a small city on the Island of Montreal. He was still sore from
being on the wrong end of a sleeper hold and from being
manhandled by a pair of thugs—and still resentful of them. He
would have dearly loved to twist their heads some 180 degrees
to the right and ripped them off their necks. As a result of
the soreness, he'd been uncomfortable for the entire flight
when he should have been comfortable, sitting in the first-
class cabin. The stewardess had fussed over him and given
him some extra pillows and made sure to refill his whiskey
glass—and he certainly enjoyed all the attention—but in the
end, it hadn't helped him much.

The flight itself, however, had given him time to think
about what had happened to him in the last twelve hours. He'd
wondered what Stance would have done had Logan simply

refused to accept the job. After all, he couldn't have forced him to comply. He supposed Stance could have put him in one of the CIA's small cells below ground and deprived him of light and food. Logan knew he could have withstood that as the hours and days passed by, while Lucky Break was making his final preparations to assassinate a head of state. However, that option would have been unrealistic for Stance because the clock was ticking away, and his people apparently didn't have anyone else. He'd concluded that Stance hadn't had a backup plan. Stance must have been sure that after Logan listened to him and understood the situation the world faced, he would gladly get on board. And he'd been right.

Logan was looking forward to seeing his old pal and former boss again. He'd phoned Max from the airport in Washington to make sure he'd be free from his duties as a professor at McGill University to see Logan on such short notice. Griffith Maxfield Oberon was the man who'd recruited Logan a year and a half before the United States entered the war and who was responsible for having turned him into a spy. Max had trained him personally, cursed him when he made mistakes, and slapped him on the back when pleased with his performance. Logan would never forget his penetrating eyes, fixed in a stare. He could never read them—could never tell what was behind them. Logan shined during training partly to avoid incurring the older man's wrath.

Max had taken over as the consul general in Paris from Logan's father just before the war started in Europe. When the Nazis invaded France, the mayor of Paris as well as most of the foreign diplomats fled the city. But not Max. He stayed to secure the US embassy, burning all the sensitive documents, and watched as the German tanks moved slowly up the Avenue des Champs-Elysees to the Arc de Triomphe. Shortly after that, President Roosevelt recalled him to Washington to organize a network of spies that the president called his "Twelve Apostles," of which Logan was part.

The two men had kept in touch after the war, mostly by phone, but hadn't seen each other since the funeral of Logan's parents nine years ago. When Logan had decided to accept Stance's assignment, the first person who had come into his head was Max. In addition to his knowledge of spy work, he knew more about Egypt than anyone in the West.

Max and Logan gave each other bear hugs at the door and then settled into comfortable leather chairs in the den. Max reached to his right and grabbed a bottle of whiskey and poured some in two glasses. Both men reached for their pipes inside their pockets.

Max handed Logan a glass humidor filled with a Virginia and Latakia blend of tobacco. "Try this one, Alex," he said. "It's a local mixture I get from Blatter's in Montreal. I think you'll like it."

Alex put his tobacco pouch back in his suit jacket and filled his straight black Dunhill bulldog from the jar. Using a lighter from the end table next to him, he lit up at about the same time Max lit his own pipe. A cloud of smoke formed between the two men, momentarily obscuring their faces. As the smoke cleared, they reminisced about Logan's father and about Max's and Logan's time together in North Africa. At one point during the conversation, Logan noticed that Max's eyes had mellowed and were quite warm.

They chatted away, Logan looking for an opening. When he found it, he turned the subject. "You're right. It's great," he said, blowing out a stream of smoke. "The Latakia's top-notch. I'd love to continue on all day like this, but I'm here for a particular reason."

"I figured as much. We talk on the phone frequently enough. When you called from Washington and wanted to see me right away, I deduced you had something cooking on the old stove again. Let me guess: you're thinking about joining the CIA and want my advice."

"No, it's nothing like that," Logan laughed. "Well, almost nothing."

Max was sixty-one years old. Slightly shorter than Logan, he'd put on a few extra pounds since Logan saw him last. His face was narrow, and his hair, which had turned white already, was a wild nest on his head. Max had always kept his hair short and neatly combed. He seemed to have transformed from a lean, fast-moving diplomat-spymaster to a grandfatherly, professorial gentleman.

"You're right about the CIA, though. I'm contracted out with them for one specific job. When I leave here"—he glanced at his watch, for he had a plane to catch soon—"I'm taking a plane to Alexandria, Egypt, to hunt down an MI6 agent and kill him. I need your help."

The two men had always been frank with each other, never pulling their punches. Each of them admired that quality in the other. There was a deeply felt bond, a binding trust, between them that neither time nor distance could break, experienced only among men who have shared secrets and experienced danger and death. If Max was surprised by Logan's revelation, it didn't show on his face.

"Go on," Max said as he puffed on his pipe and sipped his whiskey. "I trust you have more to say on the subject."

Logan set his pipe down on the end table and took a deep breath. He explained the last twelve hours, supplying Max with every detail of his assignment. "What I want to know is this: how do I go about finding Lucky Break in a city of four million people when I don't know whom I'm looking for? He uses a disguise—or more accurately, disguises—that not even MI6 can detect."

Max stared at him for a long minute before saying anything. He raised his eyebrows several times and puffed a little harder on his pipe. He took another sip of whiskey and then put it down. "Well, it certainly sounds like a tricky situation you've gotten yourself into. I have two responses to your dilemma," he said, adjusting himself upright in his chair. "A short one and a long one. The short one is rather easy. Rely on the skills and knowledge you acquired over the years. You possess the best of both that I have ever seen in my career with the government. They'll eventually lead you directly to this rascal, even within the short time frame in which you have to work. Make use of that intuition you have. It always served you well." He paused a moment and then went on. "The longer response is slightly complex." He relit his pipe and blew a cloud of smoke around himself. Logan picked up his own pipe and lit up.

Max continued. "Alex, from 1951 to 1952, Egypt was ravaged by violence and anti-British protests. There were armed clashes between British troops and guerrilla squads composed of students, peasants, workers, and radical intellectuals. During that time, the government's attention moved away from the ethnic, religious, and foreign minorities to the British. In early 1952, the Brits attempted to disarm a troublesome auxiliary police force barracks in Ismailia because the force there had been supporting the protestors. It resulted in the deaths of forty-one Egyptians. This in turn led to anti-Western riots in Cairo as well as Alexandria, resulting in heavy damage to property and the deaths of several foreigners, including eleven British citizens. Many British-owned stores, cinemas, hotels, and offices were damaged during protests and riots." He took a sip of whiskey and then continued. "The Union Flag was burned, and foreign shops were destroyed. Expatriate accommodations were attacked, as was Shepherd's Hotel, a favorite of British expatriates— and mine as well, if I say so myself. At the Turf Club in Cairo, a number of expatriate members were beaten to death, and the club was destroyed. In all, over seven hundred buildings were decimated. It's generally accepted that this outbreak of violence was not planned but was a spontaneous outpouring of anger by people who'd been treated as second-class citizens within their own country. I happen to share that view. Few Egyptians could afford the luxury goods that existed at places like Shepherd's or the Turf Club, as well as most British businesses. Those who could were invariably associated with the corrupt government of King Farouk, who was out the door that same year.

"A great number of British fled the country during that period—perhaps the majority of them, but that's difficult to prove. The question you should ask yourself, Alex, is who stayed and who came into the country after 1952. The Egyptians are experts at keeping track of their foreigners living there. They have records of all foreign nationals residing within their borders, and they keep them updated. Everyone coming and going is diligently recorded. You might consider them paranoid for doing this, but they have legitimate security concerns. Even the British spies and our own CIA officers have their names on those government lists. Of course, if they're not working under the cover of a diplomatic corps, those names would be aliases. If Lucky Break is indeed in Alexandria now, as you say, you could find him. He most assuredly is using an alias. You have no small task ahead of you. I have no idea just how many British foreign nationals are living in Alexandria, but it could be in the hundreds or even several thousands. Do you have any contacts in Alexandria besides family members?"

"I have a cousin on the Alexandrian police force who's the chief of criminal investigations," Logan said.

"Ah, yes. I remember you telling me about him. Shakir is his given name, if I remember correctly."

"Yes."

"Perfect. Perfect!" Max was nearly jumping out of the chair. Logan could see he was excited to be involved, if only to give some advice.

Max puffed on his pipe and then tamped the ash down. "He should be your starting point. He would have access to the list of names of British nationals living in Alexandria. Lucky Break's alias would be on that list. His cover might be that of a journalist, but I doubt it. I would lean toward either an academician or an owner of some kind of business, but nothing too big. He wouldn't want himself known by a great number of people. That should narrow down the numbers. I would certainly look at other possibilities, but only after you have first exhausted those two. Can you trust Shakir?"

"With my life."

"Coming from you, Alex, I find that significant. Then trust him with everything. Confide in him and see whether he can free up some people to help you. You have only seven days. You can't do this one alone. Remember our missions in Casablanca? You liked to work alone, and you were good at it. But whenever time was a critical factor, I always provided you with help—insisted on it, really. You'll need help with this one too. You'll spend most of your time tracking him down. Once you find him, you should have little trouble killing him."

"This all seems overwhelming," Logan said to the spymaster. His eyes moved to the window behind Max. The top edge of the frame cut the sun in half. Several sparrows were flittering around an arborvitae, oblivious to his problem. He focused on Max again. "Frankly," he said, "I'm not certain I can do this in seven days."

Max stared at Logan, now with the same piercing eyes Logan had known during the war. "You can, and you must, my friend. There's an urgency here. There's too much at stake. We simply cannot engage in a nuclear war with the Reds, now can we?"

Chapter 8
A CHANCE ENCOUNTER

Alexandria, Egypt
Friday, July 20
8:05 a.m.

THE AIRCRAFT FLEW LOW OVER THE CITY OF Alexandria, heading north toward the sea. Logan had a window seat and looked down at the place of his birth. It was difficult for him to believe that thirty-nine years ago, he had been an innocent babe somewhere down there, being introduced to the world around him. He had been born during a catastrophic war and had participated in another a little over two decades later. Yet despite some significant changes in Egypt, life had gone on pretty much as it always had for Alexandrians.

How different it must have looked to Alexander the Great when he founded the city so many centuries ago. From the plane Logan could see Pompey's Pillar, the Roman triumphal column, on an ancient acropolis, not far from the hotel where he'd be staying. Although he'd been to the pillar many times, he always marveled at seeing it from the sky. He imagined a god throwing the pillar down like a spear from the heavens and sinking it deeply into the sand, marking a holy spot in the universe. But the spot wasn't particularly holy. It was just a place in the sand to put a monument commemorating the victory of a Roman emperor over an Alexandrian revolt. Impressive as it was, he wondered why the Alexandrians held it in such high esteem, considering what it represented. Maybe it was just for the tourists, he thought.

He shifted his eyes to get a better view of the city. It extended for twenty miles east and west and was the largest city to lie directly on the Mediterranean coast. He saw block after block and mile after mile of buildings that from this height looked all the same to him. But somewhere down there among the multitude of people, somewhere in the wide, busy avenues and the crowded, narrow passageways, somewhere in the thousands of cafés and hotels and restaurants, walking among the Alexandrians, walking among the French and the British and the Italians and the Greeks and the Turks and the Jews, was Lucky Break.

Logan had to stay focused on what he must do in order to find the rogue agent, rather than on all the obstacles he would encounter. If he didn't, he could easily slip into an inertia because he still looked at his mission as overwhelming. Surely, he had cause to believe that. In order to stay focused, he needed an outside force to act upon him relentlessly, to press him forward, hour after hour, day after day. That force would be Lucky Break himself.

Logan would hunt him down and then kill him. The thought of that was exhilarating, and he began mentally preparing himself.

The aircraft continued to fly over the city and the airport until it reached the edge of the Mediterranean Sea. It flew for another mile, and then like a giant, graceful gull, it made a wide, sweeping turn to the left until it was again aligned with the city. When the runway was in sight, the pilot lowered the landing gear and set the plane down smoothly. After exiting the plane, Logan processed through immigration and customs quickly and without incident. The officer who stamped his passport with a tourist visa recognized him from other visits and welcomed him back to the ancient, cosmopolitan city.

Whenever he returned to Alexandria, he always felt as if he were coming home, even though he had been too young to remember much about his early years. It was only on subsequent, frequent visits here after the war had ended that he had gotten to know the city well, nearly as well as a native. Having family here made it that much easier for him. He knew the neighborhoods and the different ethnic quarters. He knew the better parts of the city, and he knew which areas to avoid. He knew Alexandria so well that he considered it his second home. His Egyptian birth had been the result of his father's government job here. Notwithstanding, he loved his relatives and felt extremely close to them—especially to Shakir. They considered each other brothers rather than cousins. The distance between their two countries had only made them closer. *Shakir will be surprised to see me today*, Logan thought.

He left the airport along with other passengers through the main exit, carrying one medium-sized brown leather suitcase. He felt a blast of heat and heard a barrage of shouts. Dozens of taxi drivers stood by their cars with their hands up, vying for the travelers' attention. Each was shouting a mixture of Arabic, English, French, Greek, German, and Italian. Because his skin was the color of café au lait, something he'd inherited from his Egyptian mother, Logan could pass for any number of nationalities. The drivers exploited the use of language to make weary foreigner travelers feel more comfortable as they listened for the sounds of their own tongue. In reality, an Alexandrian taxi driver would know his native Arabic, of course, and perhaps a second or even a third language as well, but the drivers had all learned the basic greetings of languages they couldn't speak at all. It was something they had to do in order to survive in this cosmopolitan city.

Logan looked at the row of taxis in front of him and picked one that he thought could get him to his destination without breaking down. He got into the Morris of a short, stout man in his fifties with a thick, bushy mustache who could pass for Italian, Greek, or Egyptian. Logan told him the address in Arabic, and the taxi jerked away in third gear, perhaps the only gear that worked.

From the airport, it was generally a twenty-minute drive to the city center—Logan's destination—but the morning traffic would make the trip considerably longer. The driver immediately started beeping his horn for no particular reason as he pulled out into traffic. Logan knew he would continue to do so all the way to the bank and then to Logan's hotel. He peered at the one hand grasping the wheel, the palm of the other hand over the horn, the intense look. The drivers all took this position. *Here we come! Out of the way!* Logan thought that in theory, this approach wasn't a bad idea, but it never made the ride shorter. The reality was this: you had bumper-to-bumper traffic in urban congestion, with everyone beeping their horns, going no faster than they otherwise would have without the horns.

The traffic became denser as the driver made his way through it. Along the way, he maneuvered the taxi around slow-moving trams packed with passengers, some clinging to the outside on the running boards; disabled cars being drawn by donkeys; several black American limousines with wealthy pashas in the back seats; horse-drawn gharries, those omnipresent carts belonging to peasants; and other cars and taxis. As if that weren't challenging enough for him, the driver had to watch out for sheep, goats, and camels, who were all competing with the motor traffic. And most assuredly, before he found his destination, there would be a few cars or trucks in his way that had refused to go any farther, camped in the middle of roads with steam hissing from their radiators. And of course, there were people—thousands of people. The driver took all this in stride, and so did Logan. The beeping went on.

Alexandria was a city of noise, but to Logan's ears, it was music. Tram bells rang continuously, and taxi drivers tooted their horns even, like his driver, when they didn't have to. Men with carts yelled loudly at their livestock to keep them moving. Shop and café owners turned their radios up to full volume, playing Arabic music. Dogs barked, and kites screamed from up high. Adding another layer of sound was the occasional drone of airplanes taking off from the nearby airport, and of course, there was the continuous hum of voices speaking different languages, Alexandrians and tourists alike. The cacophony of sounds was so unlike American cities that had Logan been taken here blindfolded without knowing where he was going, he easily would have identified it as Alexandria. The city had a certain rhythm and movement unlike any other.

The taxi finally pulled up in front of Barclays Bank. Logan told the driver to wait, and he got out with his suitcase. A crippled beggar was sitting on the pavement by the door of the bank with his hands extended toward Logan. He was dressed in dirty rags, the original color of which was impossible to discern. His head was covered with a cotton turban that perhaps once had been white. His legs were two twisted wooden vines beneath him; their only use was to prevent him from toppling over. Logan had brought some Egyptian money with him, so he reached into his pocket and pulled out a piastre and placed it in the man's hand before going into the bank.

"Allah is great," the beggar said.

As Logan entered the bank, a young Egyptian man—thirty,

perhaps—dressed in a neatly pressed dark suit approached him. He sported a whiff of a mustache and had a pleasant manner. Logan explained to him that he wanted to get into his safe deposit box. Logan followed him to a counter, where the bank employee pulled out a long rectangular drawer and asked for his name. Logan provided his name but was suddenly worried because he knew he would have to sign his name on a sheet, which would then be compared to the signature card on file. If they didn't match, he would not be able to get into the box.

The employee pulled out his signature card and gave Logan the sign-in sheet. Logan signed his name and then gave the sheet back. The employee held the card next to the sheet and compared the two signatures for what seemed a little too long. Logan detected a slight frown on his face—or was it just his imagination? The young man narrowed his eyes, and Logan watched them jump from one signature to the other. Finally, he told Logan with a reassuring smile to follow him to the vault. Stance must have somehow gotten Logan's signature and had it sent to the CIA officer who had initially rented the box in his name with a phony identification card. Stance had all the bases covered. But why wouldn't he?

Once in the vault, the employee inserted the bank's master key into the box's lock and turned it to the right. Logan did the same with his key. Logan slid the box out and was led to a small private space adjacent to the vault. The employee told Logan to please let him know if he could be of further assistance. Then he left.

Stance placed his suitcase and the deposit box on the metal countertop, side by side, and then he opened both. There were three stacks of money, each bound with a rubber band. One was US notes, and the other two were British and Egyptian. They looked to contain roughly five thousand each, in dollars and pounds. Information was bought and paid for with cash.

Stance had had the foresight to provide it, but Logan didn't think he'd need it. He'd probably use part of the money for his own expenses and nothing more. Cosmopolitan Alexandria was an expensive city, and tourists always paid a premium price for everything. He took some pound notes from a stack and put them into his wallet and then placed the three stacks in his suitcase.

Next, he picked up the gun and examined it. It was a High Standard HDM. Logan had used a pistol like this many times during the war. Stance must have known that. *Damn, what doesn't he know about me?* Logan thought. *The last time I fired it ...* He stopped the thought. He had told himself he would no longer think about that. Not now, not anytime. He had to stay focused on the present. The past was dead. It was Lucky Break who was alive. For now.

He put the gun into the suitcase along with a silencer and three boxes of full metal–jacketed .22 LR rounds. He couldn't understand why Stance had provided so much ammunition. If things went well, he'd need only one bullet.

He closed the suitcase and called for the bank employee. Together, they locked the deposit box. Once in the taxi, he told the driver to take him to the Hotel Cecil.

The driver took the coastal road to avoid heavier traffic and pulled up to the hotel. A muezzin high in a nearby minaret was calling out the *adhan*, summoning the faithful to prayer. Logan, who was not Muslim and not particularly religious generally, enjoyed listening to the voice. It was as much a part of the city as were its ancient structures.

The Hotel Cecil had stood on the same corner since 1929 and overlooked the Corniche, a waterfront promenade that ran along the eastern harbor and that was lined with restaurants, cafés, and nightclubs. The building was a mixture of different architecture that Logan had always admired. The six-storied structure had lancet arches over the top-floor windows,

Islamic ogee-shaped arches on the bottom-floor windows, Moorish-style balconies, and an art deco entrance.

The hotel was located in the heart of the business district and was convenient enough for Logan to use as a base from which to move about the city. It had been, and continued to be, a popular place for wealthy Egyptians to stay, as well as foreigners. The British Secret Service had maintained a suite on the top floor during the last war, and Somerset Maugham, Agatha Christie, Winston Churchill, and Al Capone had all, at one time or another, graced the hotel with their presence.

Directly in front of the hotel was Zaghloul Square, a small park with benches and the former site of Cleopatra's Needle. One of three 240-ton, nearly 69-foot ancient Egyptian obelisks, that single shaft of red granite was now sitting in New York City's Central Park, a gift to the city from a khedive. On previous visits to Alexandria, Logan had sometimes sat in the square, even when he wasn't staying at the hotel, to watch the sun setting over the Mediterranean. He wouldn't do that on this visit.

Logan paid the driver and gave him an extra five pounds for waiting for him at the bank. The doorman immediately reached for his suitcase to carry it inside for him, but Logan hung on to it and thanked him. The lobby was full of American and French tourists, and Logan got behind one of the queues at the front desk. He waited about fifteen minutes before he reached a desk clerk dressed in the hotel's gray uniform smartly trimmed in red. The clerk, young and serious, asked to see Logan's passport, recorded some information, and handed it back to him.

After registering and getting his room key, Logan walked to the elevator. He watched the overhead arrow as it passed the third floor and then the second and ultimately reached the lobby. When the doors slid back and the elevator attendant opened the gates, a woman appeared. She was tall with shoulder-length black hair and wore a white European dress of lightweight material. She wore black high heels, and a gold chain with a pendant at the end hung between her breasts. She carried an expensive cloth bag with the word "Harrods" in bold letters across the top. What Logan noticed most were her stunning green eyes, almost emerald in color, which were staring straight ahead at him.

"Excuse me, but don't I know you from somewhere?" she said to him in Arabic.

"I'm not sure. Do you come here often?"

"I live here."

"In the hotel?"

"Oh no. In Alexandria. I stay in the hotel on occasion."

"Maybe so then. I travel to Alexandria a lot and have stayed here many times."

"Ah, then perhaps we passed each other sometime. Are you staying long on this trip?"

"As long as I need to."

"Good. Then we'll see each other again. The next time, we'll have a coffee together and perhaps a brandy," she said with poise and self-assuredness. With that, she crossed the lobby—her heels clicking on the marbled floor—and left the hotel without looking back.

"Perhaps," he said as his eyes followed her out the door.

He then took the elevator up to the fourth floor and found his room. He set the suitcase on the bed and immediately picked up the phone to call his cousin, Shakir. As he'd anticipated, Shakir was surprised that Logan was in town. Yes, of course, he would have dinner with Logan, but not at a restaurant, Shakir said; they should dine here at his home. His family would be pleased to see him again. Logan explained that he had something important to talk to Shakir about, but it must be in private. So they agreed to meet at a restaurant early that evening.

He set the receiver down and opened his suitcase. He took out the money, gun, silencer, and ammunition, carried the items to the room safe, and locked them inside. He was fatigued by the long trip and needed to rest. Just fatigued? Ha! He was dead on his feet. On the plane, he'd gone over what he would tell Shakir. He would be straightforward with him, as he'd always been. He knew Shakir would do his best to help him. Logan wondered whether that was going to be good enough. Looking for Lucky Break was going to be like looking for a pebble in the ocean. He laughed. *Looking* wasn't quite what he had in mind. One *looked* for something that was misplaced. Lucky Break wasn't misplaced; he was hiding. Logan was determined to hunt him down and kill him, but the odds were not in his favor. Alexandria and its environs covered a large urban area, and Lucky Break was a master of disguises. Somehow he had to reduce those odds. But how?

He poured himself a whiskey from the small bar and sat down in a well-padded armchair, putting his feet up on the ottoman. Then he took out his pipe, filled it, and lit up. *And perhaps a brandy*, the woman from the elevator had said. *What utterly gorgeous and penetrating eyes*, he thought. Yes, he looked forward to seeing her again.

Chapter 9
ALL THINGS TO ALL PEOPLE

10:35 a.m.

DONATELLA MARINETTI LEFT THE HOTEL CECIL and walked down a block to catch the tram that passed by her mother's apartment. As usual, she had money on her mind. More precisely, she was thinking about how she could acquire more of it in the next week. She would do whatever it took to get as much as she could, for it would eventually provide her mother and her with a new life. Her mother had suffered enough. This was Donatella's opportunity to see that whatever time her mother had left on this earth, she would spend it in comfort in the land of her birth. She hated Egypt for what it had done to both of them.

Whenever Naguib was in Cairo, which was the majority of the time, Donatella took the opportunity to use the hotel to look for rich European and American men. After she found one, the snare usually was set at the hotel bar with drinks. In little time, he would invite her to his room. After an hour, she would be in the elevator again, counting her money. She was known quite well by all the hotel staff, who would never dare to interfere with her business transactions because they knew she belonged to Naguib, Nasser's closest minister. And

75

of course, they'd never think of telling him what she did when he wasn't there because no one wanted to experience the rage of a jealous lover who was being cheated on.

Now with only a week before her job with Addison was complete and with her departure from Egypt imminent, she had become bolder. She had decided to seek those rich men out while Naguib was there at the hotel. After all, he never left his suite while he was visiting her. The man she'd just met at the elevator, she determined, must be a wealthy foreigner—perhaps an American. His Arabic was very good, but it must have been a second language for him because he had used a phrase that one rarely heard in Alexandria these days. He would be the one she would tie her leash around first. But this one seemed different from the other men she'd encountered. He was handsome, yes, but there was something magnetic in his eyes to which she'd been drawn immediately. That had taken her by surprise. The eyes were the part of a man Donatella noticed first. That was where the power was. All else would flow naturally from them. But there were few who had power over her. *I must be careful with this one*, she thought, *or I might find myself falling in love again.*

Her body was sore from last night. It always was after she made love with Naguib. He was grossly overweight and enjoyed handling her body roughly. She'd thought about complaining to him when they first began their relationship but then thought better of it because she didn't want to take the risk that he would stop seeing her and seek out someone who enjoyed sex the way he did. There were plenty of beautiful women who would find his money and position attractive. So she'd endured it for the last five years. Her reward was well worth putting her body through this, though. He'd provided her with a lifestyle that she could not have obtained on her own, at least not in Egypt.

When Addison had recruited her in Cairo, her first

assignment had been to lure Naguib into a relationship and become his mistress. Her beauty was the bait, and he'd fallen for her at their first meeting. She'd stalked him out one fine, sunny day in Cairo. He was walking down Nubar Pasha Street near the Ministry of Interior building. She was walking in the opposite direction, going toward him. When he'd gotten within a few feet of her, she pretended to twist her ankle. He reached out to her to prevent her from falling. There was an empty table on a nearby terrace, so he helped her to a chair so that she could get off her feet. Knowing he'd been struck by her beauty, she insisted he sit down as well and have some tea. She'd stroked his ego for the next hour, and before he left (her ankle miraculously healed), she'd accepted his offer to have dinner that night.

In short time, he'd set her up in a flat, and after they'd become close and settled into a routine, she began to probe him discreetly about his job. Kamal Naguib was President Nasser's minister of the interior and also the director of intelligence and internal security services. Next to Nasser himself and very few others in Nasser's circle, he was one of the most powerful men in Egypt. Fortunately for her—and for Addison—Naguib was also a very talkative man, at least to Donatella, who was now his mistress. Words flowed from his mouth, including some on matters of sensitive government intelligence, which she in turn passed on to Addison.

Last month, Donatella had moved back to Alexandria, telling Naguib that her mother had fallen ill, and she needed to be closer to her. Of course, it had been a lie. She needed to be in Alexandria to work closer with Addison in preparation for the assassination. Naguib had been greatly disappointed, but he was willing to make the two-hour drive on the weekends to be with her. After all, this would be just temporary. Over the last five years, he'd come to rely on their intimacy, something that he never had with his wife, so he looked at the drive as a mere inconvenience.

For this latest visit, he'd arrived the night before, and they'd had dinner at the hotel where he kept a permanent suite on the sixth floor. After that, he'd enjoyed her body far into the morning hours. Now she was tired and sore. She'd left him in the suite, telling him she'd return after checking on her mother and doing a few errands. The truth was that she could take this fat, little man only in small doses before needing to breathe fresh air again. Besides, she had many important things to do.

She walked a block to where the tram stopped and waited on the corner. There were others milling about— all young men—talking and laughing at each other's jokes. Donatella ignored them, but she could feel their occasional glances in her direction. She knew they lusted after her, as most men did because of her beauty. She'd experienced this whenever she was in public—this lust. But Egyptian men were mostly reserved, especially the religious ones. They would never make her feel uncomfortable by staring at her. That treatment was reserved for foreign women—especially the blonde-headed ones. Sometimes she wished she'd been born ugly and deformed. Perhaps she could then move about the city without all those eyes secretly glancing at her every movement. But then again, had she been born repulsive, she never would have been recruited by Addison Davies to be a government minister's mistress, and she would have been stuck in this city forever.

Donatella considered Egypt a prison and Alexandria her cell. Although born in Alexandria thirty years ago, she'd never felt Egyptian, even though she was as much so as anyone else here. She felt isolated and disconnected. If her mother had never left Italy, she would have been born in Bologna. That was the place she felt part of and belonged to. Since she was a small girl, her mother had told her stories of Italy, of its rich history and culture. When Donatella was in her midteens, her mother had returned to Bologna to visit relatives and had taken her along. Her mother showed her the house she'd grown up in and all the places that had been part of her childhood. For the first time, she had met her grandparents, her uncles and aunts, and all of her cousins. They'd stayed for three months, and it had been the only time Donatella could remember being truly happy. That had been fifteen years ago, and now the fire within her burned again to return to Italy for good.

Her job as Addison's informant—his spy—was her means to that end. She'd saved every pound she'd made from him, as well as all the money Naguib had lavished upon her, spending only enough to support her mother and herself. In another week when her job ended, Addison would give her the remaining money he owed her. Together with the money from the coin, these earnings would allow her and her mother to return to Italy and start a new life, and in her mind, Egypt would disappear from their lives like a single grain of sand vanishes in the desert.

Donatella heard the tram bell ringing up ahead. As always, it was crowded, so she had to stand and hang onto the railing near a door, which she did awkwardly in her heels. The tram was slow and made frequent stops, but that was fine with her. She had to see her mother first, and she was in no hurry to return to Naguib.

The tram took an hour to arrive on rue Fuad and in front of her mother's flat. There had been a delay along with way because a camel had sat down on the tracks, and its owner could not convince the beast to move. At first, the man had talked to the animal nicely and gently pulled the beast by the rope attached to its halter, trying to coax it along. When that hadn't worked, he'd tried yelling at it, but that too had failed. Out of frustration, he'd grabbed a crop handle and hit it severely a half dozen times. The camel had just calmly looked about, unfazed by the tumult it had created. Clearly, it had no respect for its master. As a last resort, the poor man, who felt personally responsible for blocking traffic on one of the busiest streets in Alexandria, had asked a nearby food vendor for some hot coals, which he had then set under the animal's flank. In short order, the beast had made some horrible sounds and risen. Pleased with himself, the owner had then pulled it off the tracks, and the camel had followed behind him willingly, but not without a certain amount of resentment.

Upon entering her mother's building, Donatella passed the stairs leading to the flat and went down a short hallway to a small cubby built under the staircase. She opened the door and went inside, leaving the door ajar so that she could see by the light of the hallway. She reached into her Harrods bag and pulled out a plain black dress, the kind that many lower-class Egyptian women wore. She slipped it over her head. It went from just below her neck to nearly her feet. She patted it down so that it hung freely. She then took off her black heels and put on leather sandals, placing the heels inside her bag. She couldn't very well wear them and her white European dress to visit her mother, who had never seen her daughter dressed that way. Donatella wondered what her mother would have said had she suddenly appeared in that attire. She left the bag in the cubby and shut the door.

She climbed the stairs to the fifth floor. Her mother was sitting on the small balcony as usual, watching the continuous flow of people and traffic below on one of Alexandria's busiest streets.

"Ciao, Mama. How are you feeling today?" Donatella asked in Italian.

"My legs ache, but I'll be fine," she said.

"Come in, and I'll make us some coffee."

Donatella's mother got up and moved slowly to the kitchen table and sat down. "Where have you been all night? I worry when you don't come home."

"I've been out, Mama, just out. You don't have to worry about me. I'm a big girl now," Donatella said, leaning down and giving her a hug.

Donatella put some water on the single-burner stove to boil and then started to gather the ingredients to make koshari. She would use the lentils, rice, and macaroni that she'd cooked the day before and kept in a small ice box that she'd bought.

"I worry that you will get into some kind of trouble. I don't know what you do or where you go. You tell me nothing," her mother said weakly, almost pouting.

"There's nothing to tell. I work at the market, that's all."

"The market is closed at night."

"Then I go out. I'm still young enough to want a good time."

Donatella chopped some tomatoes, garlic, green peppers, and onions and pushed them aside. Then she made some coffee and gave a cup to her mother.

"Don't worry, Mama. We'll be leaving for Italy soon, and then you won't have to be concerned about me. We'll be living together, and you can see me every day." It had been so much easier for both of them when Donatella was living in Cairo. She could come and go as she pleased without worrying her mother. But returning to Alexandria had made things different. Her mother worried constantly about her seemingly erratic behavior, and she felt guilty about it. She never wanted to be the cause of any hardship to her mother.

She reached for a frying pan and set it on the burner, putting some oil in it. When it was hot enough, she cooked the vegetables separately, putting each batch of chopped cooked vegetables on a different plate when they were done.

"How did you get that much money for us to move back home? You never told me."

"I did tell you, Mama, but you've forgotten. I saved it. I've been saving my salary for a long time for this." It would kill her mother if she knew how Donatella was really earning her money.

"I still don't understand how you could save that much. Cairo is an expensive city to live in. And you were working at a market there too," she said, sipping her coffee.

"I just did, Mama. In a short time, we'll be in Bologna with family again, and we'll both be happy. Isn't that what you wanted?"

"Yes, I miss the old country so much, but I always thought returning there was just a dream of yours. And now you say we're going soon," she said, lost in thought.

"We'll be home again in a week, maybe two at the most." Donatella looked at her own cup of cooling coffee. She'd forgotten to drink it.

When all the vegetables were cooked, she took a larger pan and began layering it, first with the rice and then the macaroni. Next, she poured the lentils on top and then added a layer of onions and green peppers. She mixed some cumin, salt, and garlic into the tomatoes and poured it over the entire dish, carefully working it in. Finally, she took the chickpeas she'd cooked the day before and dropped them evenly across the top with the tips of her fingers. She lowered the flame and let the koshari cook slowly.

"We'll be happy, Mama. You'll see. We'll be part of a family again. You'll see."

"I hope you haven't been doing something that's going to get you into trouble."

"At my age? Don't be silly, Mama."

While Donatella cleaned up the pots and pans, her mother reminisced aloud about the old days back in Italy. Donatella typically could listen to her mother's stories about Italy for hours, but not today. When the koshari had cooked long enough, she put it in the ice box and then wiped her hands on a cloth.

"There, Mama, you'll have something nice to eat for a few days. I have to leave now, but I promise to return later, and we'll talk some more."

"When will I see you again?" she asked, looking up at her daughter with sadness in her eyes.

"In a few days. We're very busy at work. I'll stay with a friend who works there too. She lives a block away from the market. I'll be back soon. We'll need to start packing some things when I return." She embraced her mother, told her she loved her, gave her a kiss on the cheek, and then left.

Donatella had something important to do in preparation for July 26, before returning to the hotel and to Naguib, so she took the tram across the city again and went to the catacombs.

Chapter 10
OFF THE RECORD

6:30 p.m.

LOGAN AND HIS COUSIN, CAPTAIN SHAKIR EL Mahdeya, sat in the back of the dining room of the Hotel Claridge, having their dinner and catching up on each other's lives. The last time they'd seen each other had been the previous summer, so they had much to talk about now. Logan was restless and eager to tell his cousin about his reason for being in Alexandria, but unlike in America, business and other formalities came second to casual conversation in Egypt. So he continued to listen as Shakir updated him about the last year, detailing several amusing incidents he and his family had experienced.

The hotel was located near the intersection of rues Fuad and Nebi Daniel, and though it was quite acceptable in every way, it had seen better days. Its decline had come in subtle stages and over time. First, there was the paint that was peeling away in the corners of rooms that should have been scraped, sanded, and repainted but were, in fact, ignored. And then there were the worn spots in the carpets in the lobby and in the hallways. The management simply placed cloth mats over them. The menu in the restaurant, once the finest in Alexandria, no longer offered dishes that had made the restaurant famous. The food was quite delicious, but it had lost that certain exquisiteness that had made the restaurant— and by extension, the hotel—stand out above the rest. As a result, it no long attracted the same kind of people as it had back in its heyday of the twenties and thirties, and tourists themselves were now staying at the more fashionable hotels such as the Hotel Cecil and the Metropole, both of which had made recent renovations. Now the Hotel Claridge was no more special than the multitude of other mediocre hotels and restaurant available to people with limited incomes. That was precisely the reason Logan had chosen to meet Shakir here, knowing they would be able to have an intimate conversation without a horde of people around them. The restaurant had only a few others in it, but those guests were sitting near the entrance, so the two men were free to speak without fear of being overheard. Shakir sipped his wine and put down the glass.

Logan noticed that Shakir had failed to mention his sister when he talked about his family. He knew it was a touchy subject with Shakir, but curiosity got the best of him. "And Aria—how's she doing?" he asked.

Shakir looked away for a moment and then back at him. "I don't know how she is. None of us do. We haven't seen her in over a year." He looked down at his glass briefly and ran his tongue over his lips. "You know she's always had a wild streak in her. I fear that's gotten her into trouble now."

Logan was sad to hear that because he'd always liked her, even though she was the one family member he didn't know well. He'd seen her wild streak as simply her natural inclination for independence, and he'd admired that in her. It was far more difficult for a woman to be independent in Egypt than it was in America. Women here had to contend with many more restrictions and taboos. It was easier for them to conform to familial and societal expectations, which most did. He looked up at Shakir and saw that his eyes had watered up.

"Have you looked for her?" Logan asked.

"My father asked me not to, and I agreed. She's not a child any longer. She has to be responsible for herself. We can't help her if she doesn't want the help. If I found her and brought her back, she would only leave again." He ran his hand over his eyes, and in a voice just above a whisper, he said, "I think she's selling herself."

There was a long, uncomfortable moment during which they looked down at the table and said nothing to each other.

Then, without warning, Shakir broke the silence in a loud voice. "So are you going to tell me what your mysterious visit is all about, or are you going to sit there like a lump of bread and keep me wondering, my brother?"

The two men had always referred to each other as brothers and never as cousins. Shakir was as tall and handsome as Logan. He combed his black hair—short on the sides and longer on top—straight back and parted it on the left side, and he had the demeanor of a military officer. Except for Shakir's thick mustache, Logan thought he looked much like Rudolph Valentino and had often teased him about it. Rather than wearing the uniform of the Alexandrian police, tonight he wore a white cotton suit because from here, he had to perform undercover duties at another location.

"Yes, I'll tell you," said Logan, "but first you must assure me that what I say to you goes no further than this table." Logan trusted Shakir with his life, but this mission was so important that he needed to hear Shakir's words spoken so that there would be no chance of the slightest of misunderstandings. Logan was quite aware from past experiences that when he passed on secret information to another person, it increased the chances of a leak. The person with whom he trusted the information could always slip up and reveal it to another, unaware that he'd even done so. Or—as likely, perhaps even more so—the confidant could tell just one other person, with the admonition that the other person not reveal it to anyone else, which, of course, that other person usually did. The best of spies fell prey to this because it was a grim task to keep a secret to oneself. There was a certain inclination that compelled a person to want to share it. The consequences not only were serious but could even be deadly. Logan hoped he hadn't insulted his brother with the demand.

"Of course, Alex, you have my assurance," Shakir said, unfazed by his brother's secrecy. "But first, let's order some drinks."

Logan caught the attention of the waiter, and after they ordered two cognacs, Shakir took a cigar from his suit-coat pocket and lit up. Logan could not relax enough to light up his pipe. He remembered Max's advice about telling Shakir everything, leaving nothing out. Shakir needed to know every detail of the mission if he were going to be of any use to Logan. Under these circumstances, it made little sense to tell him only a few details.

For the next hour, Logan explained why he was in Alexandria, pausing only when the waiter returned with their drinks. Shakir sat listening to him, his attention fully focused on his brother. He interrupted Logan only twice, seeking clarification on some details. When Logan finished, Shakir picked up his drink for the first time and finished it all at once.

"My first response, Alex, is that we need to inform Nasser's security unit in Cairo immediately. This operation is too big for one man to handle. How could your handler in Virginia possibly think you could do this by yourself?" He puffed on his cigar slowly, having gone through only half of it in the last hour.

Logan hadn't expected this reaction from him. "Shakir, we

can't tell the security unit or any other agency about this. I'm adamant about that." Did he not understand the importance of secrecy? It was imperative that Logan convince him of this. "If we inform them, and Nasser cancels his trip to Alexandria on the twenty-sixth, Lucky Break will plan another assassination attempt. He's highly skilled at changing his appearance, so he is free to move about the city at will. And from what I've been told about him, he's a very patient man. But we both know that Nasser will not hide from his enemies. He's never done so in the past, and he won't do that now. He always rides about wherever he is in an open car with crowds of people around him. If the authorities were to conduct a mass search for an assassin, Lucky Break would eventually find out. Have no doubt about that. Then he would blend into Alexandria like a chameleon even more so. At most, they'd only scare him off temporarily. But I assure you, he'd be back. We can't take that chance. I have to find him by myself and kill him in the next week, but I need your help." Logan wiped the sweat from his forehead with a napkin. He began to wonder whether his cousin would do something crazy on his own but immediately felt guilty about the thought because he'd never known Shakir to act impulsively or irrationally. Shakir had a cool, methodical brain, quite suited to the work he did.

"I see your point. But if you fail to find him and he succeeds, and if someone finds out that we knew about this beforehand and didn't inform Nasser's security, we will both be hanged within the first twenty-four hours of being discovered." Shakir looked at Logan, waiting for his response and calmly blowing smoke.

Logan hadn't thought about this possibility. He'd involved Shakir the second he started to explain the mission to him. Now he began to wonder whether that had been a wise thing to do. After all, Shakir had a wife and children to consider, which Logan didn't. In Casablanca, he'd always put his missions above his own personal safety. There had been risks he was willing to accept to ensure their success. But he and the men he had worked with had been eager volunteers. Shakir wasn't. Then he remembered the words he'd heard just yesterday: *Rely on the skills and knowledge you acquired over the years. You possess the best of both that I have ever seen in my career with the government. They will eventually lead you directly to this rascal even within the short time frame in which you have to work.*

"I'll have to take that risk, Shakir. If you don't want to become further involved, I'll understand, and it ends here. If I were to fail and be found out, you know I'd never reveal your name." There it was. He'd provided Shakir a way out.

There was silence at the table for a long minute. Logan could see that Shakir was considering his options. Suddenly, Shakir turned around in his chair quite abruptly and threw a hand up toward the waiter. He ordered two more drinks. When the drinks came, Shakir broke the silence. "How can I assist you?" he said.

Logan knew that once Shakir decided to do something—anything—he would follow it through to the end.

"Lucky Break has an informant who's been providing him with intelligence that could only come from someone in Nasser's close inner circle. The informant must be either a cabinet minister or someone who has close access to one. If he's a member of the cabinet, who would be the most likely person? Perhaps someone who doesn't fully share Nasser's vision for Egypt." He leaned over the table. "Think of one single person, Shakir. If we find that person, I'll do what's necessary to find out from him who Lucky Break is and where he is."

Shakir thought for a minute while sipping his cognac. "As you know," he said, "our president has been plagued by assassination attempts. Because of this, Nasser has had the

Cairo police investigations unit keep track of every move his ministers make, both day and night. Of course, they are the ones closest to him, and most have been at his side in different capacities since he was prime minister, before he became president. The surveillance has been going on for the last year. Though he's aware that the British and French have been behind many of the past attempts, Nasser fully understands that coups are often initiated by those closest to a president."

Nasser should know, Logan thought.

"The head of investigations in Cairo reports directly to Nasser himself. This is all done in secrecy. Very few people know about this—certainly not the ministers—and the chance of a leak is zero because the consequence would be extremely severe."

"So how do you know about this?"

"I'll get to that. As I said, Nasser's ministers have been and continue to be under constant surveillance. None have shown any unusual behavior that would make us suspect they are not loyal to the president. Because we have less than a week to find Lucky Break, I don't think it would benefit us to focus on that angle. I don't doubt the intelligence that there is an informant, but it must be someone other than a cabinet minister." He relit his cigar and puffed gently.

Logan had never engaged with Shakir in his role as Alexandria's chief of investigations, and he was impressed by the calm, disciplined way in which he thought. However, he was not going to exclude the possibility of a minister being an informant quite yet.

"Now to answer your question as to how I know all about this. One of the ministers Cairo has been monitoring is Kamal Naguib, Nasser's minister of the interior. He's also the director of intelligence and internal security services. You might even say that he's my boss," he said, smiling. "Needless to say, he is in the president's inner circle and is a very powerful man in the government. As I said, Cairo has found nothing concerning any of the ministers that would suggest disloyalty, and this, of course, includes Naguib. He's had a mistress for at least the year he's been under surveillance—a woman by the name of Donatella Marinetti, an Egyptian of Italian descent. This, too, is nothing unusual because all the ministers have their mistresses. The security branch has investigated the backgrounds of each one and has cleared them. None have criminal records or suspicious behaviors.

"A month ago, Marinetti moved to Alexandria, her birthplace, to care for her ailing mother. Naguib changed his habits and now comes to Alexandria to be with her frequently, mostly on the weekends. That's how I became involved in the president's security. When Naguib leaves Cairo, I get a phone call from a certain man in the investigations unit. I personally monitor Naguib when he's here. We tapped his phone at the hotel in which he stays. When he's in the city, that's all I do— watch him. He stays at the Hotel Cecil by the Corniche, and Marinetti is there with him. Naguib has a suite permanently reserved for himself. He pays for it whether he's in the city or not. My job has been very easy. He almost never leaves the hotel when he's here, and his phone calls are usually to his subordinates in Cairo. They discuss government matters and nothing more. I should be at the hotel right now. He came in earlier than usual, and I was involved in a case when I got the phone call, but I couldn't leave what I was doing. I sent one of my men to sit in the lobby. That's where I'm going when we're finished here, to relieve him.

"Marinetti comes and goes freely, but I don't keep track of her. My job is Naguib. However, I did have one of my men shadow her in the beginning. We know that she lives with her mother. We also know where she buys much of her food. Apparently, she enjoys British imports because she goes to a particular shop several times a week to buy provisions.

Tracking her became repetitive, so I pulled the officer off. As far as we know, she doesn't work. I'm sure the minister provides for her and her mother. Naguib is just another powerful minister who can afford to keep a mistress. He's a short, fat, bald man, and he's very wealthy. Marinetti is a young, gorgeous woman who sees nothing but his money. She flatters him, and he's willing to pay for it. As you know, this is very common here. Very boring from an investigative point of view."

"You know, I'm staying at the same hotel."

"Excellent, my brother. Then perhaps you can mind Naguib for me," he said, laughing. Then he became more serious. "I told you all this about Naguib and his woman because I know you eventually would have found out. I would forget looking for someone who's close to Nasser. I don't think you have time for that. I would focus what little time you do have on another strategy. Do you have another one?"

Logan considered what Shakir had just told him, and he had to agree with him. If he'd had more time, he would have considered that angle. Instead, he decided to work the advice Max had given him. "Yes. What I need right away, Shakir, is a list of British nationals who've lived in Alexandria since 1952, especially those who've come here recently."

"That's easy enough. When we're finished, we'll swing by police headquarters, and I'll get it for you. Then we'll drive back to the hotel together, if that's where you're going."

Shakir drove east on the tree-lined Canopic Way, the ancient thoroughfare of Alexandria. He turned left at the Moharrem Bey police station on rue D'Aboukir and parked on the side of the street. Known as the Caracol by all in Alexandria, the headquarters was situated at the intersection of the road that led to Rond Point and looked more like a castle than a police station, with its high stone tower at the corner. At the bottom of the tower was the main entrance, and at the top was a clock, a present from Britain for Edward VII's coronation.

Logan had vague memories of this area. He remembered the tower on the corner because that was where the tram turned on its way to Rond Point and to El Shallalet Park, where his parents had often taken him on Sunday afternoons. Within the park were the ruins of the ancient city walls of Alexandria. As a young boy, Logan had climbed about the structure, while his father would explain to him what it was. Of course, at the age of four, he couldn't understand, but as an adult, he'd since discovered its historical significance. He hadn't been back to this area of the city since he was a child, and he decided that he would like to see the park again before he returned to Georgetown, but now was not the time.

Logan followed Shakir into the building and down a long hallway to his office.

Shakir pulled a folder from his files in a cabinet and set it on his desk. "Here are the names of all British nationals residing in the city. The lists are updated as people come and go. There are also passport photos. If you lose the file, it would place me in an embarrassing situation with Cairo," he said, smiling at Logan. "As you know, when tourists arrive at their hotels, they're required to show their passports. The hotels send us their names, their countries of origin, and their passport numbers daily. When they leave, they also notify us, at which point their names are scratched. We keep that information in a different folder. Would you have any use for it?"

"I'll have my hands full with this list," he said, looking down at the thick folder of the British nationals. "But I may have to look at the tourists if I come up empty."

During the drive to the police headquarters, Logan had thought about what Shakir had told him about the minister and his mistress. In Casablanca, it had been relatively common

to arrange for a woman—and on the rare occasion, a man—
to have an affair with a Vichy official and to spy on him. He
remembered that some very important information had been
obtained that way. Of course, he also remembered ...

"Do you have a picture of the mistress of that minister ...
what's his name?"

"Kamal Naguib?"

"Yes, Naguib."

"I don't. If there is one, it's probably in Cairo. My brother,
I know exactly what you're thinking. You're staying at the
same hotel as Naguib, and so it would be convenient for you to
do a little snooping around. I'm telling you, don't waste your
time with that. As I already assured you, all of the ministers'
mistresses have been thoroughly investigated and have been
cleared by our unit in Cairo. None had any criminal records or
any behaviors that could be considered suspicious. Your time
would be better spent looking through the names in that file."
He paused a moment. "Ah, I get it! You don't think you're going
to have enough work to do with them."

Shakir was probably right. Logan couldn't afford to waste
any of the little time he had left. "Okay, point taken," he said,
returning the smile that Shakir had given him earlier.

"For the time you're here," Shakir said, "I'll be in the lobby
of the hotel for the remainder of the weekend and in my office
here most other times. If I'm not, they'll know where to find
me. If you need to contact me, tell them you're my brother,
and it's urgent that you talk to me. I'll let them know myself
that you may call. Otherwise, you can reach me at home. Let
me know how else I can help you. Should you decide you
need extra eyes and ears, I'll make some men available to
you. I'll tell them that we're after a common foreign criminal
who cheated business owners out of money. That happens
frequently enough here in Alexandria, so the story won't
arouse any suspicion."

Logan thanked him for his help, and before they left, they embraced each other in a way that solidified their commitment to finding Lucky Break.

They drove to the Hotel Cecil in silence, for they'd already done much talking this evening. Along the way, a persistent thought kept stabbing at Logan's brain. He had no idea how long he could ignore it. He just couldn't shake those green eyes of the woman he'd met at the elevator at his hotel. Had she not said that they would have coffee together soon? And maybe a brandy?

Chapter 11
KNOWING WHICH WAY
THE WIND BLOWS

Saturday
2:15 a.m.

LOGAN SAT AT THE DESK IN HIS HOTEL ROOM and set a match to his favorite pipe: a straight, black, sandblasted Dunhill bulldog. Once the tobacco caught fire, he watched the flame dance about the top of the bowl from his long and controlled draws. He blew smoke out; at the same time, he lightly tamped the ash down. He then repeated the ritual with another match, as if it were some ancient, sacred, pyrolatric ceremony.

He wasn't depressed. He would say so himself if you asked him. It was true he wasn't very happy, but that was a far cry from being depressed. Depression suggested a loss of interest and a loss of hope, neither of which applied to him. Alexander Logan had a monumental task before him, and the clock was ticking away. The immediacy of it all, along with the dark knowledge of the consequences if he failed, made him feel like a two-ton boulder was on his back. He imagined what it must have been like for Sisyphus to roll his own boulder up a hill, only to have it roll back down again. At least Sisyphus didn't have to carry it on his back. The pressure weighed on Logan greatly, but it also served to spur him on. During the war, he'd been a problem solver. That was what he had done best: he'd solved problems. As a spy, he'd relished the challenges set before him. Now he had the biggest problem of his life to solve—knowing which way the wind blew.

Earlier that evening, he'd gone through the file Shakir had given him, separating the people he could eliminate right away—females, dependent children, the elderly. He'd spread the others across his bed: fifty-three male British nationals remained. Each sheet listed the man's age, address, phone number, marital status, profession, and place of employment and included a copy of a passport photo. First, he'd scrutinized each photo to discern whether anything stood out—anything that drew his eyes to some facial feature that seemed unnatural. They were all would-be assassins to him. Lucky Break's photo *had* to be among them, and he most assuredly would be wearing a disguise in the photo.

Some of the men wore glasses and had bushy eyebrows. A number of them had mustaches, and a few wore beards, but most were clean-shaven. Some had long hair, some had short hair, and a half dozen or so were bald—or nearly so. Their hair color ran the spectrum. There were men in their twenties and men in their sixties, with the majority falling somewhere in between. He took a closer look at the photos of the older men, looking for signs of anything that might point to someone younger in disguise. Lucky Break's face was looking back at him from one of these photos; he just couldn't tell which one. All of the faces looked quite natural to him. *This guy is good*, he thought. *Very good.*

Logan was good at reading faces and body language. Max had taught him well. During training, Logan had had to interrogate prisoners, with his own fellow trainees playing the role of prisoners, as he himself did for them. In these scenarios, the other trainees had been given a secret to keep and had been told to lie to him. Max had wanted them to use their own natural instincts to cover the lie. When lying, everyone displayed certain universal mannerisms, speech patterns, and body language that were nearly impossible to hide. Logan had learned what those were.

But those interrogations had been done with actual people, not photos. The idea of interrogating a photo made Logan chuckle to himself. These photos told him nothing. Any one of them could Lucky Break.

If he'd had a month in which to track them all down, he would have done so, but even then, the task would have been daunting enough. But he didn't have that kind of time, so he set his pipe down on the desk, leaning it against a thick glass ashtray so that it wouldn't fall and spill the ash, and got up and walked over to the bed. He bent over and began reviewing the data on each man, one by one, eliminating the ones who he thought were least likely to be a British intelligence agent capable of assassinating the president of Egypt.

He'd done something similar to this once before, in North Africa during the war. In his main duty station of Casablanca, an Italian spy who'd been deeply embedded in a cover had somehow gotten information concerning food shipments arriving in the port and had begun feeding the information to the Gestapo and the Vichy authorities. Logan had been monitoring those shipments because hidden among the food were small arms that were to be eventually used against the Vichy government. What tipped Logan was that the authorities suddenly began searching the ships far more carefully than they'd done before. Previously, they'd simply pried the tops off the crates and rummaged around a bit until they were satisfied. Now they were emptying the contents of the crates and searching them, as if they were looking for something specific. In no time, they found the handguns, although there was no way they could trace them directly to the vice consuls.

Eventually, Logan had found another way to get the weapons into the country; but in the meantime, he had to find the informant because he feared that the spy would be used in another capacity to undermine his team's covert operations. There were a dozen Italians whom he suspected; all had something to do with shipping and receiving at the docks, and all had some contact with the US consulate office. Time was critical, so he drew up a list of names using specific criteria he'd devised and put the most likely one at the top and the least likely one at the bottom, with the others arranged somewhere in between, depending on how closely they met the criteria. He then took two at a time and watched their every movement, looking for suspicious behaviors.

In three days, he had his spy—an affable young man who'd been overly friendly to everyone: coworkers, German guards, French bureaucrats, and even Logan himself. At the docks, he'd been constantly telling jokes in several languages that made everyone laugh. Logan planted some false information in a cargo manifest and watched the man as he looked it over and then passed it on to a guard. That same night, Logan lured him out of a bar, into a dark, adjacent alleyway, and broke his neck. The spy had been number two on his list.

He decided to use a similar strategy here. He gathered up all the files and began examining them. He pulled those who worked in a diplomatic capacity or as academicians or who owned or worked in a small business and set them aside in three piles. He then went through those piles and eliminated anyone who had a family with children living with him here in Alexandria because it was improbable, though not impossible, that an MI6 agent would have his family with him. But Logan had to admit it would be an excellent cover. Stance had never said whether Lucky Break was married, and Logan realized that Lucky Break could have acquired a family here to add to his cover. Logan gambled that he hadn't.

The number of files now numbered fourteen; that was something Logan could handle. He no longer felt overwhelmed by them. He went back to his desk, relit his pipe, and reviewed his notes:

Culverton D. Duncan, age 58. Married. Children grown and living in England. Owns Stanley Bay Jewellery. Seventeen years in Alexandria.

Rowland Crichlow, age 54. Single. Hotel manager at the Metropole Hotel. Ten years in Alexandria.

Patrick Murphy, age 66. Single. Professor of French and English literature at Alexandria University. Twenty-one years in Alexandria.

Clive Middleton, age 34. Married. No children. Works for a British development agency. Three years in Alexandria. Worked two years in Cairo before that.

Humphrey Porter, age 47. Married. No children. Operates a small retail business. Five years in Alexandria.

Daniel Dexter MacGregor, age 59. Divorced. Worked at the British consulate for six years in Alexandria.

John Campbell, age 39. Single. Vice consul at the British consulate. Worked at the

British embassy in Cairo for five years, then transferred to Alexandria three weeks ago.

David Derek Hallows, age 61. Married, no children. Professor of biological sciences at Alexandria University. Twenty-five years in Alexandria.

Willoughby Jones, age 43. Single. Works at the British consulate. Seven years in Alexandria.

Simon Honeyborne, age 52. Single. Assistant professor of languages at Alexandria University. Five years in Alexandria.

George Sedgewick, age 49. Married. Family in London. Owner of a British importer/exporter wholesale company. Ten years in Alexandria.

Thomas Aldwinckle, age 58. Married. Professor of Egyptian history at Alexandria University. Eighteen years in Alexandria.

Addison Davies, age 63. Single. Owns and operates Davies Imported Foods. Five years in Alexandria.

Neville Carter, age 54. Single. Works at the British consulate. Two years in Alexandria. Six years at the British embassy in Cairo.

Those over fifty years old went to the bottom of the pile. He decided to choose four names from the fourteen as his first set of prime targets. It was going to be guesswork. He stared at each name. *Which one are you, Lucky Break?* He went from one file to the next, his eyes jumping to each picture as he did. He puffed and tamped his pipe. *Where are you, you bastard?*

He finally separated four files: Campbell, Jones, Sedgewick, and MacGregor. Three of the four worked in the British consulate, with one being the vice consul. The other one owned a small business. One was over fifty, but he could be using a disguise. He had a perfect cover working in the consulate and had been there for six years. He would be fourth on Logan's list of suspected assassins.

It was 4:10 a.m. when he looked at his watch. He was dead tired, but he knew he wouldn't sleep. Thankfully, Logan could function with little or no sleep for long periods. He drew on his pipe and blew the smoke out and then set it down. He went over to the more comfortable armchair and sat down, putting his feet on the ottoman. He rested his arms on the chair and closed his eyes. He pictured a lit candle in his mind. He focused on the steady flame and emptied his mind of everything, including Lucky Break, and let the tension melt away from his body. For thirty minutes, he breathed deeply, imagining his muscles relaxing as his mind drifted to the point that separated consciousness from unconsciousness. When he finished, he felt as if he had slept for eight hours.

He opened his eyes. His first thought was of Lucky Break, who, like Faust, had sold his soul to the devil. Logan would dearly love to know what Lucky Break feared the most. He could use it against him. He hoped that Lucky Break *did* fear something because a man who feared nothing could do anything he pleased.

Logan stood up, slipped into his jacket, and walked to the safe. He opened it and got out his gun and silencer. He dropped the magazine, checked to make sure it was full, and slammed it back in place. He placed the silencer in his jacket pocket and tucked the gun into his belt at the small of his back. He then went to the desk and picked up the files, looking at the top one. In less than an hour, he would be seeking out his first target: John Campbell.

The game was afoot.

Chapter 12
HUNTING SEASON

5:15 a.m.

ASSOCIATE PROFESSOR ALEXANDER RASHIDI Logan walked across the lobby of the Hotel Cecil wearing a tan seersucker suit. His shoes echoed off the shiny greenish-black marbled floor, attracting the attention of Captain Shakir El Mahdeya, who stood at the front desk, leaning an elbow on the counter and talking to the hotel clerk. The two men glanced at one another out of the corners of the eyes, but neither acknowledged the other's presence. Logan thought that Shakir must have made arrangements with the hotel when he first began his surveillance here to play the role of house detective; otherwise, staff would have begun to ask too many questions about his continued presence on the weekends.

As Logan passed Shakir, a pang of guilt shot through him for having involved Shakir in this mission. When Stance had read off the names of Logan's Egyptian relatives during their encounter in Virginia, he hadn't mentioned Shakir's immediate family—his wife and two children. The children now were adults in their early twenties and were enrolled at the university. Maybe Stance hadn't known Shakir had a family. That was unlikely because he'd known everything thing else. But Stance hadn't involved Shakir in this mission; Logan himself had done that.

If it all went down the drain and Nasser was assassinated, the president's security detail would investigate. They'd eventually find out that Shakir and Logan had known about the threat a week before and hadn't notified the authorities. They had ingenious methods of finding out information. Such a discovery would mean the death penalty for both of them. However, the government would almost certainly go after Shakir's family as well. That was how they operated. It was always the families. Before hanging Shakir, they would torture him in front of his family, or vice versa, and then they would kill them all. They'd feed the press the lie that Shakir had been the mastermind behind the plot.

Logan didn't have to go through with this mission; he didn't have to risk Shakir's family. He had the power to stop it now. He could tell Shakir to notify the right person, who in turn would then notify Nasser. If the president then decided to give his speech and was assassinated, at least Logan and Shakir would not be culpable; Shakir's family would be safe.

However, should the assassination attempt fail, Lucky Break would just lie low and wait for another time, and the stakes would be the same: Soviet nuclear warheads aimed at London and Paris and the beginning of World War III imminent. No, Logan thought, he had to go through with the mission. He had to find Lucky Break and kill him before any of that could happen. He could no longer afford to entertain thoughts that would compromise what he had to do. He swallowed some phlegm that was caught in the back of his throat as he opened the door of the hotel and stepped outside.

The weather was cool at this time of the morning for Alexandria. Fighting back his fears, he did nevertheless feel refreshed and energized and eager to start his pursuit of the man who could change the world. He also felt more self-assured after having narrowed down the names to just fourteen. He couldn't have done any better than this, and he hoped it would be good enough. He had to keep in mind what Max had told him two days ago in Westmount: Logan was the best Max had seen in his career. Logan had always hated accolades because they'd always put pressure on him to continue to live up to them. The pressure was on him once again.

The city was stretching its arms, trying to wake up. This was Alexandria at its quietest, and the streets took on an eerie hue. Logan could smell the sea from where he stood, and this always had a calming effect on him. The few people who were out were probably going to their jobs, their long, decisive strides suggesting they were going somewhere in particular. The motor traffic was beginning to perk up, and in the distance, he could hear the harsh braying or moaning of an animal, most likely a recalcitrant donkey or a camel. Logan started walking west, passing shops that were still closed. He could see their owners through the windows, busily preparing for the day. A half-empty tram went by him, but he ignored it. He was looking for a taxi.

Normally, there would have been a half dozen taxis at the hotel parked along the forecourt, but it was a little too early for them because few hotel guests were up at this time of the morning. Those who were would be eating breakfast rather than looking for a taxi to take them to a tourist site or to the airport. It would take Logan thirty minutes or so to reach Pompey's Pillar, where he'd be sure to find one. The slight breeze on his face felt good. In a few hours, it would be much hotter, and there wouldn't be any relief until much later that night, breeze or no breeze.

He crossed a street and continued southwest toward the pillar while thinking about his first target. If anyone fit the profile of a would-be assassin, John Campbell did: thirty-nine, single, and vice consul—an excellent cover for an MI6 agent and killer. He'd arrived in Alexandria three weeks ago from working at the British embassy in Cairo, where he most likely had recruited his informant. How long had he been ignoring MI6's cables? Logan couldn't remember, but it must not have been more than three weeks. Perfect.

Physical attributes: six feet tall, 165 pounds, medium-cut blond hair, mustache, and—Logan pulled out the passport picture and looked at it—long ears that stood out like an elephant's. He glanced at the picture several times while he was walking to commit it to memory. However, he knew that if this was Lucky Break, he was looking at a disguise. If Campbell had changed it, that would only make his job that much more difficult.

At this point, Campbell would stay clear of the consulate office. However, Logan couldn't understand why he would have registered a private address with the local police. It would be too easy for someone to find him there. The address could be a ruse—he had to put down some address—but it did leave a doubt. What if it was Campbell's real address? The more he thought about it, the less sure he was becoming. If Campbell was not Lucky Break, then the address should be legitimate. However, this was not the time for Logan to be second-guessing himself. Campbell's profile had placed him at the top of the list, so Logan had to check him out. If it turned out that Campbell wasn't Lucky Break, Logan would go on to the number two person on the list, and then the number three person, and then the fourth, and so on until he found him.

As he approached the pillar, the nearby sphinx looked down upon him. Pompey's Pillar was the only remaining sign of an ancient temple colonnade that had stood atop the city's acropolis, a four-hundred-ton slab of red Aswan granite. The Arabs called it Amoud el-Sawari, or Column of the Horseman.

Logan called it a Roman affront to the Alexandrians. He looked to the left of the pillar at a small garden that both Egyptians and tourists alike sought for shade and saw several taxis parked under some trees. He got into one of the taxis and disturbed the driver, who'd been sleeping.

He directed the taxi to a café across the street from what he hoped was Campbell's apartment on rue Nebi Daniel. Earlier, when Logan had first seen the address, he had known exactly where it was. He paid the driver and took a table on the sidewalk outside the café.

A short, thin man came out of the café wearing a white galabia. He was in his sixties with white hair and thick eyebrows and a pleasant face. He walked a few steps toward Logan and stopped. Angling his head, he narrowed his eyes at him with great curiosity. Logan looked at him and smiled. After several seconds, the man recognized his old American friend.

"Professor Alex," he said in Arabic. "*Salaam*, my friend!"

"*Salaam*. It's good to see you again, Ahmedy."

Ahmedy el-Shamy's café was Logan's favorite place to sit and pass the time during his trips to Alexandria. It was small and well kept, with half the seating outside. Ahmedy served two meals a day, one in the morning and one in the afternoon. Logan had at times sat there long enough to eat both. When it wasn't busy, he and Ahmedy would sit over many cups of coffee or tea and discuss the problems of the world. On a number of occasions, they had even solved several of them, if only the world would listen to them.

"Is it that time of the year once again?" Ahmedy said. "Time goes by too fast for me to keep track."

"And for me as well, my friend."

"While you were away this past year, I myself found a solution to the conflict between your country and the Soviet Union," he said with hint of humor in his voice. "I have thought hard and long about this one. I propose that the leaders of both countries come to Ahmedy's café and sit down to a nice meal. After they finish, they will be so satisfied that there will be no fight left in them. They must be friends then."

They laughed and shook hands the way Egyptian men did when a witty remark had been spoken or a story had been told, by swinging their right arms outward before bringing their hands together with a loud clap and then shaking for at least a minute or so.

"What brings you here at this time? You always come later in the morning, my friend Alex."

"Ahmedy, I'm looking for a man. I think he lives in one of those apartments across the street," he said, pointing. He took out the picture and showed him.

"But of course. That is Mr. Campbell, the Englishman. Yes, he lives there. He comes here for a coffee and a bite to eat almost every afternoon. I wonder whether it's because of the convenient location or that our food is so excellent. Anyway, he is a very pleasant man. His Arabic is very good."

"Have you seen him lately?"

"Yesterday afternoon. He sat where you're sitting now."

"How long has he been coming here?"

"Let's see now ... perhaps nearly three weeks, maybe a month. Is he in some kind of trouble?" he asked, angling his head slightly at Logan.

"Oh no, it's nothing like that. I knew him long ago and heard he's living here now. I want to surprise him, so if you see him, please don't tell him that someone is looking for him." On principle, Logan didn't like to lie to people he considered friends. But he had no other choice this time.

"Of course. And now, how about your favorite coffee?"

"Absolutely," Logan said, and Ahmedy left to get it.

Ahmedy's answer confirmed it: Campbell lived at the address that he'd given the Alexandrian authorities. He must have anticipated that someone from MI6 would eventually come looking for him. Was he that confident in his abilities to elude them? Or maybe he wasn't Lucky Break after all.

Ahmedy returned with the coffee and placed it in front of Logan. "It would be wonderful to sit and have a nice long chat with you as we used to do, but in the morning, I am very busy getting ready for customers. Perhaps if you return in the afternoon, I will be free. Maybe your friend will be here as well."

"That's fine, Ahmedy. I don't know how long I'll be here. We may get a chance to talk later."

"God is great, Professor Alex. God is great."

Logan looked over the edge of his cup as he drank his coffee and fixed his eyes on the door of Campbell's apartment building. He mentally reviewed the possible scenarios and the subsequent courses of action he would take when Campbell came out. It suddenly dawned on him that Campbell might not be in his apartment at all. Perhaps he'd left early, before Logan arrived. Perhaps he'd stayed at another location last night. Logan could be sitting there all day for nothing—valuable time wasted.

A muezzin somewhere high in a nearby minaret began his urgent cry to remind the faithful that it was time to stop what they were doing, however important it might be, face Mecca, raise their hands to their ears, and then clasp them in front—the left always with the right—bow, kneel down, and touch their forehead to the floor while reciting Al-Fatiha. Logan shifted his position forward slightly because the back of the chair was pressing against his gun. He enjoyed listening to the muezzin's voice, but he would never understand the blind obedience of the faithful.

He decided to give Campbell two hours. During that time, he would consider an alternative strategy to pursue if Campbell didn't show up. The traffic on the street had picked up, and there were more people out and about now. There was little breeze where Logan was sitting, so he felt more of the sun's warmth. It would be a scorcher today. But then again, wasn't every day a scorcher in Alexandria?

The muezzin finished. Logan sipped his coffee and then put the cup down. He fixed his eyes again on Campbell's door across the street and began humming the tune to "Que Sera, Sera." *Whatever will be, will be. The future's not ours to see— que sera, sera.*

Chapter 13
ALL IN A DAY'S WORK

6:10 a.m.

"IT'S SO EARLY, MY DARLING DONATELLA, MY beautiful pet," Kamal Naguib said in Italian, his voice as thick as syrup.

From the moment Donatella had discovered that Naguib spoke perfect Italian, she had insisted he use it whenever they were together. If she was going to spend so much time with him, she much preferred to speak the language of her own people. It was, after all, the language of love, even though she felt nothing but contempt for this man. She was with him for only one reason: to extract intelligence. She wanted to do that in Italian.

He stretched his arms above his head, with his mouth opened wide in a yawn. When he finished, he asked, "Why don't you come back to bed, my precious gift?"

Precious gift? she thought. At least he knew what her name meant. *Yet he treats me like his possession.* "We can't sleep our lives away, Kamal. Is that the reason you come to see me, to sleep?" Donatella asked as she slipped into a light blue cotton dress.

"Of course not, but I kept you awake for half the night. A

112

little more sleep would do us both some good." He playfully tried to grab her from the bed, but she took a step out of his reach, leaving his arm hanging over the side.

Donatella took her gold watch, a present from him on the occasion of their fourth year together, from the nightstand and handed it to him. It was a delicate little thing with several diamonds bordering its face. Naguib had thought it suited her. "Here, fasten this for me. It'll keep your mind on something else for a change." She might very well be the only person anywhere, besides Nasser himself, to give Naguib orders. When he was with her, he behaved like a well-trained servant.

"Your little wrist is so beautiful and fragile," he said, his chubby fingers awkwardly fumbling with the clasp. "I must always take special care with it."

Damn you, she thought. *How about the rest of my body?* Naguib had always treated her body too roughly during their lovemaking, at times leaving bruises on her arms and legs. "I ordered your favorite breakfast while you slept." She jerked her hand away from him. "It will be here soon," she said matter-of-factly, and then she left, as one leaves a room she finds repulsive.

"Good," he said. "I could eat a cow by myself." Looking up to where Donatella had been, he realized that he was indeed by himself.

The suite was one of the most expensive available in all of Alexandria. The cost of staying there one night was equal to six months' salary for the average Egyptian. Naguib had reserved it indefinitely. The main room was furnished with a soft leather divan in deep burgundy and several matching armchairs. A mahogany coffee table sat in front of the divan, and matching end tables were beside each of the armchairs, with an array of European paintings tastefully lining each wall. A thick, contrasting beige shag carpet ran throughout the suite. Donatella loved to sink her bare feet into it. For reasons she couldn't quite understand, it made her think about how her life would one day be in Italy.

A small kitchen area with a refrigerator, an electric stove, and a chrome table with glass top blended into the corner of the room in front of long rectangular windows that gave them a spectacular view of both the city and the Corniche. A television, which they never used, sat by a wall facing the divan. Their bedroom, off to the right, was equal in size to the main room. The bed was big enough to comfortably sleep a family of Egyptians along with their relatives.

There was a knock on the door, and Donatella walked through the main room in her bare feet to answer it. A hotel employee in a white uniform wheeled a metal cart into the suite and nudged it to the side of the table. He had to pull the cart across the room rather than push it because of the thick carpet. After he transferred the food to the table, Donatella gave him a tip. He bowed his head slightly, and then he left.

Naguib entered the room, stretching and yawning again. Donatella was already seated on one of the chrome chairs with black leather seats and was gazing down upon the city. He joined her.

Before Donatella had first made contact with Naguib in Cairo, Addison had given her his dossier. It had been important to know as much as possible about the man she was about to seduce. Naguib had come from a long line of landowners and was quite proud of his Egyptian heritage. However, his ambition as a young man had taken him in a different direction from that of his father. After he graduated from the Royal Military Academy in Cairo, the same institution that Gamal Abdel Nasser would also graduate from eleven years later, he had enjoyed a career in the Egyptian army, of which his father and uncle had both strongly disapproved. However, it wasn't until after he had been appointed to several government posts, the very nature of which required him to attend many functions, both officially and socially, that he'd acquired his ravenous appetite for exquisite food, especially American and European. And Donatella herself had in time assimilated his liking for the American breakfast.

Donatella watched Naguib lift the stainless-steel cover off his plate and set it aside. He looked down at the four eggs—sunny side up—and the bacon, ham, fried potatoes and tomatoes, and toast. As he did so, his neck flattened, forming three rows of flesh. He reached for the coffeepot and poured two cups, and then he ate with the same passionate enthusiasm that he had shown Donatella the previous night.

"How did your week go?" she asked, pushing her modest amount of food around the plate with her fork. He'd always talked freely about his job with her. She counted on him to continue to do so.

"I'm worried about Gamal," he said with a mouthful of food. "He's getting too close to the Soviets with their atheistic socialism. It sickens me."

What sickened Donatella was watching him eat with his mouth open, so instead she focused her attention on the water glass in front of him. "But you said that he was just using them to acquire their resources," she said, looking up at him as briefly as possible to avoid the sight of his mouth, but long enough so that he wouldn't think she was avoiding eye contact.

"Yes, yes, I did say that. Indeed, I said that, my dear. You listen well and remember. But there are always strings attached to whatever the communists give. They want a Soviet influence in the Arab world, and they're starting with Egypt. I've warned him about that many times, but he always laughs, pats me on the back, and tells me not to worry, as if I'm a mere lackey, some court jester to be tolerated, instead of his director of intelligence and internal security. If I wasn't loyal to him, I might even take matters into my own hands."

Donatella thought that if he said that in public, loyal or not, he'd be shot on sight, regardless of whether he was Nasser's close friend and confidant. But the remark—the way he spoke so freely—did prove just how much he trusted her. She bit into her toast and pretended to be more interested in that than in what he was telling her, to avoid suspicion. She'd always used small talk successfully to obtain intelligence from him. After five years, she had become an expert at it.

"Is he still planning his trip here on the twenty-sixth?" she asked. She had to say something more to him than this to deflect focus from her real interest. She didn't want to spark suspicion. He was, after all, in change of Egyptian intelligence. So she added, "His trips always mean more work for you and less time with me."

"My baby," he said, smiling across the table. The smile lingered there for a while, and then he abruptly changed directions and answered her question. "God yes, and it's going to be a security nightmare for me, worse than usual because his speech is to be in celebration of the fourth anniversary of the coup." He wiped his mouth with a napkin and then ran it across his forehead, leaving a speck of food there. "There will be more people than usual attending it, not to mention the crowds along the route to Mansheya Square. We've tried to talk him out of being so exposed, but he always tells us that his popularity comes from being with the people, not isolated from them. I believe he's pressing his luck, but who am I?" He looked up at the ceiling, his hands held high. "Nothing but his director of security, charged with protecting him."

He lowered his head and arms and, shoving his plate aside, placed his hands in front of him. He suddenly stared at her, his expression deadly serious. She couldn't remember him ever looking like that before. It frightened her. Had she slipped up and given herself away? Did he know about Addison's plot to assassinate Nasser, and had he been toying with her all along?

His eyes bore into her, and she began to shake, her stomach knotting to the point of nausea. She felt the razor-sharp blade of the guillotine dropping on her neck.

"Damn it!" he shouted, slapping the tabletop and spilling some of the coffee and water. "Doesn't he know there could be an assassin out there planning to kill him? No better time than an anniversary. He continuously exposes himself in that damn open car of his. If he were murdered, my career would end! I might even be arrested for not protecting him as I should." His expression hadn't changed throughout the tirade. "I could even be executed for dereliction of duty!"

Donatella let out a breath. His rant so upset her that she couldn't force herself to speak.

Then as quickly as he'd gone mad, he settled down again. He got up from his chair and walked to her. He took her by the shoulders and guided her up into his arms. "I've upset you. Please forgive me, my darling."

She continued shivering in his arms.

"It's just that I worry so much about Nasser's safety, and he simply doesn't listen to me."

Nasser's safety? she thought. *He's worrying about his own ass.* She stopped shaking and was calm now. The day, route, and location were all confirmed. Good. Nasser *must* take rue Fuad to the square. It was the most direct route, and no other street could handle such crowds. Addison would be pleased with this.

They sat down again and finished their coffee. Neither one could force small talk after the outburst, so they got up and went to the bedroom. Naguib prepared a shower for himself in the bathroom. Once she heard the water running, she searched in his pants for a key to his briefcase. She opened it and sifted through his papers for anything that looked like it might be important to Nasser's visit to Alexandria, but she couldn't find anything. In fact, she really didn't know what was important to Addison and what wasn't. The shower suddenly stopped, so she closed the briefcase, locked it, and returned the key to his pants. Naguib appeared in the bedroom with a towel wrapped around his waist. He looked grotesque to her with his short, fat, hairy body, his bald head, and his stomach hanging out. At least when they made love, the lights were dim, and she didn't have to look at him.

"Kamal, I must check in on my mother to make sure she's all right," she said. "I'll return in the afternoon."

"But my darling, I've come all this way so we could be together. Stay a little longer, won't you?" he pleaded. "I wanted to roll over in bed and sleep earlier, but I got up just for you. Besides, my rose petal, my passion for you is aroused again. You can't just leave me now."

She knew it was useless to argue with him when he was in this mood. It would take more time than it was worth to convince him otherwise, and she had no desire to see him sulk like a child. It was important, once every so often, to give him the illusion that he had some power over her in order to maintain a balance. She let her dress fall to the carpet and got into bed. This time he was done with her in ten minutes. He was snoring when she took her flashlight and closed the door of the suite.

Donatella was not going to see her mother. She had seen her the previous day and had even made her a meal that she could eat over the next several days. She'd be fine today. Instead, she took the tram that ran by Pompey's Pillar and got out there, and then she walked for five minutes until she arrived at the catacombs.

The Catacombs of Kom ash-Shuqqafa were the largest of the Roman burial sites in Egypt. They'd been discovered fifty-six years earlier when an unknown force with predetermining powers sent a peasant, unbeknownst to him, with his donkey to walk over the site. As the peasant did so, the tether that was around the neck of the donkey was suddenly yanked out of the peasant's hand. He looked back only to find that the donkey had disappeared from sight, having fallen into a great hole, like some cosmic joke. The force had determined that it was time, after centuries of the site being hidden, for the Egyptian people to rediscover the catacombs.

In the present day, the government had closed the catacombs to the public a month before to renovate the site above it. However, they had not begun the work yet. Addison had made some discreet inquiries and learned that the work had been rescheduled for the middle of August, and the government had decided to leave the site closed until the work was completed. Addison had thought it would be an ideal place for Donatella.

Donatella found the large stone hidden by bushes that she used to enter the catacombs and pulled it aside. Once in, she worked the stone back into position and turned her flashlight on. The subterranean tomb comprised three levels carved out of solid rock, forming a maze of rooms and passageways that she had to maneuver through. However, she'd done this so many times before that by now she had little difficulty finding her way. With the single beam of light in otherwise utter darkness, she entered the first level through a breach in a rotunda wall and descended a spiral staircase; in ancient times, the bodies of the dead had been lowered on ropes down the center of a circular shaft here. That led to the Hall of Caracalla, where the bones of humans and horses had been found decades earlier. She continued on until she reached a hallway that led to the central tomb chamber with walls ninety-one inches thick.

She made her way through more stone tunnels until she

came to the staircase leading to the second level. She shined the flashlight on a wall and saw two carved falcons flanking a winged sun. Farther on, she passed the figures of a man and a woman, perhaps the tomb's original occupants. She used these as landmarks to make certain of her direction. She walked farther and farther into the dank sloping tunnels, descending deeper into the realm of darkness and death. It suddenly occurred to her that if the batteries of her flashlight failed her, she would never get out of there. She cursed herself and thought about going back but decided against it. She would remember to bring extra ones with her next time.

Finally, at the third level, she found an antechamber with columns and pediments and made her way to an inner sanctum. She moved the beam of light across the figure representing Anpu, the Egyptian god of the dead, another landmark. She walked through the room and found what she had been looking for: a straight stone passageway that was seven feet high, five feet wide, and forty feet long. Here she gathered the many paraffin lanterns that she'd placed here a month ago, lit them, and spread them out the length of the passageway.

Then she set about her work.

Chapter 14
THE WAITING GAME

7:00 a.m.

LOGAN DRUMMED HIS FINGERS ON THE TABLE and waited.

The temperature was already increasing exponentially. It would be another hot day in North Africa. He hadn't been in Alexandria long enough to be fully acclimated, although the heat he'd experienced in Georgetown just three days before would help his body transition. He took longer than most to adapt to changes in climate whenever he traveled. Ahmedy, having anticipated his needs, had put some cool water in a ceramic bowl for him. Logan dipped a cloth into it, squeezed the excess water out, and then put it to his forehead. The water had already gone slightly warm.

If Logan knew with any degree of certainty that John Campbell was in his flat, he could wait all day for him to come out, standing on his head and humming his tune. The anticipation itself would be enough to keep him from becoming bored. But the uncertainty of not knowing gnawed at him because he could be putting his time to better use. The last thing he wanted to do was wait here all day and

121

then discover Campbell was somewhere else. It would be time wasted, and at this point, he had none of it to waste.

He supposed he could knock on his door on the pretext of looking for someone else, perhaps the last tenant who'd lived there. After all, Campbell had no idea who Alex Logan was. Logan assumed that he had above-average intelligence and a high degree of common sense. In spite of that, Campbell never would have considered the possibility that the CIA had subcontracted an American to permanently take him out of the picture. He'd be more concerned about an MI6 agent knocking on his door.

If Campbell were there and opened the door, what would Logan do then? Kill him without first identifying him as Lucky Break? Never. Foolish idea. Immoral as well. Logan could give some sort of song and dance routine about why he was there, but if Campbell was Lucky Break, he would be smart enough to become suspicious. Afterward, he might even change his routine or move to another location. Logan didn't want to do something foolish to tip him in any way just because he was impatient. He decided he would simply have to wait and observe.

Logan hated surveillance work because it invariably involved boredom. He wasn't used to inactivity. He preferred to be in motion, on the go, always doing something to relieve himself of pent-up energy, especially if it involved the added element of danger. He remembered having thrived on that during the war. However, he knew he had to sit and stare continuously in the direction of apartment building entrance—because if out of boredom, he shifted his eyes at the wrong time, it would take Campbell only a few seconds to walk through the door and disappear among the crowds of people that were now on the street, and Logan would never know it. Such was the dreadful nature of surveillance work.

So he sighed, fixed his eyes on the door to Campbell's

apartment building, drank more coffee, drummed on the table, and hummed. There was a continuous flow of people going both ways now on either side of rue Nebi Daniel, and the motor traffic was beginning to pick up. A horse-drawn cart with crates of vegetables stacked high in the back suddenly stopped in front of him, blocking his line of vision, but moved on just as quickly. As the cart passed, Logan saw a hand closing the door to the apartment building across the street, but the person himself was blocked from view by the crates of vegetables. Logan stood up to get a better look, and sure enough, he saw John Campbell walking down the street, going east. Had he taken his eyes off the door for just a second, he would have missed him.

Initially, Logan had planned to shadow him. But now he considered searching his flat for anything that might suggest he was Lucky Break. Perhaps he would find a makeup kit or some notes or correspondence from an informant in Cairo. He was still not positive that Campbell was his man, and he didn't want to live with the knowledge that he'd killed someone who was innocent. He had to make a quick decision because his target was beginning to dissolve among the crowds of people. Apparently, Campbell was still using his flat and would likely return there should Logan need to find him again. Logan was eager to discover something definite that would either implicate or clear him, so he decided to let him go on his way and search the flat instead.

He jogged across the street. Once inside the building, he took two steps at a time to the second floor. The hallway was dark, so he took a penlight out of his jacket and shined the narrow beam on the doors as he passed them. He found apartment 2A at the opposite end. He moved the light around the door frame, examining the edges carefully to see whether Campbell had placed anything there to detect whether someone had entered the flat while he was away. He found a piece of straw about an inch or so long wedged in toward the bottom of the door and took note of its approximate position relative to the floor. He jimmied the lock and opened the door a little way and then reached down and picked up the straw that had fallen. He entered the flat cautiously and placed the straw on a bookshelf to the left of the door. The curtains were pulled back, allowing enough light in for him to see.

Logan did a precursory reconnaissance of the flat to avoid any surprises later while he was doing a more complete search. From the size of the flat and from Campbell's belongings that he could see, he calculated that he would need ten minutes to go through everything.

The flat was small and consisted of two rooms. He started with the main room, which was furnished sparsely with dilapidated European furniture. He lifted the cushions off the couch and then got on his knees and shined the light under it. Nothing. He looked at the bookshelf for anything obvious and also found nothing of importance. There were about thirty books that he wanted to check, but that would require more time than he had. He didn't know when Campbell was returning and didn't want to be surprised by him.

Suddenly, there was a knock on the door. Logan froze in place. He took out his gun and quietly made his way to the door. He stood by the frame near the hinges.

From the other side of the door, a voice whispered, "John, it's Peter. Let me in."

When there was no response, the voice whispered again. "John, are you in there?" Again, there was a knock on the door, slightly faster, slightly more forceful. "Goddamn it, John, open the door." The door knob jiggled vigorously.

Logan had his thumb on the safety of his gun. After a long minute of silence, he heard footsteps going down the hallway. The event had taken two minutes away from Logan's ten. *Fuck you, Peter.* Logan stored the man's name in his head.

He went to a wooden desk and pulled out its drawers.
They were empty. Then he went into the bedroom. He lifted
the mattress and examined the pillows. He opened the drawer
of the nightstand, which also was empty. *He must only sleep
here*, Logan thought. He hadn't seen much evidence to the
contrary.

He remembered seeing a briefcase earlier, next to a small
floor safe in the closet, so he opened the door again. He
cursed himself for not having acquired the skills to open a
safe. Max had taught him much about spy work in Casablanca,
but because safecracking hadn't been useful for him to know
there, he had never learned how. Now he wished he'd learned
the skills on his own.

He put the briefcase on the bed. He tried the locks, and
they snapped open. Besides a few consulate papers, there was
nothing else inside. He scanned the sheets, and they looked
like routine correspondence for supply allocations that kept
the consulate functioning. They were different from what he
was familiar with, but the content of the papers was pretty
much the same. He arranged them in their original order
and was putting them back in the case when he noticed the
edge of a manila folder sticking up in a side compartment.
He pulled the folder out and opened it. There was one sheet
of paper in it. It was a cable marked "Top Secret" from MI6
headquarters in London and addressed to Mr. John Campbell
at the British embassy in Cairo, dated June 26, 1956, a little
over three weeks ago. There were only two words printed on
the page in capital letters: "ELIMINATE HIM."

"I got you, you son of a bitch," Logan said aloud. The British
government had been behind this all along, pretending to
have a rogue agent on its hands. Campbell must have been
transferred to the consulate in Alexandria for the purpose
of completing his plans to assassinate Nasser. He had a great
cover. No wonder he wasn't worried about protecting his

address. No one would be looking for him. It was difficult for Logan to believe that the Brits would risk World War III to get rid of Nasser, but that's exactly what they were doing. *Those fools, those goddamn fools.*

Logan decided to take Campbell in his flat. But he couldn't wait for him to return because Campbell would notice that the piece of straw had been disturbed—a warning that someone was or had been in the flat. He would most certainly flee at the sight, and then Logan would be right back to square one.

He returned the folder to the briefcase and placed it back where he had found it. He quickly checked the flat to make certain that he was leaving everything as it had been. Then he put the piece of straw in the same place where he had found it and shut the door. He looked at his watch. The search had taken him all of nine minutes.

The temperature outside seemed to have increased by twenty degrees since he'd gone into the apartment. Logan walked a little way down rue Nebi Daniel and stopped at a shop that sold clothing. He had to do this fast, so he looked at the galabias that were on display and quickly picked a white one much like the one that Ahmedy was wearing. He stepped to another counter where the taqiyahs were stacked high and found one with a deep red color that would suit him. He would have to hurry because Campbell could return anytime. He paid the proprietor and went back to the café. He told Ahmedy that he was disguising himself as a surprise for his friend and asked to use a back room in which to change. After he finished changing, he gave Ahmedy his jacket and shirt to keep and said he'd collect them later. He sat down and ordered a *qasab*, a cold drink made from sugarcane juice. It would cool him down and help restore some of the energy that the sun was taking from him.

Then he sat patiently, waiting for John Campbell to return.

Chapter 15

THE PAST IS ALWAYS
IN THE PRESENT

12:15 p.m.

ONCE OUTSIDE, DONATELLA PLACED THE STONE back in place. After time in the dark, cool confines of the catacombs, it seemed even hotter to her on the street than it was. The sun was overhead now, the humidity high as usual; she began sweating immediately, her dress clinging uncomfortably to her body. She looked around for a taxi but found none. If the catacombs had been open to the public, there would have been many nearby for tourists. Instead she walked to Pompey's Pillar, where taxis outnumbered people.

Whenever she was inside the catacombs, she could not allow any thoughts whatsoever to enter her head except those that were directly relevant to what she was doing. In the beginning, she'd struggled with that because she had many pressing concerns about her immediate future. Her thoughts would flit from one thing to another. She had come to see the effort as a mental exercise, sharpening her mind, keeping it focused on her task. It wasn't easy for her to do, but in a little time, she had gained enough control over her mind that when an errant thought entered it, she could erase it immediately, replacing it with the task at hand.

Several hours of intense concentration at a time in that dank underground tomb always left her mentally and physically exhausted. But it was necessary. What had kept her going was the knowledge that it would soon end. She was critical to Addison's plan, and he, of course, would pay her well for her skills. This would soon be over, and she and her mother would be gone. Reminding herself of that from time to time gave her fortitude and determination.

Her mind was now free to roam at will. It was like being released from a prison cell after years of knowing only four walls and suddenly experiencing the freedom and fresh air of the outside world again—not that she knew anything about prison cells herself, but she had known men who had, and they had all told her the same thing. The word they'd used was *electrifying*. In fact, she had come to look at the catacombs as a dark prison with cool death around her. Leaving them was always electrifying.

As she walked toward the pillar with her mind unrestrained, she thought of Giuseppe Lucertola. This surprised her because she hadn't thought about him for nearly ten years. It was he who had unintentionally made possible her forthcoming trip to Italy, where she would begin a new life with her mother. *How could I possibly have forgotten Giuseppe for so many years?* The mere question made her feel ashamed. In her mind she began replaying the nearly forgotten memory from the first time she'd met him.

At fourteen years old, Donatella had begun working at a vegetable market to help her mother out with expenses. Her mother, uneducated and unskilled, did what she could to make ends meet, but it never seemed to be enough. For young Donatella, the hours were long, and the pay was low, but without any skills of her own, there was no other work that she could do. Her body was strong and already the size of a woman's, and her beauty was just beginning to blossom. Her breasts, which had been small, had suddenly become full and attracted the attention of men who passed her vegetable stall. She was so naive at that young age that she had no idea why they stared at her. She asked the other women who worked with her. They also had noticed men staring at her, but whether out of jealousy or lack of concern, none of them told her why.

Each day after she finished work, she would go to the restaurant where her mother worked to wait for her to finish. Then they would walk home together, sharing their experiences from the day, both tired but both very happy with each other. One day the owner of the restaurant, Giuseppe Lucertola, an immigrant from Italy like her mother, saw Donatella sitting at a table, waiting for her mother. He approached and asked her whether she was hungry. She was shy and said nothing, but the look on her face said that she was, so he insisted that she eat. When her mother protested that she couldn't afford the meal, Giuseppe said that when he offered someone a meal, he would never expect to be paid for it. Donatella's mother was, of course, embarrassed by Giuseppe's generosity, but her daughter accepted the meal graciously and ate with relish, for she was indeed always hungry after working a full day.

The next day when Donatella came to the restaurant for her mother, Giuseppe again offered her a meal. One meal was fine to take and could be justified. Refusal might be taken as an insult. But accepting a second meal without paying for it would be taking advantage of his generosity, so her mother protested again, and again, Giuseppe insisted that Donatella eat. After all, what was a restaurant for if not for eating, he told her. This happened again the next day and the day after that. After a very short time, Donatella's mother began relying on that one meal a day for her daughter as a way to save on expenses, for indeed, they were among the poorest of the poor.

Giuseppe had taken a liking to Donatella. He began preparing her meal himself instead of having an employee do so, and he always added something extra special to her plate that he knew she'd like. He soon began sitting with her while she ate, always asking how her day at the market had gone. Donatella, in turn, appreciated his attention and soon looked upon him as a father. After a month had gone by, Giuseppe began occasionally buying nice clothes for both her and her mother, which also made their lives easier. Donatella thought that maybe Giuseppe, who was single and roughly her mother's age, might be interested in marrying her mother. She had never known her own father and wouldn't mind at all if Giuseppe planned to ask her mother for her hand. Besides, she already was looking at him as a father.

One day while Donatella sat eating and her mother was cleaning the outside tables, Giuseppe sat next to her and smiled. He leaned to her side, and in a low voice, he asked whether she would like to have a job that was much easier than what she had been doing at the market and that paid much more as well. Excited, she said yes, of course, she would. The first thing that came to her mind was that he was going to offer her a job at the restaurant. Giuseppe then told her to return to the restaurant that night at eight, but he said it was very important not to mention this to her mother. She must know nothing of this. Donatella was too timid to ask him why, but in her excitement, she agreed to this condition despite knowing that it would be difficult for her to keep a secret from her mother; she was used to speaking freely with her about all things.

When she returned that night, he took her into his apartment in the back of the restaurant. She'd never been back there before and was impressed by how it was furnished. Unlike her own small apartment, it was large, and she could tell that everything in it was expensive. She followed him into a small room that had a bed. Beside it was a table with a fancy brass lamp. A wooden chest of drawers was pushed to one wall, and there was a long mirror on the opposite wall beside the bed. He reached into his pocket and pulled out a five-pound note. It was more money than she had ever had at one time. All she had to do to earn the money, he explained to her, was entertain a friend of his who would be there shortly. He opened the top drawer of the dresser and removed a gorgeous dress made of fine linen. He handed the dress to her and asked her to put it on. She'd never seen a dress like this before, and her eyes widened with delight. She held it up to the light and could see the lamp clearly through the material. When she asked him how she was to entertain the man, Giuseppe told her not to worry, that his friend would show her how. He would provide the important details. She stood with the dress and the money in her hands and was bewildered by it all. Nevertheless, she would do her best. He reassured her that it would be very easy and not to worry, and then he left and closed the door.

She changed into the dress and looked at herself in the mirror. She had always seen herself as a girl, but now she was looking at a woman. She stood there, transfixed and admiring herself, until there was a quiet rap on the door. A man of Giuseppe's age came into the room, and she drew back from him at once. He wore the uniform of a British officer. She knew that because she'd seen that uniform many times before. She immediately became shy and self-conscious and a little afraid as well, for when she was smaller, those who wore that uniform had treated both her and her mother with disrespect. The officer smiled and told her in Arabic how beautiful she was. She had to admit to herself that she liked hearing that because no one had told her so before. He then sat down on the edge of the bed and took off his shoes. She wondered why he was doing that. Then he unbuttoned his uniform shirt and took off his pants. She became scared but was unable to say anything. He turned and faced her. She'd never seen a naked man before, let alone a naked Englishman. He smiled at her again but said nothing. He drew her to him, and she became terrified and started to tremble in his arms. She suddenly felt nauseous and thought for a moment that she was going to vomit.

When he was finished with her, he put his clothes back on and left with not so much as a backward glance. She remained lying on the bed, with blood on the sheet between her legs. At first, the experience had terrified her, but in a short time, as she lay under him, she had become indifferent to it. It brought her neither joy nor sadness. She'd blotted the act out completely as he'd had his way with her. However, what *did* bring her happiness was the five pounds and the silk dress that Giuseppe had given her.

She got up and put her clothes back on. When she was dressed, she heard another rap on the door, and this time it was Giuseppe. He explained to her that he'd tell her the next day when she could earn more money, but he repeated that she could never tell her mother. If she did, then there would be no further opportunities for her. Their business transactions would end.

Donatella continued to work at the market and go to the restaurant so that she and her mother could walk home together. The next time she worked for Giuseppe, which was two days later, there was only a small amount of blood on the sheet afterward, and she was not frightened by the experience at all. The third time, there was no blood at all, but there was a slight change to the way she felt. This time the experience brought her a small amount of pleasure.

After nearly a year, she was making more money than she had ever believed she could, her work at the market now a vague memory. During that period she'd gained enough self-awareness to understand that she didn't need Giuseppe to make arrangements for her. She was capable of doing that herself. Of course, when she told him, he became enraged, telling her that he would fire her mother if she left him. But at that point, she knew that she could make enough money to support both her and her mother, and then some.

And indeed, she did. Though only fifteen, Donatella was now a beautiful woman. She began going to the homes of men, both foreign and Egyptian, who had sought her out and who willingly paid her much more than a mere five pounds. Some of these men were important people in Alexandria, and they always treated her with respect. And throughout all of this, she managed to keep everything a secret from her mother, including the bank account to which all of her money went, except for a modest amount that was enough to provide her and her mother with a little better life than what they had had.

When Donatella was sixteen, she and her mother traveled to Bologna, the place of her mother's birth. There, for the first time, Donatella met her grandparents, her uncles and aunts, and her cousins. Her mother showed her the city, taking her to some special places from her childhood. She pointed up at the third-floor *appartamento* on Via Caprarie where she had lived as a child. She took her to the Piazza Ravegnana that she loved so much. She showed her Le Due Torri, the two towers, where she had played hide-and-go-seek many times with her friends. They would play until exhausted, her mother recalled, and then they'd form a circle, hand in hand, in front of the towers and sang, "Giro, giro tondo ... casca il mondo. Casca la terra, tutti giu per terra!" (The world circles round ... the world falls down. The earth falls down, and we all fall down!). After going around and around, they'd all fall on the hard cobblestones. What fun she must have had! Donatella saw joy in her mother's eyes as she told the story. But the piazza also brought back some bad memories for her mother. That was where she'd first met Donatella's father, who had slithered away like a snake in the grass after learning that he was going to be a father. He'd left her mother pregnant, stigmatized (they had not been married), and alone. It was at that point her mother had decided to leave Bologna for Alexandria.

Donatella had heard countless stories from her mother over the years, but now she was actually there to see Bologna for herself. She was completely enthralled by the three-month visit. In Bologna, unlike Alexandria, she felt that she belonged to something, was a part of something. For the first time in her life, she heard no other language spoken but Italian. Years later, she would remember the big meals her grandmother had prepared and the extended family sitting around a huge table, eating, telling stories, and laughing. She so much wanted to be part of the permanently. Before they left, Donatella knew that this was where she wanted to live for the rest of her life, so when they returned to Alexandria, she continued seeing men and continued adding to her bank account.

When she was nineteen and more beautiful than any other woman in Egypt, she decided that she could do even better in Cairo because there were many more rich men there. And she was right. As years went by, her reputation grew, and so did her bank account. Then one day that all changed.

She was approached by an Englishman on the pretext of his wanting her services. He told her that he could make her so rich that she would no longer need to sleep with so many different men for money. By this time, Donatella was so full of self-confidence that it bordered on arrogance. However, she was curious, so she listened to him. For the first and only time, she would be the mistress of just one man, who happened to be one of the wealthiest men in Egypt. Her decision to accept the Englishman's offer would change her life forever because from that time on, she'd be working for Addison Davies—as a spy.

And now, with only one week left before she would leave for Italy, she thought of Giuseppe Lucertola and had him to thank for everything, for he was the catalyst who had started her on the path to realizing her dream. Without him, she might very well still be in the market, selling tomatoes and zucchini, the men eyeing her as they walked by.

She grabbed a taxi at the pillar, and it let her out one block from Davies Imported Foods. She walked the rest of the way. When she entered the shop, Addison was behind the counter, and an Egyptian customer was at one of the shelves, looking at canned goods. Donatella needed a few items that she and her mother had gotten used to over the years, so she decided that as long as she was there, she could do her shopping at the same time.

The other customer continued to add a few more things to his basket, and in a short time, he took them to the counter, where Addison totaled them. The man paid him, and because he was a steady customer whom Addison pretended to like, they chatted a while about the weather and then moved on to a professional tennis match that was to take place soon in the city. After that, they said their goodbyes, and the man left. Then and only then did Addison look toward Donatella for the first time.

"Yes, madam, and what can I help you with?" he asked with an ironic grin.

Donatella looked toward him briefly and then continued shopping. *Disgusting man*, she thought. She put several jars of jam in her basket along with some Tetley tea that her mother enjoyed. When she finished, she took her basket up to the counter.

"You smell of death," he said, above a whisper. "You must be coming from the catacombs. I trust everything's going well."

She gave him a dirty look and ignored his comment. He was fully aware that things were going well in the catacombs. "The president's on schedule for the twenty-sixth, but there's going to be much security with him. He *will* be using rue Fuad to get to Mansheya Square."

"Brilliant, my dear Donatella, just brilliant!" he said.

Donatella saw frustration, restrained anger, and impatience in his face.

"I already know the chap will have security with him, and rue Fuad is the only road that runs directly to the square that could hold the crowds." He ground the words out in a steady and low voice. "What I need to know are the *details*." In a somewhat kindlier tone, he added, "It's attention to the seemingly insignificant details that I taught you to look for that will allow us to succeed, not some obvious facts that all of Egypt knows."

She stared at him and narrowed her eyes. She'd always had conflicting feelings toward him. He was just like all the other arrogant British scum, always smug and self-assured. But he *had* provided her with the opportunity to make much more money than she could have made without him. He'd used her body, intelligence, and beauty to get what he wanted. What he didn't know was that she was also using him to get what she wanted. Or maybe he did, but it didn't matter now.

"You know I can't get everything at once, or Naguib might become suspicious. He's not leaving until Monday. I'll get your *details* before then." She couldn't wait until this was all over. Then she wouldn't have to see him again. She began transferring the jars and tea from the basket to her bag.

"And the coin?"

"You have the money?"

"Soon, my dear."

"Then that's when you'll get the coin." She grabbed her bag and walked to the door without saying anything further.

"I'm sorry, madam," he said in a louder voice, "but you seem to have forgotten to pay for all the bits and bobs you put into your bag. Bad show there. We can't very well have *that* now, can we?"

She stared back at him over her shoulder with the door half open, her hand on the knob. "Then why don't you call the police and have me arrested?" she suggested sarcastically, with a hint of a smile that was more of a sneer. "They'll have me behind bars for the next six months."

"Cheeky now, aren't we?" he said.

She stood there, glaring at him, her eyes on fire. She was going to say something but didn't. She simply left the shop and disappeared into a crowd of people.

Chapter 16
A DEADLY DECISION

12:15 p.m.

IN THE DESERT AT SUNSET, MINUTES BEFORE the earth is about to swallow up the sun, the sand takes on a certain color—not quite brown or tan and not quite beige, but a synthesis of all of them. That was the color of Alex Logan's skin. Dressed as an ordinary Egyptian in his newly purchased white galabia and with a dark red taqiyah on his head, he blended in nicely with his surroundings. Because he was fluent in Arabic and spoke an Alexandrian dialect he'd acquired from his mother, he could easily pass for one of the locals.

This time he waited for John Campbell patiently, for he knew that Campbell would eventually return to his apartment. He'd sat at the same table for three hours and consumed two more glasses of *qasab*, which had made him feel cool and refreshed, but his bladder was now making him uncomfortable. Too bad. It was just one of many inconveniences of surveillance. He'd have to piss later. He couldn't afford to miss Campbell. The galabia, too, made him feel cooler. Made from lightweight cotton, it buttoned high at the neck and flowed down to his shoes. It functioned much better than a suit in this hot

Alexandrian climate. If he lived here permanently, he would certainly wear one all the time.

He'd used most of his time waiting to review what he was going to do and say to Campbell once he was in his apartment. It was all about strategy. He didn't want to leave anything to chance. With the discovery of the secret cable from London, he no longer doubted whether Campbell was Lucky Break. Before killing him, however, he needed to find out whether he'd been working with anyone else. Killing Campbell would serve no purpose if he'd been working with someone who was ready to take his place. Logan expected to be lied to. It would take an effective strategy to get the truth, and he had one. Indeed, he did.

Who was Peter? Why had he been whispering at the door? Stance hadn't said anything to him to suggest that Lucky Break had an accomplice, other than an informant in Cairo. It was unlikely, but not impossible, that the informant was also part of the assassination plot. Each one—the spy and the assassin—required a very different set of skills and needed extensive training by an expert. Some people could do both well, but not many. However, it was also unlikely that Campbell was planning this alone. There were too many details that needed to be sorted out for this type of operation for one man. He would need the help of at least one other person, maybe more. That had both positive and negative ramifications for the assassin. With help, Lucky Break was more likely to succeed. However, with more people involved there was an increased chance of someone leaking bits of information to the wrong person, which could lead to failure. The incommunicative, lone assassin was the most dangerous. But Logan had a gnawing gut feeling that Lucky Break had another person working with him. The only one who could tell him the identity of that other person was Campbell himself. He would remain alive until he had done so.

After another fifteen minutes, Logan saw Campbell walking toward the apartment building from the same direction he'd previously gone. He opened the door and walked in. Logan folded a piece of long paper he'd gotten from Ahmedy, and then he gave Campbell another ten minutes before making his move. He quickly relieved himself in the toilet in back of Ahmedy's shop and then made his way across the street.

At the door to the apartment, Logan raised his galabia above his waist and reached for his gun and silencer, which were pushed into his belt. He screwed the silencer onto the barrel, and then he knocked on the door. He heard a voice immediately.

"Yes?" The word was spoken in Arabic, and it sounded distant, as if Campbell had called out from across the room.

"I have an urgent telegram from London for a Mr. John Campbell," Logan answered in Arabic.

There was a peephole in the door, and Logan was sure Campbell would use it, so he hid the gun behind his back with one hand and held the piece of paper up to the door in the other so that Campbell could see it. A telegram for Mr. Campbell—that's all it was.

Logan waited for a few seconds and then heard the voice again. "Slip it under the door."

The tone of his voice was typical of that used by Europeans when talking to Egyptians of low status. *The bastard.*

"I'm sorry, sir. I am required to obtain a signature."

He heard a muffled "shit" in English from behind the door, followed by the sounds of the lock sliding back in its housing and the doorknob twisting. As Campbell pulled back the door, Logan reached forward fast and grabbed him by his tie while holding the silencer to his forehead, forcing him backward into the room. It all happened with such speed and determination that Campbell was left stunned and helpless.

Logan closed the door with his foot and told Campbell to sit on a chair with his hands on his head. Continuing to point the gun at the man's head, Logan reached back and locked the door.

If Campbell was frightened, his face showed no signs of it. His stunned look had quickly disappeared. What remained was simply a look of concern. "Who are you?" he said coolly.

Logan didn't respond.

"Listen, I'm a British government official. I represent the prime minister himself. You're making a big mistake. I suggest you leave now, and nothing more will be said about this."

Logan knew that Campbell, as a vice consul, didn't represent the British prime minister. Only the British ambassador did that. Campbell must have thought he was talking to a simple Egyptian thug.

"Shut the fuck up, or I'll put a bullet in your head," Logan said, switching to English.

"Good God, you're an American!" Campbell said, now clearly surprised. The areas around his mouth and eyes twitched several times, and his eyes widened slightly.

"I said shut your mouth." Logan pushed Campbell's head back a little with the silencer, leaving a small round indentation there. "Stand up and turn around. Keep your hands glued to your head."

Logan patted him down, taking a gun from the holster at the small of his back. "Turn around and sit down and don't try anything foolish. You mean nothing to me. I'll kill you were you sit."

Campbell did as told. "What's this all about? I don't understand." His voice was controlled, but Logan detected the last few words breaking up slightly.

Logan grabbed another chair and placed it backward directly in front of Campbell, five feet away. He sat on it with his arms resting on his legs, the gun steadily pointing at Campbell. If he tried anything, Logan could wound him without so much as moving an inch—or kill him, if he had to.

Logan had decided earlier to use the direct approach with him, asking questions that were backed by an imminent threat of death if Campbell didn't answer to his satisfaction. But Logan had to give Campbell hope that he could get out of this mess alive, if he only told Logan what he needed to know. What Campbell didn't know was that sometime soon, Logan was going to kill him regardless. That was the reason he'd been sent to Alexandria, and that was what he was going to do.

"You didn't seriously think that the American government was going to stand by and let you start World War III, did you?"

"You're daft. Who the bloody hell are you?"

"The person who's going to kill you if you don't come up with the right answers to my questions. I suggest you might want to take a good look at my face."

Campbell was regaining his composure, and Logan knew what was going on in his mind. If a person didn't kill you right away, then the longer it went on, the more hope you had of extricating yourself.

"I don't know what you're talking about," Campbell said. "You clearly have me mixed up with some other bloke, I assure you."

"Who's working with you?"

"I told you, I don't know what you're talking about. How could I bloody well start World War III? And why would I want to? I'm a British vice consul. Who the hell do you think I am?"

Alex decided to turn the screw. Campbell was becoming a little too comfortable and self-assured. If he was working with someone, Logan had to know now. There weren't many days left until July 26.

"No more games. You're an MI6 agent, code name Lucky Break, and you've gotten the green light from your government to assassinate President Nasser. If you tell me who you're working with right now, and if I can verify it, you'll continue to live. If you don't, you have about another minute until I put a bullet in you." Logan was quite prepared to do it, just not that quickly.

Campbell's complacency suddenly turned to agitation. "For Christ's sake, *yes,* I work for British intelligence, but I'm not Lucky Break. I've been ordered to find and kill him myself." The apartment was hot, and sweat had formed on his forehead and was now dripping down his face. "Can I wipe my face?"

Logan nodded. Campbell was beginning to break down, but he was still lying. Campbell slid his palm across his forehead, which glistened with sweat. Logan watched carefully. He could see no signs that he had any makeup on. Okay, so he wasn't wearing any at the moment. As in his picture, Campbell's ears stuck out, which made him look silly and vulnerable.

"I said no games," Logan said. Of course, Campbell would say anything to get himself out of the quicksand he found himself in, to keep from sinking deeper into the muck, so Logan wasn't surprised by his lie. For a split second, Logan thought about reinforcing his interrogation strategy by putting a bullet in Campbell's foot. He would ask him once again first. He aimed the gun at Campbell's foot. "One last time: who's working with you?"

Panicked now, Campbell exclaimed, "Christ, I said I'm not Lucky Break! I have cables from my headquarters in London that will prove it."

"I saw one cable in your briefcase already that said to eliminate Nasser."

"Damn it, that meant to eliminate Lucky Break. There are more cables in my safe that can verify that."

"Why wasn't the one in your briefcase in your safe as well?

144 «❂» John Charles Gifford

"It was in my office at the consulate. I brought it here to put with the others, but I forgot to."

"Tell me what the other cables said."

"Listen. I *am* an intelligence agent. I've already told you things what would get me in trouble with headquarters. Besides, I have no idea who you are."

Logan said nothing but simply lifted the gun to Campbell's head.

"Okay, okay. I'll have to assume you're with the CIA because you're here to stop Lucky Break and know something about what's going on."

Logan continued to stare at him but remained silent.

Campbell explained about Prime Minister Eden pulling MI6 out of Egypt temporarily after the Soviet threat, to ensure there would be no miscommunications. "When Lucky Break didn't respond to the repeated cables they sent him, headquarters contacted me, wanting to know what was going on. I told them that I have had no contact with Lucky Break. This was just before I was to leave the country and return to London. I didn't even know who he was because he's been buried under layers of cover for years. I then received a cable telling me to stay in place at the embassy in Cairo and that I would hear from them soon. Eden can't take the chance that Lucky Break is planning on killing Nasser himself, so in that final cable, the one you read, MI6 ordered me to eliminate him. Intelligence feels that Lucky Break is going to assassinate Nasser on the fourth anniversary of the coup, during his speech here in Alexandria on the twenty-sixth. They had me diplomatically transferred here to the consulate office to locate him and kill him. That's what I've been doing since I arrived. They sent two additional agents on tourist visas under the cover of academicians to assist me."

"Who's Peter?"

"How do you know about him?"

"He knocked on your door this morning, while I was visiting your apartment."

"Peter's one of the men they sent. I have no idea where the other one is."

Logan felt a knot in his stomach, the kind you get when you discover you've been wrong about something you were so certain you were right about. Spy work was fraught with that. "Do you know whether Lucky Break is working with anyone?"

"No, but he planted a local spy within Nasser's circle of advisers who's been feeding him intelligence. Maybe he's still working with that person."

"Do you know what Lucky Break looks like or what his cover is?"

"Yes, I have a picture of him, but it'll do you no good. He uses different disguises and names. I could bump into him on the street and wouldn't know it."

"Show me the other cables. If they say anything other than what you just told me, I'll put a bullet in the back of your head."

Campbell got up shakily and put his hands up where Logan could see them. Logan followed him into the bedroom. Campbell knelt down, spun the dial, and opened the safe. Logan watched him carefully in case there was a weapon inside. There wasn't. He took the cables out and stood up. "Here's the lot. Read for yourself. I'm telling the truth."

"Stand over there," Logan said, waving his gun in front of him, "and lean into the wall with your feet back. Spread 'em! Stare at the wall. Don't move."

Logan read each cable, one after another, while glancing up about every five seconds or so at Campbell. They were exactly as he'd said. Campbell's story, supported by the cables from London, placed Logan in the position of having to make a critical decision. If he made the wrong one, he could blow everything, maybe even get himself killed.

He was faced with a choice. Either he would have to trust

Campbell completely—and might even have to work with him in finding Lucky Break—or he'd have to kill him. If there was no trust, if he felt the least doubt about him, he would never be certain that Campbell wasn't Lucky Break. He couldn't take the chance of releasing him only to find out later that he *was* Lucky Break and that he had assassinated Nasser while Logan was off chasing his tail. Besides, British intelligence could have planned well in advance to use the cables as a ruse in the event something like this happened. Logan thought it was quite conceivable. The Brits were quite good at what they did.

He had to trust his instinct absolutely or not at all. And he had to decide *now!* He walked up to Campbell and placed the silencer against the back of his head, forcing his head down. Bile worked its way up into his mouth. He could hear his own heart thumping, his chest on fire. *Decide, damn it!*

Campbell's head jerked down, the silencer pressed hard against it. A surge of pain shot through his body. *He's crazy,* Campbell thought. *He's absolutely insane.*

He continued leaning against the wall spread-eagle, feet apart, hands flat against the wall, fingers spread. He had done what this intruder had told him to do; he was fully cooperating. He had given the man the cables; they verified what he'd told him. Yet this maniac seemed not to believe him. What more could he do to convince him he was telling the truth? If he said something now, anything, it might be the wrong thing, and the guy might blast his head to pieces. Was he going to do it regardless of what Campbell said? *Jesus, God Almighty, don't let it end now, not this way.*

It had been only a few seconds since the intruder put the gun to his head, but it seemed like hours ago. *The bastard must be thinking about what to do next.* Campbell's will to live was receding, like a man in quicksand. He was being completely and hopelessly controlled by the iron will of another. He could feel tremors in his body. They started in his knees and worked their way up through the muscles in his thighs and then spread through his upper body, through his shoulders and arms and finally to his hands and fingers, flat against the wall. Could the man see the tremors? Campbell felt nauseated and thought for a moment that he was going to vomit. Helpless. *Goddamn it, shoot if that's what you're going to do, and get it done with!*

Campbell had chosen a dangerous profession, and he knew there was risk with it, but he was still a young man with much more to do. He'd laid out his future for himself in the intelligence field. He'd seen himself working his way up the ladder to the position of chief of the British Secret Intelligence Service, the top dog. He had the education, the tenacity, and the instincts, and he was now gaining the field experience. After that, who knew? Politics? But this American had knocked on his door, and in a second, his world had turned upside down. His psyche suddenly changed again. He wasn't ready to die now at the hands of a lunatic who thought he was Lucky Break. *Jesus, God Almighty, no, no, don't let this happen.*

This and much more was going through the mind of John Campbell as he stood spread-eagle against the wall with his head down, forced by the silencer attached to the man's gun.

Chapter 17
IN SEARCH OF A
SNIPER'S NEST

2:00 p.m.

ADDISON DAVIES WAS NOT ONE TO CLOSE HIS shop in the middle of the afternoon for a few hours, as was the custom of most other merchants in Alexandria, who used the time to either rest or run errands. The work ethic he'd gotten from his father forbade him to do so. It was true that he'd had little in common with his father, but on the issue of hard work and persistence, they'd always agreed. "If you're going to do something," his father used to tell him from very early on, "for God's sake always make a good show of it!"

Addison had always viewed his father as a right nutter, with his constant talk of socialism and his support for the government providing free this and free that to its citizens. Hard as he tried, Addison could never make him understand that he was contradicting himself—because the society he was advocating precluded the very notion of hard work and diligence. When things were given away, he'd explained to his father countless times, people would come to see those things as their God-given right, and then they would expect even more, especially if they didn't have to work for what they received. But the conversation was useless because his father just couldn't grasp what he was saying. Nevertheless, Addison had learned his lesson well about hard work, so much so that he had to be the best in everything he endeavored to accomplish, whether he was running a small import shop of British goods as a cover for his covert activities as a spy or plotting the assassination of a head of state. He had to be the very best at both.

Today, however, was different. Not only would he close his shop, but he would do so for the remainder of the day. He grabbed his straw hat from the counter, went to the door, and opened it. He put the key into the lock, pulled the door shut behind him, and locked it, giving it a little tug. Then he pulled the security gate across the front of the shop and locked that as well. *Ta-ta for now.* He turned around to face the street and looked for a taxi to take him to the old Turkish quarter. The sky was mostly a brilliant blue, with clusters of dense, towering vertical cumulonimbus clouds here and there. These thunderheads were capable of producing dangerously severe weather. But at the moment, they hung above him harmlessly. If there was a storm brewing, he hoped that it would hold off until later in the afternoon, after he finished with what he was going to do. He wondered whether he should return and grab his umbrella. No, he decided, he would chance it. What was life without a few risks here and there? He stuck his hand out in front of him, and a taxi pulled up within seconds.

While the taxi maneuvered through crowded and narrow streets, he relaxed in the back seat and began to think of Donatella—beautiful Donatella. It seemed that whenever he had a spare moment, his mind instinctively entertained her more often than not. He didn't mind it, though. He rather enjoyed it and was, in fact, amused by his obsession—no, that was entirely the wrong word. "Keen interest" would perhaps be a better way to put it; he was amused by his keen interest in her. He had every right to be interested, however. She was, after all, working for him. But he wondered whether he was becoming the proverbial jealous lover. The notion was absurd, he thought. He wasn't her lover; he was her employer, so to speak. She herself had seen to it that he'd never be her lover. He ran a finger over his false mustache as he looked at the people going by him on the sidewalk and suppressed a smirk.

Notwithstanding, Donatella had been an effective tool for him during the last five years, feeding him intelligence she'd gotten from her fat lover. He was pleased with her work, and she in turn was content because he'd been paying her much money, and of course, she was getting much more from Naguib as his mistress. It had been a stroke of genius on his part to bring them together. Her skills at deception came to her naturally. Oh, he had had to train her, yes, but only to reinforce what she already possessed. What he had done was hone her innate skills. Naguib, that fat-ass security director, had never once become suspicious of her in all those years. How ironic, he thought. The Egyptians were pathetic when it came to intelligence work. The British had helped them set up their intelligence networks during World War II, and still they couldn't get it right, even at the very top of their agencies. *I'll show them again just how incompetent they really are.* That thought also amused him.

But this situation was different from all the others he'd been involved in. Nothing could go wrong, and Donatella would play an indispensable role in the plan's success. So far, she was performing magnificently well, but Addison had begun to wonder whether she was capable of continuing to withstand the pressures the job produced. The stakes were now suddenly much higher, and he was beginning to demand much more of her. Would she be able to handle the sacrifice he was asking of her? Even for all the money she would yet receive and for the chance to leave Egypt for Italy with her mother? Or would she crack like an egg? She was, after all, a mere woman with limitations. Would she simply collapse under the pressures at the last minute, destroying his painstaking plans for assassinating Nasser? This was one thought that did not amuse him.

Damn it! he thought. He had to stop second-guessing himself about her, he told himself as he noticed that the taxi was approaching his destination. There was little point in these noxious, torturous exercises of self-doubt because he couldn't change the plan at this late stage. He had to maintain his confidence that she would do her job as he'd taught her. If, for some reason, Donatella backed out or showed signs that she was becoming unstable and was no longer an asset to him, however, he knew that he'd have no other choice but to kill her. She knew too much about the operation for him to allow her to walk away. She was capable, if so inclined, of subverting all he'd worked for. That would be a shame, he thought, a terrible shame. Above in the sky, he heard a distant rumble. Perhaps a storm *was* brewing. He hoped it would hold off a little longer.

The taxi stopped, and Addison paid the driver and got out. He found an outdoor café and, in spite of the heat, ordered a strong cup of Egyptian coffee, to which he had grown accustomed. Mansheya was Alexandria's main square, and now that Donatella had confirmed it as the location from which Nasser would be delivering his speech, it was time to choose a sniper's nest.

La Cible Café skirted the front of the most open part of the square. Mansheya Square was, in fact, the busiest square in all of Alexandria, but the scene currently was nothing compared to how it would be on July 26. Addison had seen Nasser give speeches in Cairo and in various venues throughout Alexandria so many times that he himself would be capable of setting up his security. A wooden platform would be set up directly in front of where he now sat at the café, facing the square. The podium from which Nasser would deliver his speech would be centered on the platform, approximately eight feet from the front edge. However, Addison had rarely seen Nasser use the podium. He'd start his speech there, but in a short time, he'd take the microphone from the podium, advance closer to the edge of the platform, and then start pacing to his left and right, continuing his speech. Of course, this always made matters more difficult for his security officers because there was the ever-present threat that someone in the audience would jump at him with a knife. Nasser's personal bodyguards would be on high alert at this point—on high alert with eagle eyes.

Addison began to visualize the entire spectacle that would happen on the twenty-sixth. Nasser would be in an open limousine, standing in the back, slowly going down rue Fuad, one hand bracing the seat in front of him, the other hand waving at the crowds, utterly oblivious to his security needs. The street would be crowded, and people would be hanging out of windows in the buildings on either side of the road, shouting their love for the leader. As he made his way toward the square, the crowds would part for the car and then swarm around it again in the rear, filling up the street behind it. Security officers in plain suits and sunglasses would be stationed along the route, looking for anyone who would do harm to their president. Their job would be overwhelming. After entering the square, Nasser would pass the Palace of Justice building on the right and the statue of Mohammed Ali on his horse to the left. Reaching the other end of the square, he would get out of the car and begin mingling with his people, who had waited there for up to ten hours for him to arrive. They would reach out to touch the president's outstretched hands and tell him that they love him. Perhaps he would even say a word or two to them and look them directly in the eyes and smile. His security detail would be going crazy with concern for his safety, their eagle eyes no longer capable of watching every movement in the crowd. The young children there who were old enough to understand what was going on would one day tell their grandchildren about this day.

Eventually, he would turn and mount the raised wooden platform and go to the podium where he would begin his speech. Directly in front of him would be rows of chairs with important Egyptian and foreign dignitaries. Perhaps even Khrushchev himself would be there. Wouldn't that be *smashing*! Nasser would look down and acknowledge some of them, but there would be too many for him to make eye contact with all. Minutes after beginning his speech, he would move away from the podium and go to the edge of the platform, the long microphone cord trailing behind him. The crowd would number into the hundreds of thousands, lining the converging streets and square. There would be bodies hanging out of every window and people standing in every balcony of every building lining rue Fuad and Mansheya Square, listening to their leader's every word, which would echo through the loudspeakers that had been placed throughout and bounce off the surrounding buildings.

The optimal time for the assassination, he considered, would be before Nasser mounted the platform, while he was still in the crowd. It had two strategic advantages: the eyes of everyone, save the security detail and personal bodyguards, would be on Nasser, and the din coming from the crowd would be so deafening that it would muffle the shots fired from the rifle and thus provide an assassin an extra minute or two to successfully escape the sniper's nest and blend into the crowds below. Once it was discovered that Nasser had been shot, there would be such chaos, such confusion, that Addison anticipated a human stampede. No doubt, the casualties would number well into the hundreds. What better time to make an escape?

Sitting where he was, Addison had Nasser's view of the square. The sniper's nest would have to be located at the highest level possible. He looked up at the buildings at either side of the square for the highest ones. And then he lowered his head and began to read a newspaper he had bought earlier, while sipping his coffee. He didn't want to be conspicuous and draw attention to himself. Most of the buildings were too low, he decided. They would be filled with people all the way to the top. He looked up again at a building that had caught his attention earlier in the taxi. It was the only redbrick building on the square. It was also the tallest, with six stories, plus an ornamental parapet at the top. It was perfect as a sniper's nest and afforded suitable cover. He began to mentally calculate the distance and angle from the parapet to where the limousine would stop and Nasser would merge with the crowd, and he concluded it was well within the kill zone. The effective range of the weapon he would use was 550 yards, the approximate length of five football pitches. It was the perfect distance and angle for his scoped sniper rifle.

Before section D of MI6 merged with several other government organizations to form Special Operations Executive during the war, Addison had engaged in paramilitary operations against the Germans, and he'd functioned for a time as a sniper. Sniper rifles were made for serious men who were on deadly missions. On the advance, in contact, or in defense, the snipers aggressively pressed the battle to the enemy. Troops relied on their snipers to keep the enemy and its own snipers at a distance. An expert sniper expected and relied on perfection from his weapon.

In little time, Addison had become one with his British-made number 4 MK1(T) sniper rifle. Typically, he'd taken great pleasure in looking through his scope from higher ground at German soldiers below him. Ideally, they'd be in the open and thus exposed to him, with little or no chance of finding cover to protect themselves. He would carefully choose one soldier and fix his crosshairs on him. He preferred to shoot his victims through the heart, but if the angle wasn't just right, then he would aim at the head. From his concealed position and wearing camouflage, he would gently squeeze the trigger and watch his victim fall. Then he'd wait a few seconds or so while he gleefully observed the others trying to figure out what had happened and scramble in vain for cover. When he'd entertained himself sufficiently, he'd pick them off, one by one. Even though that had been sixteen years ago, it still brought him a certain amount of pleasure to think about it and even more pleasure to know that the same rifle was going to be used on the twenty-sixth.

As he sat on the terrace of the café, he noticed that there were tall palm trees directly in the path that the bullets would have to travel. He stood up and pretended he needed to stretch to get a better look at the angle and calculated that the trees would not block the view and were low enough for the bullets to pass overhead without touching them. The slightest obstacle in the path of a bullet—even a palm leaf—could be enough to deflect it slightly from its target. He counted on dead accuracy.

Yes, the redbrick building was the perfect site. Then, suddenly, a horrible thought occurred to him, and he cursed himself for not having thought about it before. More wasted time. This building was indeed the perfect site for a sniper— too perfect, though. He realized that Nasser's security detail would also think so. There would be perhaps a half dozen men with rifles and binoculars behind the parapet, looking down for would-be assassins among the crowds. The building would be of no use to him.

With the lack of suitable buildings around the square, the assassination would have to take place somewhere en route to the site on rue Fuad, while Nasser was in his open limousine. Addison was disappointed. The president would no longer be a stationary target. However, his car would be moving slowly because of the crowds. It would surely stop periodically for ten or fifteen seconds so that Nasser could reach his hands into the crowds. Addison had seen him do that many times. That would be ideal, but he couldn't count on it happening. He had to prepare for a moving target, slow as it might be.

He folded his paper and walked the length of the square onto rue Fuad. He had to start all over again. *Damn!* It was imperative that he find a suitable sniper's nest today. The clock was ticking away, and he had many other crucial things to do. He stopped and looked up at the buildings on either side of the street but quickly looked away because he was momentarily blinded by the sun. He looked up again, this time shading his eyes with his hand. He could tell that the buildings contained either flats or low-level government offices. One of them might have been suitable, if not for the fact that there would be people in the windows, trying to get glimpses of their beloved president as he passed them by. The roof was all wrong for a sniper to conceal himself. It wouldn't do.

The next block was the same. He walked another block and stopped again. He looked up at the top of an apartment building. At five stories, it was the highest one he could see in the area. He focused on one particular window on the top floor, and again, he calculated the angle and distance. It was even better than the redbrick building at the square. From here, he figured there would be little trouble putting a three-inch grouping into the target at less than one hundred yards. A sniper could stand at the window with the shade covering most of his body. The downward angle would be such that the muzzle of the rifle would be barely exposed. Even an inexperienced trained sniper would have no problem with a stationary target, but a moving target was another matter entirely. But perhaps all that would be required was one round expertly fired into the brain of the president after all. Regardless, this would be the perfect location.

Now all he had to do was inform Donatella that she had to make arrangements for her mother to move out of this flat immediately.

He felt large drops of rain on his shoulders. Indeed, a storm was coming soon. He stuck out a hand and hailed a taxi.

Chapter 18
AN URGENT PHONE CALL

1:45 p.m.

"PUT YOUR HANDS ON THE BACK OF YOUR NECK, turn around slowly, and keep your mouth shut," Logan said.

Campbell did as told. The two men stood five feet apart, facing each other. Logan continued pointing his gun at him, keeping his finger on the trigger. He now knew what he had to do. *I have no choice*, he told himself, but he wasn't pleased with his decision. He was still conflicted over the new information Campbell had given him. The cables were persuasive but provided him no sense of definitiveness, yet he was forced to make a decision based on them, mostly. Taking the life of a person who might later turn out to be innocent was serious business with long-lasting ramifications; so was releasing an assassin because you thought he was innocent. Either way Logan looked at it, it was a gamble.

Logan had gambled many times during the war, as new sources of information came to him, always under circumstances in which he had to make quick assessments and even quicker decisions. Sometimes he'd been wrong and suffered severe consequences, but more often his instincts had turned out to be right. Critical as those circumstances were, this one was different. If he made the wrong decision, there would be worldwide consequences. He couldn't let that happen.

"Go back to the chair and sit down," Logan said, indicating the next room with a wave of his gun. Whether Campbell was Lucky Break or not, Logan knew he would have been trained by British intelligence to get himself out of situations like this, even when he wasn't armed. "And be smart about it. There's no move you could make without taking a bullet."

Campbell followed the order without speaking a word and sat down in the same chair as before. Logan again positioned himself five feet in front of the Englishman, pointing his weapon at his head, finger steady on the trigger, ready to fire. He still had time to change his mind. He didn't have to go through with it. He considered the situation one last time and arrived at the same decision. Campbell's body tensed up, and he shut his eyes. Drops of sweat ran down his forehead to the tip of his nose and on to his chin, dropping onto his shirt one by one. He squeezed his eyes tighter.

"Put your hands down. It looks like I'll have to trust you," Logan said, lowering his gun.

Campbell relaxed his body immediately and opened his eyes. "I say there, old boy," he said nervously and with a flash of a smile, "you had me bloody well worried for a moment."

"I'd stay worried if I were you. If it turns out you're Lucky Break, I'll hunt you down wherever you are. I'll make it my life's mission. You'll spend the rest of your life looking over your shoulder."

"I assure you I'm—"

"I know. You told me already. Just remember what I said."

Logan had gotten himself into a worrisome situation he had not foreseen. He had to reveal his cover to a man he didn't truly know and didn't fully trust—someone he was going to eventually let go—the spy's one cardinal sin. What would

Max say about this? Logan had no other choice but to lay his cards on the table.

"I've been hired by an intelligence agency to find Lucky Break and kill him. My agency has been monitoring your headquarters and is fully aware of just how critical this situation is. I'm not quite sure how they missed MI6's cables to you, but they were confident that British intelligence would send its people after Lucky Break. Both our countries have a vested interest in stopping this maniac. I suggest we put our resources together and find him," Logan said.

"I couldn't agree more. The more the merrier," Campbell said. Catching himself, he continued, "Sorry, I didn't mean to make light of it."

Logan sensed that Campbell was thrilled to be alive. "Tell me what you've been doing since you arrived in Alexandria," Logan said.

"I need to get up and stretch a bit first. Fancy a shot of whiskey?"

Logan nodded and sat on the divan. Campbell stretched and then walked over to the bookcase. He grabbed a bottle and two glasses from one of the shelves and returned to the sitting area, where he poured a finger in each glass. Logan kept his eyes on him all the time.

"Peter, the guy you heard knocking on my door, arrived here along with another bloke named Derrick Smith, with a list of names headquarters had given them. At this point, they don't know which names are real and which are aliases." He spoke rather fast and edgily, apparently still recoiling from his near-death experience—now happy to be alive, happy to be cooperating with the person who had nearly killed him. "They're all British subjects, though. We've been running them down, but with little luck, I'm afraid." He handed Logan a glass and repositioned the chair facing him and sat down.

"You said you had a picture of Lucky Break."

Campbell reached into his jacket pocket, took out a photo, and handed it to him. "As I said, it's unlikely to be of any use to us. It's an official agency picture taken about ten years ago. Lucky Break's real name is David S. Deans." His lips were quivering slightly. He ran his tongue over them and then pursed them quickly.

From Campbell's expression, Logan thought he must be expecting him to take his gun out again and start blasting away.

"Like his picture, his name is totally useless to us. He obviously would be using an alias. The bugger uses disguises and makeup developed by our scientific branch. They have some of the best chemists in the world working for them." He paused a moment to purse his lips again. He looked at Logan apologetically. "It's going to be difficult to identify him."

Logan looked at the full-faced photo of the man he had to kill. He had boyish features and wore a crew cut. His skin was baby-smooth, as if he never had to shave. There were no distinguishing characteristics other than a small half-moon-shaped scar centered in his chin, a blemish on an otherwise clean face. He tried to picture him ten years older and wearing various kinds of makeup. "I need to keep this," he said. He wanted to compare it with the other photos he had in his hotel room.

"Please do. He gave headquarters so many names and covers over the years that it was nearly impossible for them to keep track of him. They believe, however, that for this assignment he settled on one cover from the very beginning and stuck with it. He always communicated with them as Lucky Break. He's smart and a bit arrogant. Headquarters gave him a free hand because he was providing what they thought was good intelligence. It just kept flowing in. Now they know that it was slanted in the wrong direction. We're going to have a hard time penetrating his cover."

"Let me see the list of names," Logan said, still uncomfortable about breaking his own cover. He wanted to compare Campbell's list with his own but then remembered he had left it in the safe in his hotel room. "I need to take it with me too. I'll return both of them later."

"Right. Just let me write down a few names first."

While Campbell was doing that, Logan thought about what Max had told him and the other eleven apostles in Casablanca during their training. *Whatever you do, never, ever disclose your cover to anyone, even if you think you can trust that person. It could get you or someone else killed.* That was exactly what Logan had done just now with John Campbell.

"How can I get a hold of you if I need to?" Logan asked, standing up.

"Leave a message at the consulate office. I call in on the hour when I'm away from my office. I don't know your name." He stood up as well and walked with Logan to the door.

Logan turned, facing Campbell. He was taller, so he had to look down at him. "My name is Alex Logan. If you've been lying to me, I'll make your death long and painful."

Campbell didn't seem fazed by this. "Right. Can I reach you at your hotel if I need to?" he asked.

Logan nodded. He returned Campbell's gun to him and left.

"Bloody hell. That's all I need," Campbell said aloud. "Working with some cheeky Yank." Although the weight of his gun seemed right, John Campbell nevertheless dropped the magazine of his semiautomatic to make certain that Logan had left the bullets in it and then slammed it back in place. He was angry. *Well, the wanker can kiss my arse*, he thought. He went back to where he had poured the whiskey. Both glasses were untouched. He picked one up and knocked it back and then did the same with the other.

He was mostly angry with himself. He'd been well trained by the Secret Intelligence Service for situations like what he'd just gone through. He should have been cool and calm, devising a plan by which to extricate himself and then acting upon it. After all, he'd been in a life-and-death trap. Logan could have easily ended his life. Yet instead of acting to save his own skin, he had frozen, shaking like some sniveling sluggard. He was more than angry with himself; he was appalled.

It wasn't as if this was the first time he'd been in a dangerous spot. But in that one moment—spread-eagle with his hands on the wall—when he was waiting to die, his training should have kicked in; instead, he had gone limp. He had been convinced that Logan was going to pull the trigger. There were several maneuvers he could have used. Perhaps they wouldn't have been any use to him—Logan had been standing too far behind him, like a professional—but at least it would have been better to try one of them than to just stand there and be shot to death by some American maniac. Thank goodness, he'd saved the cables. His brains might very well be splattered around the apartment now if he hadn't.

He went to the bathroom to refresh himself and looked in the mirror. *Imagine the idiot thinking I was Lucky Break*, he thought. Did Logan seriously think he would be found so easily if he were? No wonder American intelligence was so incompetent if this was what they had for agents. He brushed his teeth, patted his face with water, and combed his hair. *There's no feckin' way I'm working with him.* It was bad enough he had to work with the idiots London had sent him, let alone work with some tosser from the colonies. He looked in the mirror again. "By the way, old chap, well done. You're alive! Very good show."

Campbell was getting hungry, so he grabbed a novel he'd been reading from the bookshelf, *The Inheritors* by William Golding, and walked across the street to have a late lunch.

"Ah, Mr. Campbell," Ahmedy said, walking toward his table. "And how are you today?" It had started to rain, so the two men lifted the table slightly and moved it further under the awning, out of the drizzle.

"Good, Ahmedy. I'll have the usual."

"Coming right up." He turned to leave but stopped. "And how was your visit with your old friend?"

"Hmm? Friend?" he said, looking up.

"Yes, of course. Mr. Logan. He was waiting for you here. I saw him go into your apartment building, so I assumed you two met." He put his hand to his mouth. "Oh, but perhaps I spoke too soon."

"Oh yes, Mr. Logan. Yes, yes, we did meet. You know him then?"

"Yes, but of course. He's been coming to Alexandria for many years just at this time of the season—a little break from his teaching responsibilities, you know, and to visit family. But enough talk. You must be hungry. I will get your food now."

Family? Teaching responsibilities? Campbell thought about that. It must be his cover. However, if it was, it didn't make sense. If he were CIA, he'd be assigned here permanently, not traveling back and forth. But Logan had told him only that some intelligence agency had sent him here to hunt down Lucky Break. He hadn't said which agency. Campbell knew that the CIA had plenty of men already here. Why would they send someone else to do the job? He reminded himself to send off a quick cable to his headquarters and have them check Logan out.

Ahmedy brought him a plate of *ful medames*, fava beans topped off with chopped tomatoes and onions and served with oil, garlic, and lemon juice, with some flatbread on the side.

"By the way, Ahmedy, is Alex still teaching in the same place? He didn't mention it when we talked."

Ahmedy looked down at him. "Oh yes, Georgetown University. By the time his vacation is over here, he's ready to return to his students, full of energy."

"Yes, of course. Thank you."

Ahmedy left again. Campbell knew that it was illegal for the CIA to spy within the borders of America. He wondered who, exactly, Logan was working for. He had the correct intelligence about Lucky Break, so he had to be working for some agency with equipment sophisticated enough to monitor British intelligence. But which one? Headquarters would find out.

Campbell ate his fava beans and tried to read his book, but he found it difficult to focus because his mind was on Alex Logan. He picked up a bottle of water and drank, glancing across the street. He noticed that Peter was just about to open the door to his building. He shouted his name.

Peter turned his head in Campbell's direction and gave a short wave of acknowledgment. He dodged traffic to cross the street, walked to Campbell's table, and then sat down, brushing raindrops off the jacket.

"Give me an update on what you've been doing," Campbell said, without looking at him or giving him a customary greeting. He put a forkful of beans into his mouth.

"I followed the jeweler like you said to do. No go. He's not our man."

"Are you sure?" Campbell said as he chewed.

"Absolutely."

"Okay," Campbell said, patting his mouth with a serviette and looking at Peter for the first time. "I want you to check out Addison Davies next." He wrote down the address and gave it to Peter. "He owns Davies British Imports, but don't approach the shop until he closes up. When he does, wait for five minutes and then knock on the door on the pretext of needing some tins of whatever—think of something—because you're a tourist and can't live without it. Make up some story to get in. He should open the door to you without being suspicious."

"The guy's an old bugger. He's in his sixties, if I remember his file right."

"Remember, Lucky Break uses a disguise. Check him out carefully. There won't be anyone in the shop except you and him. Take your time. If you think he's Lucky Break, don't do anything. Just come back, and we'll take him together. I'll be in my flat."

"Anything else?"

"Just keep in mind that if he's Lucky Break, he's dangerous. Don't take any unnecessary chances. Either way, let me know."

Peter left, and Campbell eyeballed him as he walked down the street. *The idiot*, he thought. MI6 was just not producing quality agents like it used to. He found that the newer ones lacked the analytical skills necessary to perform covert work. They'd all get themselves killed eventually.

Campbell finished his meal, paid the bill, and then crossed the street to his flat. Before he did anything else, he had to make an urgent phone call.

Chapter 19
THE CONFRONTATION

7:00 p.m.

PETER COOK, TALL, YOUNG, HANDSOME, AND a bit self-assured, stood at a busy intersection and wiped his forehead with a handkerchief. Having arrived from London only a few days earlier, he found that his body had not yet acclimated to the oppressive heat of North Africa, which was starting to take its toll. He was wilting under the heat, withering like a shriveled leaf on a water-starved tree. First the rain, and now it was the heat again. Although he was physically fit, he'd rather be back in England, where the weather was more suited to him. But he was a loyal British subject, and when his superior at the Secret Intelligence Service had decided to send him and another agent to Alexandria to assist John Campbell in hunting down a fellow agent, he had accepted the assignment enthusiastically and without complaint.

He was exhausted now, having spent the better part of the day shadowing a man who headquarters had determined might be functioning in Alexandria under an unknown disguise and cover but who, in fact, might be his fellow agent David S. Deans, code name Lucky Break. He'd stood across the street from the man's home early that morning and waited for him to come out. When he did, Peter had followed him to the post office and then through a maze of narrow twisted streets to a jewelry shop in the center of the city. This Englishman had owned and operated the shop for a number of years, and it could very well provide a suitable cover for a spy. Peter had waited across the street to see whether the man would come out, and when he didn't, Peter had gone inside under the ruse of being interested in buying a piece of jewelry for his wife back home. He was greeted cordially by the man, who had proceeded to show him various bracelets, pendants, and necklaces. He had engaged the man in a discussion, asking a series of questions about each item he was shown, all the time assessing him with eyes and ears that had been expertly trained by his agency. He paid particular attention to the man's face to see whether he could detect any telltale signs of the agency's makeup on him.

Once he was convinced, as much as he was able to be, that this man wasn't Lucky Break, he had decided to purchase a ring so as not to raise suspicion should he be wrong. He picked one that his wife would most surely like. She wasn't particularly thrilled at his being away, so this would be a nice gift for her when he returned—something from a faraway, exotic country. After leaving the shop, he had decided to play it safe and wait across the street to see whether the man would close up the shop and leave. If he did, Peter would follow him again, as a matter of caution. After an hour or so, he decided to give up. He neither saw nor heard anything to suggest that this jeweler was anything but what he appeared to be. He had then returned to John Campbell's flat tired, but none the worse for wear.

Now Peter looked across the street at Davies Imported Foods, waiting for the proprietor to close up and pull the gate shut. He wiped his forehead again as sweat ran into his eyes, blurring his vision. *Bloody weather*. He didn't have to wait long. An older man—quite handsome, Peter acknowledged to himself—opened the door, pulled the gate across, locked it, and went back inside. Peter waited for five minutes and then crossed the street. He looked through the window and saw Addison Davies behind the counter, doing something—he couldn't make out what—with his head down. Peter stuck his hand through the gate and rapped on the door to get his attention. Addison looked up and shook his hand in such a way as to indicate that the shop was closed. Peter rapped again. He could see that the man was slightly annoyed by him, but Addison walked to the door and in a muffled voice told him that he was closed.

"I'm a tourist!" Peter shouted. "I'm dying for something British to eat. Can't take this Egyptian food, you know."

Addison unlocked the door and gate and slid the gate to the side just enough for Peter to walk through. "Can't very well refuse a fellow Englishman, now can I?" said Addison as Peter shouldered by him. The owner then proceeded to lock both door and gate again.

"Thanks much, mate," the handsome British agent said. "My innards can't take the local food. I end up in the loo half an hour after I eat."

"No problem. Have a look around. Baskets are over there," Addison said, pointing. "Take your time."

Peter grabbed a basket and began to browse the shelves, and Addison went behind the counter.

"Let me know if you can't find something," Addison said. "Here on holidays?"

"Sort of. I've been invited by the department of psychology at the university to deliver a speech on the latest state of affairs in psychoanalysis in Britain, but I'm making a bit of a holiday out of it."

"Where do you lecture?"

"Cambridge," he said without skipping a beat. Peter had in fact graduated from Cambridge with an advanced degree in psychology, so he was quite prepared to answer more questions if necessary. That was why headquarters had sent him—a ready-made cover. The other reason they'd selected him was his ability to make quick assessments of people. Peter was young and relatively inexperienced as a spook, but he was educated and intelligent and could think on his feet. Headquarters looked forward to prepping him for a fine career. All he needed was more experience in the field.

"Good show," Addison said, interested in his new customer.

"I say, might you have any digestive biscuits? Can't take tea without them."

Addison walked over to one of the shelves and pointed them out. Peter observed his gait carefully. He seemed to move on his feet a little quicker than one would expect of a man in his sixties.

"And how about a few tins of Ambrosia Creamed Rice Pudding? Can't live without that either, you know!"

Addison moved to a spot a few shelves away and showed him where they were. *The same*, Peter thought. He definitely had the movements of a younger man. No proof, just an indicator.

"Brilliant," Peter said, picking up two tins and placing them in his basket. He needed to engage him in a discussion close enough to get a good look at his face. Walking over to him, he said, "You are indeed a refuge for the weary British traveler. How long have you been here?"

"Five years now. Seems like a donkey's age, though," Addison said with a chuckle. "It takes a while to get used to things, especially the weather. It still bogs me down a bit, if I'm not careful."

Peter glanced several times at his face and then walked back to one of the shelves. "I better get a few other things to last me while I'm here." Up close, he had noticed that Addison's skin looked smoother than it should be. Farther away, it looked as if it were losing its elasticity, as one might expect of a man of sixty-three. If he was wearing makeup to conceal a younger face, it was good. MI6 scientists back home were the best.

Peter continued to look at the shelves of tins and jars, putting a few items in his basket. Then he walked over to Addison at the counter again and continued their discussion. "I'm here alone, you know. I wonder whether you could direct me to a good nightclub that stays open late. You know the kind I mean?" he said with a wink and a grin.

Addison picked up on his meaning immediately. "Well, I don't go to those places myself, not that there's anything wrong with them, but I think I know what you mean. You could try the Paris Club on San Stefano beach. That's where the expatriates frequent—tourists as well. Actually, you'll find a variety of spots along the seafront that would suit your needs, I believe. There's a lovely walk along the Corniche that you'd enjoy."

Peter watched and listened to Addison carefully as he spoke. The voice was off as well, but only slightly. Again, he sounded more like someone who was younger than what he appeared to be.

"I suppose a taxi could take me there, right?" Peter asked.

"Actually, if you're up for a little walk, it's close enough from here, maybe thirty minutes. But yes, any driver would know the area."

"Brilliant! Ah, there's one more thing I need, and then I'll get out of your hair and let you close up. I can't tell you how grateful I am to you for accommodating me. I'm sure you want to close up shop and get home."

Peter went to the side of one of the shelves near the front, where Addison couldn't see him. *Lucky Break*, he thought. He had not a single doubt in his mind. He couldn't see any point in wasting time and returning to Campbell. He decided to take the rogue agent himself. If by chance he was wrong, no harm done. But if he didn't take him now, who knows—they might never get another chance again. The stakes were high. He was slippery and could very well get away from them, and then where would they be? He pulled out his semiautomatic and placed it in the basket and then walked to the open area in front of the counter. Addison had his back to him.

"David," Peter said with absolute conviction and authority, "it's finished. Give it up."

Addison turned around slowly and faced Peter. "I beg your pardon. Were you addressing me?" he said calmly. He then caught sight of Peter's gun pointing at him and drew back in surprise.

"You're the only one here besides me," Peter said.

"My given name is Addison. What's the meaning of this? I don't keep much money here."

"Come off it now, old chap," Peter said. Setting the basket down, he closed the distance between them. "The game's up. It's been up since you refused to respond to the cables. Did you think headquarters was going let you off the hook?"

"I don't have the vaguest notion what you're talking about. What headquarters?"

"Let me have a little tug at your hair, and then I think you will. Come over to this side of the counter."

Addison did so.

"Now turn around and put your hands on the counter. Move your feet back and lean. Good. Don't move. If you try anything stupid whatsoever, I won't hesitate to use this gun." Peter had never done this before with a suspect, outside of practice during his field training. It felt good. It felt right.

Addison leaned into the counter as he was told. His jacket was unbuttoned and hung down loosely.

Peter walked cautiously to Addison's right side, holding his gun steadily. With his left hand, he reached over and grabbed a handful of Addison's hairpiece. Before he had the chance to pull on it, Addison, who had been prepared for Peter's arrival, reached under his arm for his dagger with lightning speed and in one continuous motion swung the six-inch, razor-sharp, double-edged blade to his side with a great sweeping force and slit Peter's throat from right to left.

The gun fell to the wooden floor with a thud, followed by Peter Cook himself.

Addison had placed the body in a large burlap sack and was now mopping the blood off the floor. Now that he knew for certain there were agents from the home office after him, he would have to change his disguise and abandon the shop. He had known this day would come, but he hadn't figured it would come before the assassination. His plans would still stand as they were, but with a slight modification to compensate for his pursuers.

He needed a car to transport the body, which would be a bit of a problem. He could easily dispose of the body in such a way that it would never be found. But that wasn't what he wanted. He wanted the body discovered and then traced back to him—or to his current identity, that is. He wanted the Egyptian authorities along with those idiots from London to engage in a hunt for Addison Davies. His heart raced as he thought about that. They'd never find Addison Davies. Never! But he wanted them to search for him.

And then it dawned on him. He put the mop down and went to the body. He wouldn't need transportation after all. He'd leave the body here and then make it obvious that the shop had been abandoned. When the body was discovered, the authorities would know for certain that Addison Davies was the killer. But by that time, old Addy himself would be dead, and someone else would have risen from his ashes to complete the job that had yet to be done.

Addison dragged the body to where he had killed the agent and then started yanking back the sack, fistfuls of burlap, first on the left side and then the right, until the body was free. He flung the sack behind the counter. He looked at the remaining blood on the floor and then looked down at himself; he was covered with it. He went upstairs, stripped, washed the blood off, looked at himself in the mirror, and then put on some fresh clothes. His blood-soaked shirt and suit could stay on the floor. He grabbed the case containing his makeup from behind the false wall and went back downstairs. All else could remain behind. He no longer had any use for any of it. He went behind the counter to where he kept his money. He counted out five thousand pounds in large notes and put it in an envelope and then placed the rest in his case. He addressed the envelope to the director of the orphanage. He would take it there himself tonight, for he didn't trust anyone else to do it.

He picked up his attaché case and placed the envelope under his arm. He shut the lights off, unlocked the door, hesitated briefly, and then turned around. In the dark he could still see the shelves full of canned goods and other products. The shop had been his life for the last five years. He was tired of it, but with all change, whether good or bad, there was always a certain degree of regret during the transition. He turned around again, opened the door, unlocked the gate, slid it back a few feet, and left the shop for the last time, leaving both door and gate ajar.

The chase would soon begin.

Chapter 20
THE THIRD MAN
AT THE TABLE

9:15 p.m.

ALEX LOGAN DECIDED TO SKIP THE SECOND man on his list and go after the next one, only because of convenience. The man lived at Le Metropole Hotel, which was only a ten-minute walk from his own hotel. Mr. George Sedgewick, age forty-nine, owned a British import/export wholesale business and had lived in Alexandria for ten years. He had a family who lived in London, but that easily could be a ruse and part of his cover. The time frame, however, was wrong. Lucky Break had been in Alexandria for five years, not ten, but that detail too could have been falsified. It would have been easy enough to do. Logan didn't have to remind himself that he was dealing with an experienced intelligence agent who was an expert at hiding in the open. In every other way, though, Sedgewick matched his criteria.

Like the Hotel Cecil, Le Metropole catered to the wealthiest of tourists and Egyptians. If Lucky Break was staying there, he would be paying a tidy sum. MI6 would have cut his resources off when he didn't answer the cables, but more than likely, he wouldn't have felt the impact of that yet. Still likelier, he would have been planning the assassination for quite some time and would have had the foresight to stash money both from his government salary and from his business. After the assassination, he would be an international fugitive. He would need a great deal of flexibility while on the run, the kind that only money could buy, if he wanted to stay ahead of his pursuers. One might say that the more resources a spy had, the better his or her chances were of staying alive. With enough money, most things were obtainable. If George Sedgewick was, in fact, Lucky Break, Logan concluded that money wouldn't be an issue for him.

Logan stepped into the lobby of the hotel and stopped. There were a few well-dressed people milling about at the front desk to his right and at the entrance to the hotel's café in the back. He heard French being spoken near him. No one he saw looked like Sedgewick's passport photo. The people who'd been talking to the desk clerk turned around and walked toward the main doors. Logan eyed them and then went to the front desk.

"Bonsoir, monsieur," said the clerk. "Comment puis-je vous aider?" The clerk was a tall, thin man dressed smartly in the white uniform of the hotel. He had dark features that could be Egyptian, Greek, or Italian. He was wearing thick, black plastic glasses that Logan had noticed earlier he was constantly adjusting. He seemed pleasant enough. Twenty-five, maybe.

"I'm looking for a friend of mine who might be staying here," Logan said in English. He knew the clerk would be fluent in several languages, but Sedgewick was English, so a friend of his might only speak English himself. "His name is George Sedgewick."

"Mr. Sedgewick, yes, of course. Would you like me to phone his room?" Out of the corner of his eye, the clerk noticed a few people getting off the elevator to the right. "Oh, there he is now. I'll call him over—"

"No, don't do that," Logan said, interrupting the clerk. "I want to surprise him." He turned his head slightly over one shoulder and watched Sedgewick cross the lobby and go out the front door. He looked back at the clerk. "I'll see him outside. Thanks."

"Very well then," the clerk said, somewhat confused. "Good luck." He put an index finger to the middle of his glasses and pushed them in place on his nose again.

Logan hurriedly left the hotel and looked around in three directions for Sedgewick. He caught sight of him just as he disappeared around the hotel to Logan's left. Logan jogged to the corner of the hotel and peered around the building. Sedgewick continued to walk at a leisurely pace down the Corniche. Logan followed behind at a safe distance. The waterfront promenade was full of people seeking out food and entertainment at this time of night, so he wasn't concerned about being spotted. And if he was, so what? Sedgewick, or Lucky Break, had no idea who Alex Logan was. That would certainly benefit Logan in the long run, but his advantage was compromised by the fact that Logan didn't know for certain who Lucky Break was disguised as either.

The Corniche was lined with restaurants, bars, cafés, and nightclubs that attracted both tourists and locals alike. Sedgewick was walking at a steady, determined pace and hadn't stopped or looked around him. Logan supposed that he might be going somewhere specific and just wanted to get there. He walked for another two blocks, passing an array of businesses with crowds of people standing and sitting out front, enjoying the evening, and then quickly disappeared behind a door. Logan caught up and stopped. He looked up at a neon sign that flashed "The Blue Moon." He opened the door and caught the smell of alcohol and incense.

The nightclub was dark, noisy, and crowded inside, and he had a difficult time spotting Sedgewick. There were small round tables spaced just enough apart to maneuver around, with booths lining the walls. He spotted Sedgewick being seated up front near a small open area, where he guessed the entertainment would later be. *Raqs sharqi, no doubt,* he thought. But in a nightclub, the belly dancing would be of the illegal variety for tourists, which generated legal revenue for the government, as well as kickbacks for certain officials.

Logan looked around for a table by Sedgewick and couldn't find one—not near him or anywhere else. They'd all been taken. Sedgewick must have reserved one for himself earlier. There were two empty chairs at his table. Logan made his way there and then bumped against him. "Oh, sorry," he said. "It's packed tonight. Mind if I join you?"

"Not in the least, old man," Sedgewick said. "Pull up a chair. Wouldn't mind a bit of company. You must be American."

"Yes, I'm here for a little rest and recuperation," Logan said, sliding onto a chair.

"Actually, I know what you mean, old chap. I'm in need of a bit of that myself," he said, chuckling to himself as if it were an inside joke.

The waiter came to the table, and they both ordered gin and tonics. Logan had looked closely at Sedgewick's face while he ordered his drink. It was full with a receding hairline, but in the dim lighting, it was difficult for Logan to see any details. He appeared to be about twenty pounds overweight. What was more obvious than his physical appearance, however, were the glasses he wore. They had thick lenses that made his eyes look smaller than they were. He was nearsighted. Logan recalled Sedgewick's passport photo. He wasn't wearing glasses in it. Perhaps he had been told to take them off so there wouldn't be a glare.

The lenses looked real, Logan deduced. In that case,

Logan could eliminate Sedgewick from his list. His eyesight alone would have kept him from becoming an intelligence officer working in the field. And there was no way he'd be able to function as a sniper. If Sedgewick was Lucky Break, however, and was using the glasses as part of a disguise, the look could be extremely effective—an expert sniper who was nearsighted and wore Coke bottles as glasses! Who would guess? It would surely deflect suspicion. But when Logan was following him, Sedgewick's gait had been steady and determined. If he weren't truly nearsighted, he would have had a hell of a time seeing clearly enough to navigate through the crowds of people. His vision would have been greatly distorted. He would have been bumping into people along the way.

After their drinks came, Logan engaged him in small talk. "Come here much?" Logan asked.

"Every chance I get. It's my home away from home, you might say," he said, chuckling again.

"Are you in business here?"

"I run an import/export wholesale company, one of the biggest in the country. Actually, my father started it. Benjamin Sedgewick. Ever heard of him? Possibly not because you're a Yank. He made a name for himself here. I took it over when he decided he wanted to fish every day in the homeland. I'm proud to say that I built the company to what it is today. How about you?"

"I teach history at a university in the States. I usually do some traveling in the summer months." After a pause, he asked, "Do you travel much?"

"Too much. I'm back and forth to England all the time. I'm getting bloody sick of it too. But I have a wife, and my two kids are at university at the other end. The company's booming at the moment, and you've got to make a few bob when you can. Inflation and recession—you've got to prepare for both, if you know what I mean." He gave Logan a soft pat on the shoulder and laughed harder this time.

"You must miss your wife."

"I do indeed, but actually, we see each other quite often. She refuses to live here away from her friends and family, but we can afford to fly her out here once a month. So with me coming and going too, we probably see each other more than most couples who live together." He coughed into his hand and was about to laugh again, but something caught his attention.

There was some activity on the stage directly in front of them. The house lights dimmed even more, and the stage lights went on, reflecting a soft rose-colored hue on the faces of the people seated around it. Logan didn't think that Sedgewick was anyone other than who he said he was, so he mentally checked him off his list. He decided to relax a little and enjoy the show before leaving early and seeking out the second person on his list of possible assassins.

The stage lights suddenly went out. The chatter diminished to whispers. A few coughs could be heard here and there, as well as chairs scraping against the floor—patrons readjusting for a better view, no doubt—and then there was silence throughout the club. A violin began its low haunting cry, and gradually the lights came on again, revealing a dancer at the center of the stage with her back to the spectators. Even from the back, Logan immediately recognized her as Little Egypt. He had seen her many times before at different venues.

As a rule, Logan hated belly dancing. He'd seen enough of it at weddings and at other functions he'd attended over the years. The government had placed so many restrictions on the dancers involving what clothes could be worn and what movements were acceptable that those who continued in the profession were often flabby, with their bodies covered as required by law. Their movements were often slow and boring. He had avoided seeing them whenever he could on his last few visits.

However, the nightclubs were different. One of the reasons Westerners came to Egypt was to see the romanticized images they had seen in the movies, which depicted dancers in scant clothing whose movements suggested something indecent. Because there was so much revenue to be made promoting that image, the government turned a blind eye to the nightclubs that catered to tourists. The term "belly dancing" itself was a misnomer, for the dance involved every part of the body: the hips, the shoulders, the breasts, the head, the legs, the arms, and the hands as well as the belly. It was this romanticized version of belly dancing that greatly interested Logan. And no one interested him more than Little Egypt.

He knew her routine by heart, but he never tired of seeing it. As the tempo of the music sped up, Little Egypt, her arms held above her head, began moving her knees back and forth at great speed while at the same time contracting her thighs to create a shimmering vibration of her hips and buttocks. She was thin but with beautifully proportioned, meaty hips. Her long black hair reached down to her waist, and as she stood there, her entire body began quivering in the soft lights. The music suddenly changed in tempo as she turned around quickly, body and music fusing into one. The gold *reggiseno*, which covered only half her breasts, was richly decorated with sequins and embroidery and fringed with spherical golden moons held by threads. A gold belt hung below her waist and formed Vs down the front and back of her light tan skirt, which was made of multiple layers of sheer chiffon, just transparent enough, and no more. She wore long earrings with golden leaves and on each wrist wore bracelets with golden links. When she quivered, every part of her body came to life.

She worked her shoulders and arms, undulating them to each side, with the tips of her long, elegant fingers held out, and at the same time shimmied her hips to the music. She moved from side to side, turning in small circles, the golden moons dancing on her body. All eyes were focused on her; not a word was spoken among the spectators. Even the waiters stopped what they were doing because of her presence on stage.

A third man appeared at their table. "George, you're a frightfully hard man to find," he whispered, leaning down.

"Addy, old boy. Join us. Sit down. Fancy seeing you here tonight."

"I tried your hotel," he said, sliding into the empty chair. "When I didn't find you there, I figured you'd be here."

"Addy, meet my new American friend." Sedgwick looked toward Logan. "What did you say your name was?"

Logan was facing the stage, and he turned in his chair halfway and shook hands over his shoulder, barely glancing at the newly arrived man. "Alex Logan. Glad to meet you." Then he fixed his attention on Little Egypt again.

A man, a foreigner, in a white suit at the next table leaned forward and shushed them with a disapproving look and an index finger over his lips.

As the music slowed, Little Egypt threw herself down, twisting her body around so that her back was on the floor. She spread her legs apart, her feet firmly planted on the floor near, but not quite under, her buttocks, and then she arched her back as far as she could, bracing herself on her shoulders. She then began slowly undulating her body, fluidly rotating her hips and chest and stomach. The brooch in her belly button rose and fell like a ship on a never-ending wave in an ocean of flesh. The amount of lust those movements produced among the patrons was incalculable. Those in the back rose from their chairs to get a better look. After a minute had gone by, she got up on one knee, and with the other leg bent to hold her balance, she began heaving her upper body in jerky movements, pushing her chest out and her stomach in, with her hips sinuously pulsating to the music. Then she threw herself backward with her hands to the floor, her back arched, her legs apart, and vibrated her entire body while holding that position. A waiter, transfixed, dropped a tray with fancy drinks on it, but no one heard it crash to the floor.

The music abruptly changed again, and she got up on her feet, her stomach, breasts, shoulders, and arms rising and falling, swelling, surging, and heaving in rapid serpentine movements, while her hips shimmied violently. Suddenly, she threw herself forward to the floor, facing the spectators with her head down and her black hair splayed out in front of her, forming a great fan. The music stopped, and the lights abruptly went out for just a moment, and when they came on again, Little Egypt was no longer there. There were two seconds of stunned silence, two seconds only, and then the club filled with a burst of thunderous applause and whistles and loud shouts from those who had just witnessed the spectacle.

"George, I can't stay," said the man who'd joined them during the show. "I have to go back to the shop and pack. I have a little family emergency back home. I'll be away for about two weeks."

As the men behind him talked, Logan only half-heard the conversation. He remained focused on the stage, trying to savor the experience of the dance.

"Hope it's nothing too serious, old boy."

"Not too, but it does need my attention. I have a delivery scheduled for tomorrow. Hold off on it until I'm back, will you? I'll phone."

"Not a problem, Addy, not a problem. If I'd known you were

going, I would have given you a package for Helen to mail from London. No harm done, though."

"It just came up. I didn't know myself I'd be leaving until a few hours ago."

"Just the same, it's a shame, old boy. I hope everything turns out well for you."

"I should be going now. Packing, you know. Early flight."

"Right. Shove off then, and I'll see you when you get back. Good luck. Safe flight. Ta-ta ..."

Logan looked over his shoulder just as the older man got up to leave. "Nice to have met you," Logan said, extending a hand.

"Yes, the same, I'm quite sure," the man said.

Once outside the Blue Moon, Addison began walking east on the Corniche, not quite knowing where to go. Peter Cook, former agent of the Secret Intelligence Service who'd been previously hot on the trail of Lucky Break, would likely be found sometime tomorrow, probably in the morning, lying dead at Davies British Imports, just as Addison had planned it. However, on the odd chance that the body could be discovered sooner, he had to get off the streets because there would be a citywide alert for his capture when it was.

It had been risky enough to go to the hotel and then the Blue Moon to find Sedgewick. It had been worth the risk, however, because Addison liked him and had enjoyed his company on many occasions at the clubs. Sedgewick was the only true friend he had, and he felt he owed him at least this consideration, but Addison had calculated the risk of locating Sedgewick as minimal. Ultimately, he never would have comprised what he had to do for anyone, including Sedgewick, if it had ever come to that. But Addison didn't see it that way now.

As Addison's principal wholesaler, Sedgewick had treated

him fairly, often donating food to him after Addison told him that he was helping supply an orphanage. He didn't want Sedgewick's truck anywhere near his shop tomorrow for a delivery, not out fear that he'd be implicated in any way—that certainly wouldn't have happened—but out of concern that Sedgewick himself might be questioned. He knew what the police would do. They'd interrogate him for hours. Sedgewick would reveal that they had been friends, and then the interrogation would go on for longer. Now the police would never think to question Addison's wholesaler if their investigation went that far because they would assume their relationship had been strictly business.

Addison set his attaché case down and looked around. *Where do I spend the night?* he thought. Early tomorrow morning, when there were fewer people on the streets, he would find a cheap out-of-the-way hotel in which to transform himself into a new person, but right now he needed somewhere to seclude himself. Ah, of course. He knew the ideal location, and it was a very short distance from where he stood right now.

Addison Davies picked up his case, turned around, and walked in the direction of the catacombs.

Chapter 21
THE PSYCHE OF A SPY

Sunday
4:10 a.m.

LOGAN SAT IN HIS UNDERWEAR AT THE DESK in his hotel room and rubbed his eyes with the heels of his palms. It was quiet except for the hum of the air conditioner. After leaving the Blue Moon, he had decided to return to his hotel because he was too tired to do anything else. He'd gotten about three hours of broken sleep, tossing and turning, his mind refusing to give him any rest, his mind jacked up on Lucky Break. He'd been used to the lack of sleep during the war and had few problems functioning in demanding situations, but civilian life had taken away some of his edge, a realization that was just starting to sink in. As a spy in Casablanca, he'd often scoffed at civilians back home, denigrating their soft, easy lives. He supposed now he'd become one of them.

Maybe age was catching up to him, or perhaps it was the stress of this operation and the realization of the consequences if he failed to find Lucky Break. Regardless of the cause, he was dead tired. *Too bad*, he told himself. *Push through it like always. You're going to bloody your hands eventually, so goddamn it, just push through it.*

At some point during the early-morning hours, he had finally decided to stop fighting it and had gotten up. He had ordered a pot of strong coffee from the twenty-four-hour room service and was now mulling over the names on his list.

He took a piece of the hotel's stationery and wrote the name David S. Deans on it, Lucky Break's real name. If that were Logan's name, what alias would he create for himself? He thought back to his own days with the Twelve Apostles and the OSS. He had never changed his own name while working under a cover, but there were many who did. Moreover, it was also common for enemy spies to do so. Although he wasn't an expert, Logan did have some secondhand knowledge about creating aliases. He knew, for example, that no one chose one by chance, neither his colleagues nor the enemy. Aliases were developed rather than chosen, and they were developed with a great deal of ego.

Spies, no matter what country they served, had certain personality traits that influenced their behavior, motivation, and mind-set. As a result, they had to develop just the right name for themselves. Once they had settled on one, no other would do. Logan was intimately aware of these traits because he shared them. They'd made him a good spy. But he was so revolted by them that after the war ended, he had decided to reenter civilian life with the hopes that he could suppress them to the point that they no longer influenced his behavior. He'd been successful, but now he found that if he was going to hunt down Lucky Break and kill him, he'd need those selfsame traits again.

Essentially, there were two of them. Call them personality types or personality disorders—they amounted to the same thing, and all spies possessed them to varying degrees, including Logan himself. One trait was that of antisocial behavior, but not in the sense of avoiding the company of others. There was a deeper, more disturbing, more sinister meaning to the word. Those who possessed this trait lacked remorse whenever they did something wrong. Certainly, the feeling of guilt was enough to prevent most people from engaging in immoral behavior. Not so with the spy. For the spy, lack of remorse became a necessary prerequisite—an asset. A spy who later felt sorry for what he or she did was a spy who would one day be a dead tree stump.

The other one—the second necessary trait of a spy—was narcissism. Whether they were born with it or acquired it as they interacted with others, spies had a grandiose feeling of self-worth. Putting themselves ahead of others, they lacked empathy. Combine the two—antisocial and narcissistic behaviors—and you get spies who spent every day of their lives lying, cheating, and deceiving others for their own ends or for the ends of their country.

But they, too, like everyone else, had rules to follow because they worked for intelligence agencies that existed and functioned by rules. The best of the spies, however, rejected rules outright, or if they accepted them, they believed that at least some of the rules didn't apply to them. The latter were the ones who were most effective at what they did— and the most dangerous—because their behaviors were unpredictable.

Logan had realized early on that he sat at the borderline of these traits, and he was appalled by that knowledge. He'd decided that if he were going to avoid fully internalizing them, as so many of his fellow spies had done, he'd have to leave his career in espionage and find a more suitable profession that didn't nurture that mind-set. He hadn't deluded himself into believing that he didn't like being a spy—in fact, he loved it! He just didn't like the person he'd turned into.

So Logan knew that the best spies developed their aliases with great care and forethought, often laboring for days until they had just the right one. Their narcissism—their overinflated, self-indulgent egos—combined with their complete, guiltless disregard for others would never allow them to do otherwise. Their sense of self-worth demanded that they see how cleverly they could conceal their own names within their aliases. Was Lucky Break egotistical enough to have done the same?

The most direct way to conceal one's name within an alias—and that at the same time also appealed to the ego of the spy—was to use the letters of one's own name, or most of them, to come up with a new name entirely. Simple? Yes, but also highly effective. Logan looked down at the name he'd just written: David S. Deans. Then he compared it with the names on his list. If he hit a dead end on his list, he would do the same with the names he'd gotten from Campbell.

> Culverton D. Duncan
> Rowland Crichlow
> Patrick Murphy
> Clive Middleton
> Humphrey Porter
> Daniel Dexter MacGregor
> John Campbell
> David Derek Hallows
> Willoughby Jones
> Simon Honeyborne
> George Sedgewick
> Thomas Aldwinckle
> Addison Davies
> Neville Carter

He first looked for patterns of vowels and consonants. The d's caught his attention immediately: Culverton D. Duncan, Daniel Dexter MacGregor, David Derek Hallows, Addison Davies. But spies creating aliases from their own names didn't always use all the letters. Lucky Break might not have used any of the *d*'s from his name at all, or he may have used all of them, or just some of them. *David S. Deans*, he thought again. He began to circle the *d*'s and then the vowels. He looked at the remaining consonants and compared what he had to the other names. *This was too easy*, he thought. The name Addison Davies was apparent, perhaps too apparent.

Would Lucky Break have been that stupid? At first glance, it was unlikely that anyone would notice similarities between David S. Deans and Addison Davies if they weren't specifically looking for them. Logan hadn't. Campbell hadn't, or he would have said something to Logan. Perhaps that was what Lucky Break had counted on. The name Addison Davies had all the letters of his real name plus two extra: the *o* and an additional *i*. His real name wasn't that deeply embedded in the alias. Maybe Lucky Break figured he was being so clever that no one would figure it out.

Logan took the photo of David S. Deans that Campbell had given him and compared it with Addison Davies's passport photo. His eyes darted back and forth from one to the other. Nothing. No lights went off. One was a youthful-looking man in a crew cut; the other, a reserved, distinguished gentleman in his sixties. He looked closer at the Deans photo. There was a crescent-shaped scar on his chin. He looked at the Davies photo and saw nothing there.

Logan didn't think the two men were the same; however, because one name was so easily embedded in the other, he decided he'd better go to Davies Imported Foods to check out the owner anyway. He dressed and then went to the safe and took out his High Standard HDM pistol and checked the magazine. It held ten .22 LR cartridges. They were all there. He took another magazine and put it in his jacket pocket for good measure, along with the silencer. If he ended up confronting Lucky Break, and the agent did anything other than surrender, he would have to kill him. In fact, he'd have to do that anyway.

As he left the hotel, the sun was peering over the horizon, briefly enveloping both land and sea in shades of red, orange, and yellow. There was a slight chill in the air, but he knew it would be another stifling day of intense heat. Birds chirped as they searched for food, oblivious to the conditions of humankind. A cat cried out in the distance, and Logan thought he saw a couple of rats scurrying off toward the square in front of the hotel.

He walked three blocks before he found a taxi. The city was just starting to come alive with pedestrians and vehicles. He gave the driver the address, and the taxi sped away. Along the way, something triggered his memory of the previous night with George Sedgewick at the Blue Moon. Sedgewick had introduced him to his friend. He'd called him Addy. *Damn it*, he thought. "Addy" could have been short for Addison. Sedgewick owned an import/export wholesale business, and Addison Davies owned and operated a retail import shop. Had Sedgewick actually introduced him to Addison Davies? Logan didn't quite remember what the man looked like because his attention had been on Little Egypt, but he had seemed to be in his sixties, which fit the age of the Addison Davies on his list. He also remembered something that the older man had said about leaving today for London and stopping a shipment from Sedgewick. This could all be a weird coincidence—meeting with two men that he'd short-listed as possible assassins. Logan had purposefully sought out Sedgewick, but to have a second one show up would be bizarre. Nevertheless, he still didn't have any high hopes that Addison Davies was Lucky Break. The taxi pulled up to the shop, and Logan got out and paid the driver through the window.

Logan wasn't expecting to find the shop open at this hour, but as he walked toward it, he noticed that the security gate

192 «O» John Charles Gifford

was not fully closed. He slid the gate back and peered through the door, his hands cupped around him to block out the glare. He saw the body of a man on the floor with a pool of dark blood around his head and neck. Logan looked behind him to see whether anyone was around. No one was close by, so he reached behind him and slid out his gun. He realized the door was slightly ajar, so he pushed on it slowly. Quietly, he entered the shop and stopped immediately. He stood there frozen in place, listening for sounds. After about two minutes, he walked around the body and started to check the room. He crept behind the counter and around the food shelves. No one. He then walked to the back of the shop, where the kitchen area was. No one there either. He noticed stairs to the right of him, so he started to climb them. The first one squeaked, so he used the outer edges of the stairs to ascend, slowly and carefully, his pistol extended and leading the way. As he approached the top, he could see that the door was ajar. He nudged the door with his hand and stepped into the room behind his gun. The bed was unmade, and the room looked as if it had been occupied very recently. He picked up a small white towel that had dried blood on it. He slid back a door and found a closet full of clothes on hangers. The clothing was of good quality and cared for, except for the shirt and pants that were on the floor, stained with blood. He then checked under the bed as well as under the sheets and pillows. Nothing. No one.

He went back downstairs and knelt beside the body. He didn't bother to check his pulse. He knew a dead man when he saw one. The deceased looked to be either an American or a European. He grabbed the man's pants at the waist and pulled him to the side slightly, enough so that Logan could get his hand in the back pocket for his wallet. He opened it and looked at the man's driver's license. It was issued to a Peter Cook with a London address. There was no other form of identification. The man's throat was slit, nearly from ear to ear. *Jesus.* Logan reached down and touched the man's face. The temperature along with the coloration of the dried blood suggested that he'd been lying there between eight and ten hours. Logan wondered whether this was the same Peter who had been assigned to Campbell to search for Lucky Break. He had to be, and he apparently had found him. Logan had no doubts now: Addison Davies *was* Lucky Break.

Cook must have surprised him sometime last night. But why did Lucky Break leave the body where it was and not lock up the shop? He could have hidden the body somewhere in the city, and no one would have been any the wiser. At least that would have bought him some time. Instead, he'd left things as they were, certainly with the knowledge that the body would be found sometime today. That could mean only one thing: Lucky Break was already on the move with a new name and disguise, exactly what Logan had been hoping wouldn't happen. *Damn it to hell*, he thought.

Last night, perhaps even after Addison Davies had murdered Peter Cook, Logan had shaken Lucky Break's hand. Acid rose from his stomach, and he tasted the bitterness in his mouth.

Logan needed to see Shakir first, before he did anything. He would still be on duty at the hotel, monitoring Kamal Naguib. Logan would call John Campbell later and tell him the terrible news about Cook. Then suddenly, he remembered what Campbell had asked him yesterday. He'd wanted to know whether he could get a hold of Logan at his hotel. How had he known Logan was staying at a hotel? His remark had even implied that he knew which one. Had Campbell put surveillance on him? Had he been keeping track of Logan? If he had, that meant Campbell had known about Logan *before* Logan confronted him in his flat.

Perhaps Logan's first instincts had been right. Maybe

the British government was planning to assassinate Nasser after all, and both Davies and Campbell were involved in it. Maybe Peter Cook had stumbled onto it and suffered the consequences. That would complicate Logan's mission, but it wouldn't distract from it. He still had to find Lucky Break. And what was he going to do about John Campbell?

Chapter 22
THE WHORE

6:05 a.m.

HE WAS KNACKERED.

For five years, Addison Davies had slept on a firm mattress. He had been used to that. But last night he slept in an upright position on a hard surface in the catacombs. He'd had little choice in the matter, not knowing whether the body of Peter Cook might have been discovered already. If it had been, the Egyptian police would have been searching for him overnight. Sleeping in a subterranean cemetery had been a small price to pay to avoid the embarrassment of being captured. He would one day be in the history books as the man who'd been responsible for the assassination of President Gamal Abdel Nasser, the man who had challenged the Soviet menace and ultimately saved the Suez Canal for Great Britain. But that would be sometime in the distant future, after the world came to its senses and saw him for what he truly was. But right now, Addison Davies had other things on his mind.

He now walked down narrow side streets and alleyways carrying his attaché case, not knowing where, specifically, he was going. The city was beginning to fill up with people going to their jobs, some to their small shops to sell the same things that hundreds of others were selling, some to the markets carrying fresh produce on carts and bicycles, after traveling for an hour or more from small farms outside the city. He stopped near a narrow mosque in an alley, set the case down near his feet, and angled his head slightly to listen to the call of the muezzin high above in a minaret. He wasn't a particularly religious man. In fact, he didn't believe in anyone's God. He'd lost all belief in a supreme being during the war and never regained his faith, but it wasn't for lack of trying.

As he listened to the muezzin's call, he thought about how nice and simple life would be if he could only find comfort in some kind of religion. Islam was as good as any religion to him, for they all assured their believers of certain guarantees, if only the faithful would worship their god and conduct themselves in a particular way.

After the war, he'd tried hard to be a believer again. He had returned to the one true Church, gone to confession, and recited his Our Fathers and Hail Marys. But his efforts hadn't lasted long—he had an emptiness in him that could no longer be filled with the childlike faith he'd once had. He'd seen too much of life and death to ever believe that some supreme being was guiding humanity to a peaceful and just end. When he'd finally stopped believing, he'd started his descent into the realm of absurdity, where he now dwelled. The good and innocent suffered, and the wicked reigned. It made no sense to him. It was absurd. He now believed that nothing was guiding humanity except humanity itself, so he developed his own philosophy of life. And who was to say he was wrong? Notwithstanding, he had no guarantees he was right because life offered none. The difference now was that he no longer cared.

However, every so often—like now—he would take a few steps backward and wish he had some kind of religious faith, some assurance, that his life meant something. At times, he missed the comfort that the faithful seemed to have. What sustained him now, mostly, was that he had come to realize he himself had to create that faith. He lived by his own set of values and had faith that they were right. There was no other way for him. But this, too, didn't matter, for he didn't have much time to live. Before the day ended, someone would kill Addison Davies. At the moment, he just didn't quite know who.

He picked up his attaché case and continued down the alley until he reached a main thoroughfare. He had to get off the streets now. If the authorities weren't presently hunting for him, they certainly would be soon enough. A sixty-three-year-old Englishman would be an easy catch in this city. At least for now, he'd have to stay away from the major hotels. The police would check them out first. And the dilapidated rooms in the slum areas would be no good because as a foreigner he would be too conspicuous there.

He looked both ways. The street was swelling up with traffic and people. Where would he go? *Yes, of course, that's it!* he thought. He suddenly knew where. *Perfect!* He crossed the street diagonally through the roundabout, dodging bicycles and stopping briefly to let a man in a horse cart pass by him. As he reached the curb, out of the corner of his eye, he saw a jeep coming his way from the right, carrying four armed soldiers. It was going neither fast nor slow. The speed suggested that the occupants were looking for someone. Their attention was focused on both sides of the street.

Damn it, they found Cook already. He turned his back to the street and walked toward the nearest shop at the corner, where he looked through the glass window at some mannequins dressed in the latest fashion and at a toy train racing along a circular track, as if he were interested in them. In the reflection, he saw the jeep slow down. He turned sideways just a little for a better view. The heads of two of the soldiers were turned in his direction. The jeep rolled to a sudden stop.

Jesus, he thought. He was trapped. None of the soldiers got out. *Keep calm*, he told himself. *Remember your training.* At this point, he couldn't make a mad dash for it. On this street, the buildings were virtually touching each other, far too narrow to squeeze his body through sideways. Additionally, he hadn't seen an alleyway or passage on either side of him. There was nowhere for him to go. If he tried to get away, they would shoot him—they couldn't possibly miss from that distance. He had no choice but to stay where he was and continue pretending to be interested in what he was looking at.

If they approached him, what would he do? For Christ's sake, there were four of them! Letting himself be taken was out of the question. He had to have a plan, however tentative. He slipped his hand around the hilt of his dagger inside his jacket and held it in place. If two of them approached him and got close enough, he could kill one of them easily and take that soldier's weapon to defend himself against the other. But there would still be two others in the jeep. It was possible that he could kill them as well but unlikely. Should they try to take him down, he was prepared to take as many of them as possible with him. But for the moment, he told himself to relax and see how this would play out. He was not about to force the situation by acting irrationally, thereby causing his own death.

Addison bent over slightly at an angle, seemingly to get a better look at the electric train through window. His eyes, however, were cast in an upward stare at the reflection. He tightened his grip on the hilt. Drops of sweat ran down his forehead and around his eyes, finding their way to his cheeks and then to his chin. Off in the distance, he could hear the angry words of two women arguing about something. Overhead, a gull cried out: *huoh-huoh-huoh.*

Then one of the soldiers got out of the jeep and started walking in his direction. *Good, only one.* He was confident that he could take him because the soldier would think Addison was an old man and would have his guard down. He was holding his rifle at the ready position, but the barrel was pointing downward. He wouldn't expect to be attacked by an old man with a dagger. Addison held the hilt of his dagger firmly, ready to pull it out, and waited for the soldier to come within range. He was within four feet of him when Addison heard the staccato voice of another soldier telling him to return to the jeep immediately. The soldier turned and ran back. Addison relaxed his hand on the hilt and watched them speed off. They must have been looking for someone else, Addison concluded. Still, he needed to get off the streets; otherwise, he would leave himself open to happenstance encounters like this one, and the next one might not go his way. Addison Davies was a liability. He needed to be killed off soon.

He turned to his right and walked for two more blocks and then turned left down a narrow street, passing few people along the way. He picked up his pace and walked another five blocks until he got to a shabby apartment complex. He entered the building and climbed three flights of stairs. On the landing, he knocked on the first door to the right. When there was no answer, he knocked harder. He heard a faint female voice and was relieved she was there.

"Who is it?" the tired voice said, just on the other side of the door.

"Addy. Open up."

The door swung open, and the whore stood there, her cotton robe hanging open, revealing a thin, naked body.

"Why so early? What's going on?" she said, slurring her words.

"I'm leaving for London later today. I couldn't leave without first seeing you."

"So you're abandoning me?" The words melted from her lips.

"Not for long. I'll be back in a few weeks." He eyed the whore, concealing his contempt for her. She was a mess. "Will you miss me while I'm gone?"

She was tall, about twenty-five years old, with long black hair. He knew she would be too busy to miss him for very long. Her eyes were unfocused and glassy. Laudanum again. So much the better. It would make things easier.

"Of course, I'll miss you," she said, dropping her robe to the floor and standing in front of him naked.

Addison locked the door and set his case by a table. He took her in his arms and pulled her against him. She was nothing but a prostitute, but she was beautiful, and it had been a week since his last visit. After they kissed long and hard, he walked to a cabinet and took out a bottle of whiskey he kept there and poured them each a shot. Like a good whore, she pretended that she was exclusively his, bought and paid for, but Addison knew better.

"I have a little time before I need to go to the airport," he said, taking her hand and leading her into the bedroom. "I thought we could say our goodbyes properly."

Addison undressed while she slipped under the sheets. He set his clothes on the floor beside the bed, and then he climbed in with her. They managed to make love for about ten minutes before she fell asleep. He gently pushed her aside. She now lay beside him, facing him, her breathing slow and deep—a result of the laudanum, no doubt. He was on his stomach with his arm hanging over the edge of the bed. He felt around his clothes for his dagger. He grasped the hilt firmly and slowly pulled his arm up and underneath him. Then he twisted his body into an upright position, so that he was now kneeling on the mattress.

"I have to go now. I will miss you, my darling," he whispered, as he thrust the dagger upward between her ribs and into her heart. She jerked slightly, as if in a bad dream, and settled into a calm repose, her face placid in an everlasting sleep. The death was fast and painless, with little blood to spoil the lovely silk sheets he'd bought for her only last month. With the tip of his finger, he traced her brow and then kissed her lips one last time. He pulled the dagger out of her body and wiped it off with a cloth.

He then got up, retrieved his case, and walked to her dressing table. He opened the case and pulled out a tube of special compound that removed his makeup. He sat down and began rubbing it onto his face. As the makeup pealed off, his face changed by degrees, killing Addison Davies forever. "Farewell, Mr. Davies," he said aloud. "It's been a pleasure."

After he finished, he showered and then dried himself off and dressed. He returned to the dressing table, and set the case on the top. He took a half dozen passports out of a compartment below the makeup and examined them one by one. Each passport showed him in a different disguise with a different nationality. In the event he needed to change identities quickly—as he did now—all he had to do was choose from personas he'd already developed, complete with a personal history, instead of wasting valuable time trying to come up with one.

He picked up the American passport and looked at his photo—an American tourist in his early fifties. *That will do quite well!* he thought. He looked at himself in the mirror and began the transformation. He took roughly twice the time it would normally take. After he finished, he examined himself closely in the mirror for any mistakes. He compared himself to his passport picture. Spot on! He had the hair parted on the right and the correct shade of gray. He looked into the mirror again at Henry Nelson from Minneapolis, Minnesota, a businessman on vacation, here to see the ancient history of Egypt. Spot on indeed!

He then took two visa stamps out of his case that he'd purchased on the black market. They weren't perfect, but they would do. He adjusted the date on one of them and stamped a page in his passport: *Rome, Italy – July 8, 1956*. Adjusting the other stamp, he stamped a second page: *Alexandria, Egypt – July 18, 1956*. This would be sufficient if the Egyptian authorities didn't check the airlines' manifests. *It will never get to that*, he thought.

He replaced everything in the case and then started toward the kitchen, glancing at the bed as he passed it. He would miss her. It was a shame he couldn't trust her to know his true identity. He couldn't allow himself to be blackmailed at this crucial stage.

Once in the kitchen, he put some water in a kettle for tea and put it on the electric burner. The morning had been queer, and he'd missed having his tea! It would be another hour before the shops were open. He needed new clothes and luggage—American-made, with the appropriate labels. He knew exactly where to get them. He would use the intervening time to have his cuppa and to practice the American Midwest accent he'd perfected many years ago but hadn't used since. He had been friends with an American businessman from Iowa and had listened carefully to his speech patterns; he had then practiced them until he had them just right. That had been several years ago, and now he needed to refresh himself. After he bought new clothes, he would return here and change, destroying his old ones. Addison Davies would no longer need them.

Henry Nelson would then be free to move about the city without concern.

Chapter 23
THE MATINEE IDOL

6:30 a.m.

ALEX LOGAN GOT OUT OF THE TAXI AND RUSHED through the front doors of the Hotel Cecil. He saw his cousin immediately. Captain Shakir El Mahdeya was sitting in the lobby in a brown leather armchair with one leg crossed over the other, reading yesterday's newspaper, smoking a large straight-stemmed briar pipe, and drinking an espresso. He'd been there all night, and his face showed it. He puffed on the pipe as he looked up at Logan. Logan could tell he was dead tired. He crouched in front of him.

"I feel like shit, Alex," Shakir said, "but you look like it. Where're you coming from?"

"I found him," he said, just above a whisper.

"Your man?"

"Yes, my man. But we need to go to the airport right away. I have reason to believe he may be leaving the country."

"Why would he be leaving the country now? I don't understand."

"I'll fill you in on the details on the way, but we've got to leave immediately."

Logan saw that Shakir was annoyed. He figured that

Shakir was drained and wanted nothing more than to go home and sleep.

Shakir said, "I need to make a call to headquarters first for a replacement. Then we'll leave."

Logan cocked his head to the side and grinned. "When did you start smoking a pipe?"

"After your visit last year. You've teased me often enough about looking like an Egyptian version of Rudolph Valentino, so I decided to buy a pipe and try it out. I thought it might make me look more like a Hollywood movie star. I even bought a Dunhill—like yours—the most expensive brand my cigar shop had." He held the pipe up as if it were a cigar and looked at it. "Frankly, I enjoy it, but not as much as a good stogie." He got up and started walking toward the reception desk with the pipe firmly between his teeth. "My car's out front," he said, squeezing the words out of the side of his mouth as he looked over his shoulder at Logan. "I'll meet you there in a minute."

Logan was in the passenger seat when Shakir came outside. "My replacement will be here in fifteen minutes," Shakir said. "That means there will be no surveillance on Naguib during that time. At this point, it's foolish to continue minding him, but orders are orders." He paused a moment, and then added, "He and his mistress are probably still snuggled up in a deep sleep."

There was less traffic on the road at this time of day, but Shakir used his siren nonetheless. During the thirty minutes it took them to reach the airport, Logan explained what had happened the night before at the Blue Moon on the waterfront promenade and how he'd come to find a dead British agent this morning in Addison Davies's storefront shop.

"Davies said that he had to leave for London unexpectedly but that he'd be returning in a few weeks," Logan said.

"Maybe his plans were upset when he realized that

MI6 was after him. Maybe he's not going through with the assassination, Alex. That's good news, no?"

"Maybe. But I can't imagine that a man like him, with the resources he has, is just going to give up and fly home. He must have made contingency plans for something like this. I would've done the same if I were going to assassinate your head of state. He's committed. He'll continue. He'll change disguises and press on. We'll be looking for a needle in a haystack."

"As if we weren't already." Shakir paused a moment and then asked, "Then why go to the airport?"

"To cover our bases in case I'm wrong. But I don't think I am. I found out from one of the British agents that his real name is David S. Deans, but it won't matter. I'm sure he's somewhere in the city, changing his looks. Once he's done that, he'll be free to go wherever he wants, unimpeded, with a new name and identity papers. And then we'll have to start all over again." He looked out the window, away from Shakir. "Damn it, I shook hands with him last night. We'll get the bastard for good next time."

"My dear brother," Shakir said, with quick glances at Logan, "we've got four days left. How are we going to do that?"

"I don't know, but we'll find a way."

Once at the airport, they went directly to BOAC and asked the woman at the counter how many flights to London were leaving today. She seemed distracted and appeared annoyed by the question. Shakir reached into his pocket for his badge and identification. That didn't improve her mood, but she said there was one at 9:30 a.m.

"How about the other carriers?" Shakir asked.

She sighed and checked her listings. None today.

"I'd like to see the manifest for that flight," said Shakir.

She supplied the manifest, and they quickly reviewed it. The plane was originating in Cairo and was nearly full. Few passengers were getting on in Alexandria—all Egyptian. There was no Addison Davies, and there was no David S. Deans.

Shakir was disappointed, but Logan was certain that Lucky Break wouldn't have booked the flight; nevertheless, they had to confirm he wasn't leaving the country in case Logan was wrong. Lucky Break wouldn't have put himself in such a vulnerable position at the airport. If he were actually leaving Egypt, he'd find another way out. But Logan was confident he wasn't going anywhere. He'd stay in Alexandria. He'd stay right here and continue with his plan to assassinate Gamal Abdel Nasser.

With four days left, Lucky Break *definitely* was not going anywhere. *Not on his life, he won't!* Logan thought.

It had taken them less than twenty minutes to arrive at the Moharrem Bey police station. Shakir now sat with his feet on his desk, having sent a detective and two uniformed officers to Addison Davies's shop to search the premises and arrange for the body of Peter Cook to be taken to the morgue. Logan paced the office. Neither man had said much on the way back, and they were saying even less now. In four days, Nasser would be coming to Alexandria—only four days before he would ride in an open limousine from the airport to Mansheya Square, four days before he'd mount the platform and deliver a speech to thousands of people, telling the world he was going to nationalize the Suez Canal.

Logan looked at Shakir and was about to say something when Shakir beat him to it.

With his elbows on the armrests of chair, Shakir made a triangle with his thumbs and index fingers. "Perhaps we have come to the point where we must consider notifying Nasser's security force." He reached over to his desk for his pipe and tobacco.

"No, not yet," Logan said. "We still have time. We can always notify them before Nasser leaves Cairo on the twenty-sixth. We can still get the bastard."

Shakir filled the pipe and put a match to the bowl. He puffed a few times to get it going. "I wish I had your confidence, but I'll tell you what I can do. Of course, it'll be your call." He tamped the tobacco ash down and relit the pipe, sending a cloud of smoke between the two men.

Logan reached into his jacket for his own pipe and then sat down. He knew Shakir was a good cop, and he was eager to hear what he had in mind.

"I suggest we look for Lucky Break the way we'd look for a high-profile murderer," Shakir said. "I'll put out an alert. I'm talking about a full-scale manhunt. I can have every available officer check Caucasian-looking males in the city, at least those who appear to be European. I'll have them check passports to make certain they're legitimate. If there's the slightest thing wrong with a passport or visa, they can detain the person and call us. It's a long shot, and I know it's a tall order, but it can be done." He puffed on his pipe and then added, "Of course, I won't tell my men we're looking for an assassin. If I did, it would be in the papers in a matter of hours. It'd scare off Lucky Break. I'll just tell them we're looking for someone we want for questioning, but I'll give it a high priority so they take the situation seriously. For the safety of my men, I do need to tell them to be cautious, that he may be armed." After a moment of reflection, he said, "Maybe we should have done this from the beginning."

"That's good, Shakir. Have them check all hotels and any places where foreign nationals congregate. Unless he's hiding out, we'll find him somewhere in the city." Logan took a moment to fill his pipe and then continued. "But he won't be hiding out. Lucky Break is too arrogant for that. He'll most likely want to flaunt his new disguise. He'll be out in the open.

His ego won't permit anything less. He now knows for certain that British intelligence is looking for him, and he may figure that the local police are as well. He'll make this into a cat-and-mouse game. We'll use his ego to catch him."

"How many other British agents are here looking for him?"

Logan had his pipe going now, and he puffed out an answer. "Two others, but they know even less than we do. I'll inform their lead agent that Peter Cook is dead. He can identify the body."

Following a moment of silence, Shakir asked, "So ... what do you think?"

"I think it's a last resort, but it may very well—"

"No, no, not that," Shakir said, interrupting him. "Does the pipe make me look like a Hollywood movie star?"

"Right, a real matinee idol."

Chapter 24
THE LAST BIT OF INTELLIGENCE

10:25 a.m.

THE COFFEE WAS HOT AND BITTER. DONATELLA looked across the table at Naguib. He brought the cup to his lips a second time, tasted it, and then winced. That was her cue to reach for the milk.

"Here, my darling," she said as she leaned over the table and poured. "This will be better."

This was part of their morning ritual after eating a hardy breakfast whenever he was in the city—he winced, and she poured. She hated it as much as she hated him. How many more times would she have to engage in this silly playacting? How long would it be before this became just a bad memory? *Fool!* she thought, referring to herself. He paid her well for her performance. She had nothing to complain about.

"I'm paying a great deal of money for this suite," Naguib said matter-of-factly. "Why is it that this hotel always serves my coffee too bitter? You would think—"

"But darling," Donatella interrupted, "perhaps most people enjoy their coffee bitter. I myself do. Besides, if it weren't bitter, you would have no need for me to pour your milk. You would throw me out into the street and cast me away." She lowered her eyes as a servant might do. This, too, was one of her parts in their ritual: feign self-deprecation and then wait for his rescuing words of recommitment.

"You are my beautiful gift, my jewel," he said, frowning. "Why would I ever do such a thing?"

"I don't know. Would you?"

"Of course not, my pet. I would do many things, but never that."

"Then what would you do?"

"I would shower you with gifts and keep you close to my heart."

She stared at him, pleased with his answer. She played her part well.

"But I must now tell you something that you will not be pleased with." He glanced at his coffee, then out the window, averting his eyes from hers as he always did whenever he had unpleasant news for her. "I must cut this trip short and return to Cairo. I need to finalize the security for Nasser's trip on Thursday."

"When will you leave?"

"When we're finished here. There's still much to be done in preparation."

Donatella pouted. Naguib twisted in his chair. She could tell he felt guilty for abandoning her. She got up, walked to him with her hands on her hips as if she were hurt, and then sat on his lap, her lower lip protruding in an exaggerated way.

"You see, this is a big security operation," he said, continuing his justification for leaving early. "I must be there to check and double-check everything. We can't have anything go wrong."

Donatella placed her long fingers on his bald head and gently pushed his head back, and then she kissed him with an open mouth, her tongue finding its way in. It was a hard kiss and long. He could never resist her when she initiated lovemaking. When she finished, she placed her hands on either side of his fat face. "Tell me how much you will miss me, Kamal. Tell me how much you will long for me."

"I will, I will. I will long for you greatly," he said, nearly out of breath.

She got up and walked to the window, where she looked down at the Corniche and at the sea, her back toward him. "And when will you return to me?"

He stood and walked to the window beside her and placed his arm around her waist. The waves below were crashing against the wall of the promenade. The sun was reaching high in the sky.

"The security forces will start arriving here tomorrow. I will come with Nasser on Thursday. After the speech there will be a reception for the dignitaries to celebrate Egypt taking control of the canal, and he will return to Cairo immediately after that, but I will give him some excuse for why I have to stay here, instead of going back with him."

She did all she could to restrain her joy. He wouldn't be back until Thursday. Today would be the last time she'd have to see him. She would no longer have to play the part of mistress. No longer would she have to endure those grubby little hands on her body. No longer would she have to listen to his sickening words that he thought were as sweet as chocolate. But there was one additional piece of information that she needed from him before this was over forever. She turned to him and lowered her eyes. "I have to tell you that I don't look forward to all those security people patrolling the streets. They always treat me with disrespect. How many will there be this time?"

"About five hundred, plus the local police. Just stay clear of them, and you'll be fine."

"But where will they be?"

"Mostly on rue Fuad, along the route. Many will wear civilian clothing, but they will be armed and always on duty. The uniformed men will make themselves conspicuous around Mansheya Square and along the route. Just stay clear of them while they're here."

"But rue Fuad is where my mother lives, and as you know, that's where I've been staying. Her health is bad. I need to look after her."

"Then stay here at the hotel, my dear. You know that this suite is permanently reserved for me. You can stay here and not have to go out. Hire someone to look after your mother for a few days."

Donatella smiled at him.

"So it's settled then," he said. He reached into his wallet and pulled out several large bills—Egyptian pounds—which he then placed in her hand. "This should take care of your expenses until I get back."

She folded the bills in her hand. "You're too good to me, Kamal. Certainly, you can spare a little time now so that I can show you my appreciation." She took his hand, and he followed her into the bedroom.

Chapter 25
ANOTHER BODY

1:15 p.m.

SHE STARED AT HIM, HER HEAD RAISED slightly, her eyes hooded and provocative, her lips full and red. She lounged lasciviously on a straw mat, arms opened. She was barely clothed in a gauzy black fabric that emphasized the allure of her curved breasts. Logan stared back at her. She had a magnetism that he found difficult to resist.

"You like her?" Ariane Baudrot asked him, speaking in her native French. She was sitting across from him at a small round table. "All men like her. Women as well. Many fall in love with her. But she has no name. We must give her a name. What do you think? You have a name for her?"

Logan shifted his eyes from the painting on the wall to Ariane. "How about *The Lustful Girl*?"

"But that's no name. And besides, she's a woman, not a girl. Just look at those breasts!"

"How about *Aimée*?"

"Don't be ridiculous. That's French. This woman is clearly Egyptian." She spoke her words with directness and authority. She took a pull from her cigarillo, angling her head slightly to

213

keep the smoke from getting into her eyes, and then added a further pronouncement. "She needs an Egyptian name."

"I suppose you're right. I'm at a loss then," he said, shrugging his shoulders.

Earlier, Logan had phoned the British consulate office and left a message for John Campbell to meet him at Baudrot's, a combination tea room, restaurant, and American bar on rue Cherif Pasha. Logan had first met Ariane Baudrot, its owner and *femme du monde*, through a friend at the British information office nearby, which shared office space with the consulate. They'd liked each other immediately. Logan admired her strength and womanly independence. She was flamboyant in dress and quirky in habit. Her hair was always tied up with a bright colored ribbon, and her makeup was always overdone. She had never married, but she had no lack of men around her—or women. She was attractive in a garish sort of way, and her ubiquitous cigarillo made her look a bit erotic. Logan liked her, but he didn't desire her. She was aging. Crow's-feet were beginning to appear around her eyes where there had been none, and the broken capillaries on either side of her nose were new since he last saw her. Nevertheless, Logan found her attractive and, he had to admit, somewhat exciting.

"I've never known you to be at a loss for anything," she said. "You look pale. You didn't sleep last night. Someone kept you awake?" Ariane had the habit of wrapping everything in sexuality. Perhaps that was also why Logan found her exciting.

"Something like that," he said.

Ariane glanced at the door. "I think the person you're waiting for is here," she said, getting up. "Be sure to visit me again before you return to America. Longer next time. We need to settle on a name for the lovely lady before you leave." She leaned down, and they kissed each other's cheeks, twice. She started to walk away but stopped. She turned around, returned to Logan, kissed him hard on the lips, and then left. "Longer next time, Alexander," she said over her shoulder.

Campbell saw Logan sitting at the table and joined him. A waiter came immediately. Campbell ordered a coffee. Logan ordered another one.

"I got your message that you wanted to see me," Campbell said. "Is this about Lucky Break? It sounded urgent."

"Peter Cook is dead," Logan said flatly.

"What?" Campbell exclaimed.

"I found him early this morning at Addison Davies's shop. His throat was slit."

"Jesus."

"Davies is Lucky Break. He was on my list. Yours too."

"I sent Cook to his shop yesterday late in the afternoon to check him out. I gave him explicit orders that if he sensed something was off with Davies, he should contact me, and we'd both return later and take him. When he didn't contact me, I thought he had eliminated Davies from the list."

"Cook must have surprised him. Lucky Break didn't care whether the body was found. He didn't try to hide it. He even left his shop open. That means he's changing disguises. He's done with Addison Davies. That identity is no use to him now. It's going to be even more difficult to find him."

"Damn it! I really didn't think Davies was our man. I sent Cook simply to verify that. Damn it!" Campbell said, hitting the table with a fist.

The waiter came with the coffee and then left. They both sipped from their cups, Logan eyeing Campbell over the rim.

"Here's where we're at," Logan said. "I've enlisted the help of the chief of criminal investigations of the police department. He can be trusted. He's put out a citywide alert. The police will be stopping all white males, checking for fraudulent passports."

"That won't be of much help. It'll drive him underground. We'll never find him."

"Listen," Logan said impatiently, "we have few options, and time is running out. If you have a better plan, spit it out."

Campbell made eye contact for a moment and then lowered his head. "I suppose you're right." He looked back at Logan. "Deans has very good language skills. He knows French like a native, and he can speak English with a French accent that would fool most people. He also knows a half dozen British dialects, as well as Canadian and several American dialects. MI6 trained him well."

"He speaks Arabic, of course."

"Of course."

"I disagree with you about driving him underground. I believe he'll have enough confidence in himself to move about the city safely. You said yourself that he's arrogant."

"Yes, very."

"Then he won't hole up in some hotel room for the next four days. He'll be in the open, flaunting himself."

Reconsidering, Campbell said, "I apologize. I was wrong. Checking passports seems to be the only recourse we have. Let's hope he maintains his sense of confidence."

"Fuck your apology. Finish your coffee. We need to go to the morgue so you can identify the body."

They both gulped the last bit of coffee in their cups, hurried outside, and hailed a taxi outside the bar.

The three men stood over the body of Peter Cook, Shakir having met them there. It was covered with a sheet, leaving the head and neck exposed.

"He must have used a dagger," Shakir said, pointing at Cook's neck, "with a very sharp double blade. The cut suggests an upward movement. Look here." Shakir pointed with his index finger, nearly touching the wound.

Logan and Campbell lowered their heads for a closer look.

"Cook must have been standing behind him and to the side. He probably had him leaning against something and was about to check him for a weapon when Deans reached for the dagger and swung it to the side."

"He's got a wife and kids," Campbell said. "They're going to be devastated."

Shakir pulled the sheet over Cook's head. "You need to sign some papers before you leave."

The phone on a small desk in the corner of the room rang. Shakir walked over to it and picked it up.

Logan looked at Campbell. "You said that there was another agent here who came with Cook."

Behind them, Shakir was standing with the receiver to his ear, nodding and saying, "Yes, yes, I understand."

"He's checking out a few names on our list," said Campbell. "As soon as he checks in, I'll tell him about Cook and update him on what we're doing."

Shakir put the phone down and rejoined the other two men. He looked shaken. "It was my office. They told me that a woman called them to report that she had discovered the body of her neighbor late this morning. The body is a female, and it looks as if she was murdered." His face was drawn and pale.

"Does it have anything to do with Lucky Break?" Logan asked.

"I don't know, but I have to go there immediately. Please come with me, Alex."

They left the morgue. In front of the building, Campbell got in a taxi and sped off. Logan and Shakir got into Shakir's car.

Shakir put the key in the ignition but didn't turn it. He

looked at Logan, his eyes glistening with tears. "It's Aria, Alex. She's been murdered."

Three uniformed police officers were at Aria's flat when they arrived. After talking with the officers, Shakir sent them back to the station. They'd already interviewed the woman who had called them. She'd told one of them that she was supposed to have met Aria at noon so that they could go to the market together. The door was ajar when she got there, so she walked into the flat. That was when she'd found Aria on the bed, naked, with blood on her stomach. The officer who'd interviewed her asked whether she'd seen or heard anything suspicious. Her flat was next to Aria's. She told him that earlier she'd heard someone knocking on Aria's door. She peeked out and saw an older man standing at the door. She heard Aria ask who it was and heard the man say it was Addy. The neighbor hadn't thought anything about it because she'd seen that same man there many times before.

Logan stayed in the kitchen, looking around, to give Shakir time alone with his sister. He could hear the sobs, the muted grief of his cousin coming from the bedroom. Logan himself had never been close to Aria and in fact had not seen her for—he did know how long, but it must have been years. His last memories of her were from when she was a teenager: defiant, independent as much as she could be at that age, and always in some kind of conflict with her parents. Shakir, the older brother, seemed to always be the bridge between her and their parents, trying to resolve this and that peacefully. Eventually, the situation at home had become worse. Aria, unprepared for the world alone, had left her parents and set out on her own. Neither her parents nor Shakir could ever keep track of her for very long.

Shakir joined Logan in the kitchen. "The wound was made by a dagger," he said. "It was pushed up into her heart. She would have died almost immediately. I don't need an autopsy to tell me that." He paused for a moment to collect himself. "It was probably the same dagger used on Cook."

"From the neighbor's interview," Logan said, "we can assume that it was Lucky Break who murdered her." He looked at Shakir's face and saw a grieving brother rather than a police inspector. "Are you able to continue? We should search the flat carefully. Maybe he left something behind that could help us."

Shakir rubbed his eyes dry with the heels of his palms. "I'm a professional police officer," he snapped. "Of course, I'm able to continue." There was much sadness in his voice—and anger, but not toward Logan. "I'll take the bedroom, and you can look in the kitchen. We need to do this carefully. From what the neighbor said, Lucky Break was a frequent visitor here, so there might be something he left behind." He shook his head. He was repeating what Logan had just said. "I have no idea how this is going to help us find the bastard."

They spent the next two hours scouring the flat from top to bottom. They pulled out drawers, looked over things, and looked under things. They got on their hands and knees and examined every inch of the flat.

"Nothing, goddamn it," Shakir said. He looked toward the trash bin under the sink in the kitchen and then at Logan. "Did you check the trash?" he said, pointing to it.

Logan walked over to the bin, picked it up, and dumped it out in the sink. There wasn't much in it: a few tin cans, a banana peel, and coffee grounds. He picked out a wadded piece of paper, brushed off the grounds, and opened it. The paper looked relatively new. "It's a receipt from a men's store. It's dated today. It lists a suit, shirt, tie, hat, belt, and shoes."

"Thank God we found something," Shakir said. "Would

you go there and interview them? I need to wait here for the morgue to come. I can't leave her alone. If they're reluctant to talk with you, tell them that the chief of criminal investigations will be pissed as hell if he has to come himself."

"Yes, this morning. An English gentleman came in just as I opened up. He bought the things listed on this receipt and left. He was quite pleasant. Is there anything wrong?" The owner of the men's store was an American in his middle to late fifties. He had a full head of gray hair and a neatly trimmed mustache. He was impeccably dressed in a white suit.

"Describe his face. Clean-shaven? Beard? Mustache?"

"Clean-shaven, short brown hair, combed to the side. His face was ... well, normal-looking."

"Which side? His hair ..."

He thought a moment and then said, "Part on the left, hair combed to the right." He frowned. "No, I mean part on the right, hair combed to the left. Yes, that's it."

"Are you certain?"

"Yes. If I close my eyes, I can see the part."

"How old would you say he was?"

"Fifty. Fifty-five ... no more than that."

Lucky Break's makeup, Logan thought. "I need the exact description of the suit he bought."

The store owner's eyes flashed. "He bought the exact same kind as I'm wearing. He liked it so much that he refused to look at any other. It's made of fine white linen, as you can see." He lifted an arm to Logan and fingered the material. "Imported from America. You see, we specialize in clothing made in the States."

Logan thought the suit looked like any other white suit he'd seen. "What's the brand?"

"Brooks Brothers. We sell nothing but the best."

"And the shoes—color and brand."

"We stock only Florsheim shoes. The gentleman purchased a pair of brown ones." He looked down at his own shoes. "Like these."

"What kind of hat did he buy?"

"A white Panama."

"What style?"

"A smart-looking fedora with a black band."

"Do you sell many of these—this particular kind of suit and the shoes?"

"Between the tourists and expats, I can't keep them in the shop. For some reason, the British really like them. I mean, they should like them because of the quality, but the British shops have some very good brands themselves. Just last week, this Englishman came in and bought four of them—all white. And he left with four pairs of brown shoes to boot—different styles!"

"That's wonderful," Logan said wryly.

"Is there something wrong?"

"There is, but nothing that you can do anything about. Are you certain of the accent? Could he have been an American? Maybe Canadian?"

"I know an English accent when I hear one," he said defensively.

Logan left the store thinking about Lucky Break. He had changed his appearance—new clothes and presumably a new face. So now he was going to look just like a few hundred tourists or expatriates in Alexandria. Or a few thousand.

But why had he visited this particular shop that sold only clothes made in America? Was he going to assume an American identity? Logan remembered that Campbell had said that Lucky Break knew a number of American accents. So why not use one at the shop? He'd changed his face, after all. Maybe when he realized that the man in the shop was American, he had decided not to risk a conversation about things back home (a common topic of conversation among expats) because his knowledge was limited. So he had continued with a British accent instead. It could all be a coincidence, however. Maybe he just stopped at the first shop he came across.

Logan couldn't very well ask Shakir to have his people stop every Caucasian male in a white suit and brown shoes and check him for a Brooks Brothers label and Florsheim stamped into the bottom of their soles. This wasn't a police state, not really.

But he had no choice. It was the only thing they could do now. Logan didn't have much hope.

Lucky Break was on the loose and in full control.

Chapter 26
THE MAN FROM MINNESOTA

7:30 p.m.

DAVID S. DEANS STOPPED SHORT OF THE entrance to a café on rue Rosette in the Greek quarter, stretched his neck slightly to the left, and peered inside. It was small and crowded with local men, mostly middle-aged, some older, one younger. A few were eating while others smoked shisha. Most were engaged in lively discussions. Two sat off to the right, playing a game of Senet. Arabic music played softly in the background. At the back, in a small cubbyhole, he noticed a man talking on the phone that hung from a wall. After a minute or so, the man replaced the receiver and joined others at a table. Deans went inside and in Arabic ordered a tea at the counter. When the tea was ready, he paid for it and took it to the back of the room to the phone, setting his new brown American-made Samsonite suitcase (with his attaché case inside of it) on the floor next to him. He sipped the tea and then placed it on a three-legged stool next to him. He looked over his left shoulder. Was anyone giving him more attention than he warranted as a Westerner? Any quick, furtive glances? No. He picked up the receiver, put a coin into the slot, and dialed the Hotel Cecil. In Arabic, he asked to be connected to room 504. It was picked up after the second ring.

"Yes," Donatella said.

Switching to Italian to reduce the possibility of anyone in the café understanding him in spite of his hushed voice, he said, "This is room service. I want to confirm your dinner at nine o'clock tonight." That was his code whenever he needed to contact her at the hotel. He seldom did. Tonight was different.

"I can speak freely. Naguib won't be back until Thursday."

Deans turned his head to the left while still holding the receiver to his ear. A man who was forking some beans into his mouth glanced up at him and then resumed his conversation with the person across the table from him.

"I need to meet you at the entrance to the Montazah Gardens in an hour. There shouldn't be too many people there at that time of night. If there are, they will think you are a common prostitute hired for the evening." At that, he grinned, knowing he'd just stirred some hot coals under her.

There was a long pause before she spoke. "Why so far away? It will take me at least an hour and a half to get there."

He looked at his watch. "Okay, then meet me there at nine and try not to be late."

He hung up the phone and then picked up his tea and finished it. He looked at a mirror hanging on the opposite wall. It was old, and his image was somewhat smoky. He nearly didn't recognize himself. His physical appearance had changed drastically, and he wasn't used to it yet. He needed a little time for his mind to catch up—time and a bit more practice in his new persona as a wealthy American tourist, enjoying the sites of Alexandria.

He picked up his suitcase and tea glass, went to the counter, set the glass down, and nodded graciously at the man who had served him. Then he left the café and walked out into the crowded street and disappeared.

Deans arrived early at the Montazah Gardens. He strolled around the paths, dotted here and there with doum palms. It was dark now, but there was enough indirect light from the far eastern part of the Corniche promenade and surrounding buildings for him to see. He took this time to mentally prepare himself for this new identity. After all, he'd been Addison Davies for the last five years and Henry Nelson from Minneapolis for less than a day. A good actor would need more time than that to prepare for a role. But Deans considered himself to be more than just a *good* actor. Henry Nelson had to be his pièce de résistance. His mission depended on it. So did his life. Still, he wondered what he would do if someone suddenly shouted out, "Addison! Oh, Addison!" He suddenly felt lighthearted and saw himself turning around. "You're looking for Addison, Addison Davies? Last I saw of him, he was on rue Fuad and simply rode off into the sunset." That's how an American might put it—that last part. Cowboy talk. He was proud of himself for thinking of it so quickly. That was what one might call thinking on your feet! Deans had always been good at that.

He was alone as he walked, so he felt safe enough to practice an American midwestern dialect, albeit quietly, for voices could easily be picked up by the breeze and carried far. He was good at this particular vernacular with its sometimes flat, sometimes singsong qualities, but he hadn't used it for quite some time. He had planned to use it with the American who'd sold him his new suit but had felt it too risky. He needed to rehearse it first. In a hushed voice, he uttered some greetings and introduced himself to an imaginary person in front of him, and then he engaged in nonsensical conversations with himself, playing the part of both parties. *Yes*, he thought, *I still have it!* He reminded himself not to use British idioms. As good as his American dialect was, those nasty little British words and phrases could give him away, especially to someone who already might be looking for any abnormalities in his American speech pattern, picking away at every vowel and consonant and expression. It would certainly be a bit embarrassing now, wouldn't it, if he gave himself away by saying "Bob's your uncle"?

It was eight forty-five by his watch, so he walked back to the entrance of the gardens and crossed the street. He stood in the shadows of two buildings and watched for Donatella to arrive. He was hoping she wouldn't be late, but if she was, it wouldn't be a catastrophe.

Five minutes later, a tram rolled up and stopped. When it continued down the tracks, he saw her walking toward the entrance of the gardens, her back to him. She was wearing his favorite green dress. He liked it because it matched her lovely eyes and formed a brilliant contrast to her shiny black hair. She sat down on a bench and looked into her purse. He strolled back across the street carrying his suitcase and walked up to her. She looked up at him, surprised by his sudden appearance.

"Well, excuse me, ma'am," he said like a polite Minnesotan. "I'm a tourist here in your lovely city. I was wondering whether you could direct me to a good old Italian restaurant nearby. I love the local food, but I've had a craving for a plate of rigatoni all day."

Deans knew that Donatella spoke enough English to understand what he was saying and just barely enough to give him directions. She stood up and pointed across the street to where he'd been standing. "You go here. Go two block, turn down street this way." She waved her hand to the right. "Go one block. She's a there."

"Why ... thank you, ma'am. I appreciate your help." He turned to go but then suddenly stopped. "Oh, by the way, the guy you're waiting for—he told me to tell you that he'll be here in a jiffy." *Jiffy.* Another good American word!

Donatella cocked her head to the side and furrowed her brow, and her eyes narrowed in a look of confusion and suspicion. Davies never, under any circumstance, would have had anyone, especially a stranger, deliver a message to her like that. He knew she'd know that—if she'd understood him, that is.

"Relax," he said, switching to Arabic. "It's me."

She scrutinized him more closely. He had allowed her to see him as Deans only once when they'd first met, and for the five years since, she'd seen him only as Addison Davies. Hearing his familiar voice but seeing an entirely different person now had to be a shock to her.

"Why have you changed your looks?" she asked.

"I had a minor setback. My cover was discovered."

"But how? By whom?"

"Let's walk into the gardens a way, and I'll explain."

They walked beyond the entrance about a hundred yards and found a bench and sat down.

"It doesn't make any difference how I was discovered, but it was by a British agent I'd never seen before. Of course, I had to ... eliminate him. I can't return to the shop. British intelligence is looking for Addison Davies. The police will be involved. But Addy died this morning. They also have an old photo of me, but it'll do them no good. It will throw them off, make it more difficult. We have to be more careful than we've ever been." Jokingly, he added, "I'm afraid you'll have to find another shop to buy your marmalade."

"But I don't understand why they're looking for you at all."

"If you recall, I told you that British intelligence pulled all of its agents out of Egypt and sent them back to London. When I didn't respond to their cables, they must have gotten nervous and sent agents to find me. They must think I'm up to some mischief or something." He chuckled. "But don't worry, my dear Donatella, they'll never find me now. And they have no idea that you even exist. Besides, I have someone looking after me, an *insider*, as they say on Wall Street. I didn't tell you about him, but he's been with us from the beginning, helping us prepare things. He tells me that an American by the name of Alex Logan is looking for me. More than likely, he's with the CIA, and he's here to stop the operation."

"Why didn't you tell me someone else was involved with us? You don't fully trust me, do you?" Her pout was genuine.

"How can you say that? Of course, I trust you. I've arranged a place for you to meet him. I'll tell you where and when as soon as I talk to him again."

"Do you know what this American looks like? Do you have a description of him?"

"I was introduced to him by a friend of mine last night at the Blue Moon. It was a chance meeting. The room was dark, and I didn't see his face up close. I don't think I could recognize him. But it doesn't matter. He has no idea whom he's looking for."

"I don't like the way this is going. It's beginning to be more complicated than you said it would be."

"Donatella, you can start worrying when you see me worrying, and that'll never happen. Besides, think of all the money you will have when we're finished and of your new life in Italy." He stopped talking for a moment and looked around them. Money had always been an effective carrot to motivate her. Reminding her of that from time to time was important. "Have you been going to the catacombs?"

"Everything is fine there and going as planned. Please stop

asking me about that." A moment later, she added, "Things are excellent, if you want the truth. You don't have to worry about my part." She ran her fingers across her forehead, bushing a few strands of hair from her face.

"Good. Do you have any more useful information from that fat man of yours?"

"Yes. Tomorrow his security people will start arriving in Alexandria. Most will be spread out in the area around Mansheya Square. The uniformed security and the Alexandria police will be at the square. Many along the route will be wearing civilian clothing. There's been no change in their plans."

"I anticipated that. You now need to find somewhere for your mother to stay for the week as we planned."

"I'll do that tomorrow. That will be no problem. Alexandria is full of hotels."

"I'll have to find a place to stay until Thursday. I don't want to be seen at your mother's apartment at all, in spite of my disguise. It would be too risky."

"Stay at the Hotel Cecil with me. As I said, Naguib won't be there until Thursday. The hotel is packed with tourists. With your disguise, you'll be just another one. No one will pay attention to you. I can order food from room service for you, and you won't even have to leave if you don't want to chance it."

"I have no intention of staying cooped up in a hotel room. No one will see me as anything but another rich American taking time away from his business for a vacation. But yes, I think staying with you is a wonderful idea. The person planning the assassination of the president of Egypt staying in the personal suite of the minister of the interior and security would be the ultimate irony." He laughed heartily. After a few moments, Donatella couldn't resist, and she laughed as well.

Deans had wanted to get Donatella in bed since they

started working together. This might be his best opportunity. He had envied the fat man for long enough. Now it was his turn to really know Donatella the way he wanted to. "Let's go to the hotel. Both of us need to get a good night's sleep," he said.

They walked to the main road and hailed a taxi to take them back to the Hotel Cecil.

"She wasn't always like that, you know," Shakir said.

"Of course, she wasn't."

Logan and Shakir sat in Shakir's office at the Caracol, the Moharrem Bey police station on rue D'Aboukir. Shakir was leaning back in his wooden swivel chair with his hands behind his head, fingers laced, legs stretched out on his desk. Logan was parked on a chair beside the desk. A bottle of Bushmills sat between them.

"She was quite an easy kid, growing up—always happy, always with a smile on her face," Shakir said. "She brought joy to the family."

"I only started to come to Alexandria when I was finished with graduate school. I never really got to know her well."

"Yes, I remember. I was long gone by that time, married with children. But before that, when she was younger ... I can still hear her laughter in my head. She would laugh about anything. She didn't need a reason. It was so infectious that it always got my father and mother going; and then with the three of them laughing, I couldn't resist either, even when I couldn't figure out what they were laughing about. I would ask her, 'What's so funny, Aria?' She wouldn't answer but would laugh harder, and soon she had me rolling on the floor."

Logan reached for the bottle and poured some more whiskey into their glasses.

"I can remember that as if it were yesterday. You should have seen the pure joy in her eyes as she laughed away, Alex. It would make your heart melt. And then one day, the lights went out of her eyes. It happened that fast. She changed into another person. Instead of being filled with laughter and joy, she became this brooding, angry, contentious little girl who was unrecognizable. I felt great sorrow for my parents because they had to contend with that every day. We tried to talk to her. Perhaps something had happened at school or with some of her friends, but she would never talk about it, not with me, not with my parents. She isolated herself from everyone. Then one day she left, taking her clothes with her, while my mother and father were away from the house.

"My parents wanted to keep this in the family, so I didn't have the department search for her. However, I did search on my own. It took me months to locate her. She was living in squalor, selling herself to live. She'd always been beautiful, but when I saw her, much of her beauty was gone. I could tell right away that she'd been drinking and putting some kind of drugs into her body. She looked terrible. I told her that I was going to take her home—arrest her if I had to. She became wild, lashing out at me with her nails. She told me that if I did take her, she would only leave again. I'd have to put her in jail or chain her up. Well, I could do neither. Perhaps I should have, but as her brother, I just didn't have the heart to do it. But she was right; she'd only leave again—eventually. I felt worthless that I couldn't help her. But now I wish I had done something. Maybe it would have made a difference."

"You can't help someone who doesn't want to be helped, Shakir."

"I know, I know. But it doesn't reduce the pain." He gulped down some whiskey. "Over the years, I would see her in various parts of the city now and again. She'd cleaned herself up, but it was obvious what she was doing with her life. She was a prostitute, and I couldn't do anything about it. I kept that from my parents. It would have killed them to know what their daughter had become. I told them that I'd been actively searching for her. People go missing every day in Alexandria. Most of them are never found. She was just one of them.

"Today, after she was taken to the morgue, I drove to my parents' house to tell them the news, but I never made it. I'm a coward. I didn't have the guts. Perhaps they're better off believing that their daughter is simply missing. I managed to keep the situation out of the papers."

"They deserve to know, Shakir. Your parents are strong. It'll hurt them, but they'll survive because they'll have some degree of closure. I think it would be far more painful for them to continue believing she's just missing. They'll cling to the false hope that she'll one day return. And when she doesn't, the pain will continue to grow."

Shakir knocked back the whiskey and poured some more. "We've got to find this maniac who murdered her, Alex. I'll rip him apart with my own hands. He's killed two people that we know of in the last few days. We must stop him before he kills a third."

A third, Logan thought. *Nasser.* How were they going to stop him when they didn't know whom they were looking for? Lucky Break was now wearing a white American-made Brooks Brothers suit and brown shoes. There must be hundreds or thousands of men in the city wearing the same clothes and probably even more wearing something similar. And who was to say he wouldn't change clothes again? "We're not going to find him sitting here," Logan said.

The two men got up, finished their drinks, and then walked out of the police station into the warm, dark night.

Chapter 27
THE CAT AND TWO MICE

Monday
9:15 a.m.

LOGAN CLIMBED INTO THE TAXI, RAN HIS PALM across the sweat on his forehead, and told the driver to go to rue Bab El Akhdar.

Addison Davies was dead—that much he knew. He also knew two other things for certain: David S. Deans would be using another disguise to remain undetected in Alexandria—what wasn't certain was whether he was posing as an American—and Deans's passport under his new identity was going to appear authentic. As an intelligence agent, Deans knew what the authorities would be looking for. Any mistakes that might have been made on the document would be minute. Deans was going to be difficult to find.

Furthermore, it was unlikely he'd disguise himself in any other way but as a Westerner. An Englishman dressed as an Egyptian would attract unwanted attention, so there was a possibility that he could be identified during a random stop by a police officer. But that was a long shot Logan couldn't count on. Shakir had almost all of his own officers spread out in the city, stopping males who appeared to be either American or

European and checking their passports. He actually didn't have the authority to call for a citywide manhunt, and he couldn't risk asking the chief of police to do so. The chief would want to know why. They had to keep quiet about Deans for the time being if they were going to catch him. Shakir had enough men under his command to make a decent go of it. Besides, a citywide manhunt—the press would have a field day with that—might just be the one thing that would drive Deans underground.

Deans was savvy enough to anticipate that the police force would be on the alert for him, and Logan was counting on his arrogance. He was hoping that Deans would be supercilious enough to stay out in the open and parade himself in front of the authorities. However, with only roughly seventy-eight hours before Nasser was to stand in the heart of Mansheya Square and give his speech to the Egyptian people—and to the world—Logan was beginning to lose heart.

Logan pointed out the window at a warehouse up ahead. "Stop just there," he told the driver. He got out of the taxi and then reached back into the window with some piastres. The sign on the building read "G. Sedgewick Wholesalers & Co." He opened the door and walked into a large room that appeared to be the main office. Beyond a front counter, five women, British and Egyptian, sat behind desks, busying themselves with typing and calculating. He approached the counter and asked one of the women whether George Sedgewick was in. She smiled at him shyly and got up. He passed through a short swinging gate and followed her to the back office.

Sedgewick was behind his desk, sipping tea. Logan saw him looking over the rim of the cup at him. He lowered the cup to its saucer. "By my Aunt Fanny's good looks," he said with a genuine expression of delight on his face. "Aren't you the Yank I met at the Blue Moon Saturday night?"

"I am. I need to talk to you. Can you spare five minutes?"

Logan was unshaven, his tie was pulled down, and his suit was wrinkled.

"Of course, of course. I can spare more than five minutes. Come in and get the weight of the world off your feet," Sedgewick said, showing him a chair. "I want to tell you again how lovely it was to chat with you." He cocked his head to the side. "I must say, you look at bit knackered. The women in our fair city must be giving you a run for your money. Vacations for a bachelor can be beastly. Tell me your name again. I'm afraid I had one drink too many that night to remember."

Logan sat down, dispensed with all the niceties, and got to the point. Making eye contact with the man, he said, "Listen carefully to me, Mr. Sedgewick. I'm working with the local police here. Don't ask any questions because I can't answer them. I have to ask you some questions, and I need you to answer them truthfully. If I think you're not, then Captain Shakir El Mahdeya, chief of criminal investigations, will come and ask you them himself."

Sedgewick stared at him, his eyes appearing small behind his thick lenses. He tried to move his lips but failed. He swallowed once and then twice more before any words came out. Hesitantly, he said, "Blimey ... I was just going to offer you some tea."

"Do you *understand* what I just said?"

"*Yes*! Yes, yes, yes."

"Explain to me how you know Addison Davies."

Sedgewick flinched slightly at the name. "Addy? Well ... he's a ... he's a customer of mine." He got that much out, but he had to swallow again before anything else would follow. "Has been for five years. He's a shopkeeper." He moved his head forward, closer to Logan. "Is he in trouble with the police?"

"Do you know him socially?"

"Somewhat," he said, clearly confused and disturbed by Logan's sudden appearance and the barrage of questions.

Logan didn't want Sedgewick to feel threatened by him. He actually liked him. But he had to convey to him that he wanted his complete cooperation—now. "I could take that as you being evasive. Be more specific."

Sedgewick adjusted himself in his seat, sitting upright as much as he could. Perhaps his words would flow more readily. "Well, we meet up from time to time for a drink and a little entertainment."

"Where?"

"Just one of two places: either the Blue Moon or the Ramleh Casino in San Stefano, if we feel like gambling."

"Does Davies like to gamble?"

"Far more than I. To tell you the truth, I wouldn't go there myself if it weren't for him." He considered what he'd just said. "At least not as much. Is he in trouble?"

"What else can you tell me about him?"

Sedgewick thought about that for a moment. "Not much more. If he's in trouble with the police, then I think there must be some kind of mistake. Addy's a right old chap. He's very generous. He supports an orphanage in his neighborhood, with money and food. He even got me to go in with him."

"Which orphanage? There are a lot of them here."

"I actually don't know. I send him extra boxes of canned goods along with his orders every so often—you know, the kind that children would like, puddings and such—and he delivers them. Been doing it for years. But it won't do you any good to know which one because he does it anonymously. The people who run it don't know where the donations come from."

"Are you expecting to hear from him?"

"Oh, he's off to London for a fortnight. He said he'd phone me when he's back so I can make a delivery to his shop."

"Addison Davies is in serious trouble with the law. If the police find out you've been anything but truthful with me, you're going to be as well. That includes tipping him off about this conversation. Am I clear about that?"

Sedgewick ran a chubby hand across his high forehead. "Oh my, yes, yes, very clear indeed. Very clear ..."

━━➤◄❂►━━

12:00 p.m.

Deans stood in front of a full-length mirror in Kamal Naguib's bedroom in the Hotel Cecil and admired himself. He wore a lightweight brown sports jacket, a lighter shade of brown trousers, a contrasting green and yellow tie, black shoes, and a felt fedora, tilted slightly to one side. After buying his first new set of clothes and shoes, he had returned to Aria's flat for one purpose: to throw the crumpled-up receipt in the trash bin, knowing that the authorities would find it. He was convinced that they would eventually link Aria's murder to Addison Davies. He was also convinced that the CIA officer, Alex Logan, would learn about it as well. They would be searching the city for someone wearing a white linen Brooks Brothers suit, a Panama hat, and brown Florsheim shoes. After leaving Aria's flat, he had gone to another shop across the city and bought the clothes he was now wearing. It wasn't a foolproof scheme by any means, but with just a few days now before Nasser's arrival, it would buy him some time.

Earlier that morning, he and Donatella had ordered breakfast from room service and discussed the operation while they ate. The crucial hour would be here soon enough, and there mustn't be any miscalculations. After a second coffee, he'd had her return to the catacombs to spend the day—perhaps for the last time. He was pleased with how this was working out. Naguib's suite had turned out to be perfect. The only disappointing aspect was that he'd slept on the couch last night while Donatella occupied the bedroom. He had been planning to seduce her—he'd thought about it long and hard and planned it out mentally—but with the operation only a few days away, he'd thought better of it. He didn't want to take the chance of antagonizing her. Perhaps another more propitious opportunity would arise before they parted ways for good. In the meantime, he would have to control the desires of the flesh.

There wasn't much more he needed to do before Thursday—if he wasn't ready at this point, he'd never be—and the thought of being cooped up here, even in this luxurious suite that someone else was paying for, left a sour taste in his mouth. He did admit to himself that there was a risk in going out in public, but it was a slight one, and he'd never been one to shrink away from any kind of risk, big or small. So with that thought, he looked himself over in the mirror one last time, adjusted his hat, and then left the suite.

When the elevator doors opened into the lobby, he took two steps out and then stopped dead in his tracks. His breathing became shallow and fast. He felt lightheaded, and he noticed a tingling sensation in his fingers. His body was reacting instinctually to the sight of three uniformed police officers checking the passports of guests. He had little control over the initial automatic reaction of his body, but he could control its duration. He took a few more steps from the elevator and stopped. He purposely slowed his breathing down, inhaling deeply and then slowly exhaling. After a few minutes, his breathing was back to normal. He proceeded to the main doors of the hotel, anticipating that he would be stopped as well, and he was.

"May I see your passport, please?" The officer spoke to him in English since there were many foreign tourists staying at the hotel.

"Certainly," Deans said, taking it out. "Is there a problem?"

"Just a routine check. What's your name?" he said, looking at the passport.

"Henry Nelson."

"Place of birth." The officer looked up at Deans and then back down at his picture in the passport.

"Minneapolis, Minnesota," he said, and then added, "America."

"What's the purpose of your visit?"

"Just a vacation to see the ancient sites here, like the catacombs." Deans's mouth angled slightly into a grin, which went unnoticed by the officer.

"When will you be leaving?"

"Oh, probably in three or four days. I'd like to listen to Mr. Nasser's speech before I leave." Another slight grin—a cheerful countenance for the authorities.

The officer looked up at him again, and the look lingered for a few moments this time. He glanced down at Deans's picture once more and then returned the passport to him. "Enjoy your stay, sir."

Deans turned around and walked a few steps before the officer called out to him again. "Mr. Nelson," the officer said. "Please return."

Control, control, he told himself. Deans walked back to him. "Yes?"

"The catacombs ..."

A cold sweat broke out on Deans's forehead. *Control, control ...*

The officer seemed to momentarily scrutinize him, or at least that was how Deans saw it. Finally, the officer said, "They're closed for the season."

Deans relaxed at once. "Thanks, officer. I'll remember that." And then he turned again to leave.

He made his way through the crowded lobby and went outside into the hot, humid air and chuckled to himself.

Incompetent fool, he thought. He walked a few blocks east to the Ramleh tram terminus, passing a five-story Venetian-style building with an enormous round white metal sign made to resemble a pill displayed on its roof. The word "BAYER" was printed on the pill in large, bold capital letters, both left to right and up and down, with a single Y joining the two in the center. Underneath it was the word "REMEDIES." Davies glanced up at it briefly and continued on his way. Once inside the terminus, he checked the schedule on the wall and then purchased a ticket at the window. He went outside to wait for the tram that would take him to San Stefano and to what he hoped would be a delightful afternoon of gambling.

———◉———

3:30 p.m.

Even though the trip lasted only forty minutes, the jerky movements of the three-car tram lured him into a kind of semiconscious state. He remained that way until the tram squealed to a stop at San Stefano, as air entered the brake lines. Alex Logan shook the cobwebs out of his head and stepped down from the tram. He could see the facade of the Ramleh Casino from a distance in front of him. Hordes of vacationers swarmed around the area. He hadn't expected so many people on a Monday, but it was July, after all. The absurdity of looking for one man among all these people whose appearance wasn't known to him suddenly hit him. A sharp, sudden pain in his side reminded him that he could be wasting valuable time here. However, if he were to leave and return to Alexandria, what would he do there? He'd be faced with the same problem. According to Sedgewick, the casino was one of Deans's haunts, so he decided to stay in spite of the poor odds of spotting him.

Logan walked through the crowds to the building and went inside. It had been built as a summer hotel by the sea in 1886 and gradually over time had been expanded into a complex that housed a theater, a concert hall, tennis courts, and a private beach, in addition to the gambling hall. Logan was somewhat familiar with the layout because he'd been here several times before, but not for the last two or three years. He made his way through the lobby and discovered as many people inside as out. The only thing in his favor was that he was looking for a Caucasian male wearing a white suit and Panama fedora, sporting brown shoes. At least that would eliminate a good chunk of them.

There were two large doors to the casino room. He opened one of them and went inside. The room was crowded but not packed. Logan swept the room from left to right, looking for white suits. Most of the men seemed to be wealthy Egyptians, Greeks, Italians, and Turks. A few appeared to be American or European. As far as he could tell, half of them were wearing white or off-white suits and brown shoes. *It must be some sort of uniform*, he thought. On a Monday afternoon, Logan figured they were on vacation and staying at the hotel.

He walked around the room, focusing his attention on the Caucasians. He needed to get close enough to see their shoes. They were spread out around various gaming tables. Because the casino catered to foreign tourists as well as locals, there was a wide variety of games. Besides two roulette wheels, there were tables for craps, ratscrew, stud poker, blackjack, and Trente et Quarante. Logan spent the next hour going from table to table. The ones who wore brown shoes were too old and the wrong body type. No disguise was that good.

He was hot and needed a drink, so he went to the bar, ordered a gin and tonic, and then took the drink over to a plush, dark green leather chair and sat down. There was a table between him and a matching leather chair, on which sat a man in a brown jacket. The man held a drink in one hand and a felt fedora in the other. Logan was absolutely exhausted. He didn't know when he'd last slept. He was trying not to become discouraged but was finding it difficult. He was sick of looking for a needle in a haystack, and he had to resist becoming indifferent to the whole thing. Fatigue was becoming a major obstacle.

He swung his head around to the man next to him. "Any luck?" he asked in English.

"Not so far," the man said, slurring his words slightly. "I'm taking a break. I'll have another go at it later before I leave." He took a sip of his drink.

By his accent, Logan could easily tell the man was an American. He reached a hand over to him and said, "Frank Sullivan. It's good to hear an American voice once in a while." For some inexplicable reason, the name just spilled from his lips. He hadn't planned on using an alias. Frank Sullivan had been a childhood friend of Logan's.

"Henry Nelson," the man said, shaking Logan's hand. "Yes, we're a rarity here. You here on vacation or business?"

"Just a short vacation from teaching during summer break. How about you?"

"Same here—a little holiday to see the sights. I own an accounting firm in Minneapolis."

"Oh, Minneapolis! Great city. Where in Minneapolis?" Logan had friends there and knew the city fairly well.

"Across the street from Dayton's on Nicollet ... right downtown."

"Ah yes, I know exactly where that is."

At this point, Logan had to force himself to stay awake. The lack of sleep since his arrival in Alexandria was catching up with him. In fact, he was approaching drowsiness, aided unintentionally by the gin and tonic and by having sat down.

Nevertheless, he took a swig of his drink and sat upright in the lounge chair, as much as it was possible.

"What sights have you seen so far?" Logan asked.

"Oh, many. They're all extraordinary. Just before I came here, I saw Pompey's Pillar and the Sphinx next to it. Very simple in design, but when you think about how old they are, well, I find it incredible. Hah, we Americans think something is ancient at a few hundred years. But this pillar's been around since AD 297, and it's a monolith! How they got it up is beyond me."

"Amazing," Logan said, only half-hearing what the man said.

"Did you ever hear the story of a British commander by the name of John Shortland?"

When Logan didn't respond right away, Nelson asked, "Are you okay?"

Startled, Logan said, "Yes, fine. Go ahead. What about ..."

"Shortland. Well, as I was about to say, he flew a kite with a rope on it over the pillar. It was sometime in the nineteenth century—can't remember the exact year. Anyway, this enabled him to get a rope ladder up. So he climbs up the pillar with the Union flag and a flask, drinks a toast to King George III, and gives three cheers. Ain't that something?"

"Amazing," Logan said again, trying his best to keep his eyes open.

"As if that wasn't good enough, a few days later he climbs it again, puts a weather vane up there, eats a steak, and toasts the king again. Cheeky, wasn't he? A right old nutter." Nelson threw his head back and laughed. "He toasts the same king who gave the American colonies a hard time." He laughed again.

"Truly amazing," Logan said. He couldn't fight it any longer; if he continued to sit, he'd soon find himself asleep, so he rose from the chair and extended a hand to Nelson.

"Sorry to have to cut this short, but I've got to get back to Alexandria."

Logan gave Nelson one last look as they shook hands. The man was pleasant enough. He wished he could continue the conversation a bit longer. Nelson looked to be in his fifties, but he had a younger, smoother face. His only flaw, if one could call it that, was the small half-moon-shaped scar centered in his chin. "Good luck with the rest of your visit. There's lots to see here."

9:37 p.m.

Donatella had taken a taxi back to the Hotel Cecil from the catacombs because she was exhausted, having spent the entire day there preparing for Thursday. She was wearing a khaki shirt and pants, with brown ankle-length leather boots. She was hot, dirty, and sweaty, and the only thing she could think of now was a cool shower. She might not be able to get back to the catacombs before Thursday, so she'd spent some extra time there. Deans had told her earlier this morning in the suite that he was going to arrange for her to meet the third person in their cabal because they'd be working together on the day of the assassination. She'd felt uneasy about that meeting the whole day.

Donatella entered the hotel and crossed the lobby. Only a few people, probably tourists, were milling about. A police officer was leaning an arm on the counter to her left. As she approached the elevator, she noticed a man walking in the same direction from the restaurant. She recognized him immediately. She really didn't want him to see her this way, but she had little choice at this point. They stopped at the same time in front of the elevator. He pressed the button and glanced at her.

"Hello," she said in Arabic. "We met the other day, right here."

The man turned his head again, paused briefly, and then said, "Oh yes. I remember. How are you?"

"After a good shower, I'll be fine. I spent the day in the desert, so you'll have to excuse my appearance."

The elevator door opened, and they stepped in.

"Floor?" he said.

"Five."

"Four and five," he said to the elevator man.

"I think we met when you checked in," she said. "Are you enjoying your stay?"

"I always enjoy Alexandria. I'm Frank Sullivan, by the way."

"Donatella Marinetti. It's a pleasure to meet you. I believe I told you that the next time we met, we'd have coffee and a brandy. As you can see, I'm not quite dressed for that. Perhaps you can give me a rain check."

The elevator stopped on the fourth floor, and the door opened.

The man looked as if he could sleep standing on his feet, but before he exited the elevator, he managed to say that he'd be pleased to give her a rain check anytime she wanted one.

The doors closed and then opened again on the fifth floor. Donatella got out and walked to her room, wondering whether Deans was waiting for her.

Chapter 28
ZIGZAGGING THE CITY

Tuesday
10:15 a.m.

LOGAN TOOK A TAXI TO MANSHEYA SQUARE. The assassination would take place here at the square or en route on rue Fuad. There were no other suitable places in Alexandria—none. If Lucky Break decided on rue Fuad, the chances of Logan stopping him were nil. There were simply too many miles to cover, even for Nasser's security force. But if he selected the square, then Logan at least would have a fighting chance. Logan knew the area well. But this was different now; it required another perspective. He had to view every inch of the square with the eye of a sniper hell-bent on killing the president.

After a good night's sleep, he felt both mentally and physically refreshed. But something was wrong; the feeling kept gnawing away at him, and he couldn't shake it loose. All morning, he'd thought about the guy he'd met at the casino in San Stefano the day before. What was his name? Something simple—common. Smith? Jones? Ah yes, it was Nelson, Henry Nelson, and he was from Minneapolis. They'd talked about it.

Logan had been looking for someone in white; this man had been wearing brown.

Logan remembered feeling sleep-deprived and only half-listening to what Nelson was saying. He had been so tired, he could have slept standing up. He vaguely remembered Nelson talking about working downtown in an area of Minneapolis that Logan was familiar with, and he remembered Nelson telling him some story about the pillar (although he couldn't remember enough details to retell it), and that was about it. He was a friendly guy with a warm demeanor, and Logan had enjoyed the chance encounter, in spite of the fact that he'd been so tired.

Yet something was troubling him about this guy, and he just couldn't pinpoint it. Maybe it was nothing more than his lack of sleep as of yesterday. Certainly, his brain hadn't been processing things the way it should. Maybe he sensed something was wrong when everything had been fine.

Logan found an outdoor café in front of the most open area of the square. There were hundreds of people at the square now, perhaps even thousands. In a few days, there would be a hundred thousand or more here to see Nasser give his speech. *Roughly fifty-three hours from now*, he thought. A waiter came to his table, and Logan ordered a coffee and a bottle of cold water. After the waiter brought both to his table, Logan asked himself the important question: *If I were an assassin, where would I set up shop?* He looked to his left. Nasser's limousine would enter the square from rue Fuad. The convertible would be traveling slowly because of the crowds, and Nasser would be standing up, making himself an easy target. If Deans believed that in order to assassinate Nasser, he'd have to sacrifice his own life in the process, then it wouldn't matter where he was because an escape route wasn't necessary. If that were the case, then no one could do anything to prevent the assassination. There were just too

many places from where Deans could fire a sniper rifle. He'd
have to remain undetected only until he could fire a round
or two, and then it wouldn't matter. If he were going to use a
pistol, then Deans would have to be in the middle of the crowd
up front, near the podium. That would make detection almost
impossible because he could dress like an Egyptian with a
robe and turban of some sort, hiding in the open.

From the little he knew about this man, Logan didn't
think that Deans would sacrifice himself. From his training
and experience, Deans would be confident enough to know
that he could not only assassinate Nasser but also escape the
area unharmed and undetected. That meant he would choose
his sniper's nest carefully. An escape route was absolutely
necessary. Not just any building would do.

Logan looked around him at the buildings fronting the
square. Nasser would have to pass by the Palace of Justice
building on the right and, opposite that, the statue of
Mohammed Ali on his left. Most of the buildings around the
square were too low and would be full of people standing
on the roofs and hanging out the windows. One building,
however, stood out. It was redbrick and the highest of the
buildings at six stories. Logan looked up and saw that it
had an ornamental parapet at the top, perfect for a sniper's
nest and cover. The only problem with that, Logan thought,
was that he was certain Nasser's security force would use
the building. Two uniformed men were up there right now,
walking around, pointing down at various locations below
them, with the same idea.

Logan sipped his coffee and then took a long swig from
the bottle of water. He wiped his mouth with the back of his
hand. He suddenly realized that there were other uniformed
men around, armed with automatic weapons. They were
spaced apart and walking leisurely, probably just to show
their presence as a deterrent. He determined that if he were

the sniper, he'd stay clear of the square. There would be too many people crowded together and too many security police in the area to pull off the assassination successfully. Logan couldn't see any way for Deans to escape. It would, however, be the perfect place for an insane terrorist bent on killing and then committing suicide. But that wasn't Deans. He also considered that a bomb could be used, but he disregarded that immediately. The wooden platform where Nasser would deliver his speech would be constructed soon, and the security forces would be inspecting every stage of it. They would be standing guard before and during the speech. Deans wouldn't have the opportunity to plant an explosive.

Logan finished his coffee, got up, and put a few piastres on the table. He walked around the square to rue Fuad and then proceeded down the street. As always, it was crowded. After walking a few blocks, he stopped and looked up. Deans would have to use one of these buildings along this street. They too would be packed with people. It was impossible to estimate the number of buildings along the length of rue Fuad. If just ten percent of them were suitable for a sniper, the number would be in the hundreds. Logan was becoming discouraged again.

He continued down the street for a few more blocks and stopped again at an unexpected sight. He stepped back into a doorway and looked across the street. People were passing by on both sides. The woman he'd met at the hotel was standing in front of what looked like an apartment building, talking with a man—John Campbell. What was the woman's name? Yes, Donatella something. He couldn't remember her last name, but it was Italian. Why would Campbell be talking to her? How did they even know each other?

And then it hit him like a ton of bricks. He remembered the night at the restaurant with Shakir. His cousin had told him that when the minister of the interior and director of intelligence traveled to Alexandria, he was assigned to keep an eye on him. Naguib was his name, and he came here to be with his mistress. Her name was Donatella. Logan couldn't remember her last name, but it was also Italian. This woman must be one and the same.

Logan had to talk to Campbell—today! This woman he was talking to was the mistress of the man who was responsible for Nasser's security. What the hell was going on? He intended to find out. He made note of the location and then continued down the street.

------------>◄(❶)►◄------------

The morning had been lovely, so he had decided to take advantage of it. He'd taken an early tram to San Stefano to attend a flower show he'd read about in one of the newspapers. The show was well attended by people of all nationalities dressed in their very best. Besides the flowers, he'd greatly enjoyed mixing with the young women there. After that, he'd taken a taxi to Stanley Bay and had a nice, leisurely stroll along the beach. Following a light lunch in a nearby café, he had taken the tram back to Alexandria again. He hadn't wanted to return to the hotel quite yet, so he had next gone to the Corniche and walked the promenade until his feet couldn't take him one step farther. By that time, he was weary but very content with life.

David S. Deans had worked up an appetite by evening, and now he was sitting at a corner table by himself in a Greek restaurant called Pastroudis on rue Fuad. He'd always heard good things about it, but never in his five years in Alexandria had he ever been here. Since he'd be leaving the country soon, he had decided to give it a try. What harm would that do?

He started with an appetizer, the Florina peppers stuffed with feta cheese and herbs and dressed with olive oil and vinegar. *Heavenly*, he thought. As he ate, he considered how things were going. He was pleased in spite of the recent setback. Old Addy was dead and buried, and he had to admit to himself that he missed him in a certain way. And Donatella had been acting rationally and was very much focused on her part of the mission. That was always positive, so he was indeed pleased.

After he finished the peppers, the waiter brought him a salad called *dakos*, made with dry barley rusks soaked in olive oil and topped with diced tomatoes, herbs, and capers. *Crunchy!* He decided to forgo the soup.

He was also pleased with himself. The idea of throwing his pursuers off the mark with the receipt for the clothes he'd left in the whore's flat had been brilliant. And he'd conceived the idea on the spur of the moment as well! Everything was running smoothly now. The train was on the right track and on schedule. He was glad that he'd decided to take the day off and enjoy life a little.

His thoughts were interrupted by the waiter again. Ah, the main course! One of his former customers had recommend this dish—*kreatopita*—a meat pie with lamb and goat, wrapped in pastry, with a light tomato sauce and a side dish of rice. He ate with relish!

Thursday would certainly be a busy day for him. He'd be tied up the whole day, so to speak. He chuckled at the thought. But Wednesday—what would he do tomorrow? He wasn't about to sit in the hotel room all day. It would be his last full day before the chaos began. He had to think of something interesting to do. It was unlikely he'd ever be in Egypt again, let alone in Alexandria. There must be something to visit that he hadn't seen before.

The meal had been satisfying. He was on the last drop of his coffee when he noticed another patron enter the restaurant, hesitate at the door, and then walk toward him.

The man was Egyptian—maybe Greek, since this was a Greek restaurant—and he didn't look well. He was unshaven and looked as if he had slept in his suit. The man took the table next to him and nodded in his direction, and out of courtesy, Deans greeted him politely but said only what was necessary. He wasn't in the mood for a conversation with a stranger.

He got up, placed some bills on the table, and left.

Logan knocked several times on the door of Campbell's flat on rue Nebi Daniel. When there was no response, he left the building and walked down the street to rue Fuad and then turned left. It took him ten minutes to get to rue Toussoun Pasha where it intersected with rue Cherif Pasha. The British consulate was housed in the same building as the British information office a few doors down the street. He walked until he came to the building and was about to open the door when he heard his name called. He turned around. Directly across the street, John Campbell was sitting in an outdoor café. Logan crossed the street, dodging the traffic, and stood over him.

"I assume you're looking for me," Campbell said, setting his book facedown, open to the page he'd been reading.

"One of your agents is dead, we have two days left to find Lucky Break, and you're sitting on your ass, reading a book and having lunch," Logan said. "You British really do need your tea time, don't you?"

Campbell smirked, looking up at him.

"Wipe that smug look off your face, or I'll wipe it off for you."

"Jesus, what's got under your skin, mate? Don't get your knickers in a twist. Sit down here, and we'll have a proper chin wag."

Logan could tell that Campbell was no longer intimidated by his American counterpart—if that was, in fact, what Logan was. He stared down at him, trying to control his temper. Finally, he sat down opposite him.

"For the record," Campbell said defensively, "I've been chasing my arse around this city trying to come up with something. If you don't eat properly, you're of no use to anyone. This is the first time I've sat down since six thirty this morning. My legs are dead tired!"

"What have you come up with?"

"Unfortunately, nothing. Looking for Lucky Break is like looking for a pebble in an ocean. I wired headquarters that they've given me an impossible job with few resources."

"Why don't you just go home then?" Logan's question had the force of an imperative.

Campbell's face hardened. He pointed an index finger at Logan. "Listen, Yank. I have a mission to do. I'll do it the best way I can. If you don't like it, then you can feck off."

"Where's the other agent that Cook came here with?"

"Hillary? I'm meeting up with him later."

"How do you know Donatella?"

"Who?"

"The woman I saw you with earlier today on rue Fuad."

"Are you talking about Donatella Marinetti? What were you doing, spying on me? Jesus H. Christ ..."

"I asked you how you know her."

"If you think I'm accountable to you, then you're barmy." He narrowed his eyes at Logan and started to say something more but stopped. After a moment, he scratched his head and said, "But I'll tell you anyway, since you brought her up. I've known her for years in Cairo. The whole damn city knows her. She used to be a high-class prostitute; I can personally attest to that. But now she's the mistress of one of the ministers in Nasser's government. She moved back to Alexandria to be with her mother. She's sick or something. We bumped into each other this morning. Does that satisfy your curiosity?"

"She's the mistress of the minister who's in charge of Nasser's security here," Logan said. "Does that ring any bells for you?"

"If you're implying that she's connected in any way to Lucky Break, you're daft. I've known her for a long time. She's nothing other than what she is—a minister's whore."

"And you're sure of that?"

"Listen, you just accused me of wasting my time by taking a break to eat. Now you're suggesting that a whore is somehow involved in an assassination plot. If you ask me, I think your judgment's a bit off. I assure you that if you have any notions of following up on her, you'll definitely be wasting *your* time."

Logan stared at him for a long moment, and then he got up and walked away. *He's probably right. Asshole.*

———————

Shakir had done all that he could do, but he had serious doubts as to whether it was going to be enough. He could put an end to this now by simply informing Nasser's security team that he'd heard rumors that an assassination attempt was in the works. But there were always rumors. They might not take him seriously. They would surely question him about his source. If he told them the truth, they'd want to know why he hadn't informed them earlier. He could tell them that he had just now discovered it. Still, they would push him for his source. He had to keep Alex out of it.

Nasser was the only one who could cancel his speech, something he rarely did. There'd been so many attempts on his life that Nasser now looked at them as *normal*. He would never change how he ran the country, and he would never let his security interfere with how he communicated with his people.

At least if Shakir told Nasser's security, they might be on heightened alert. Whether or not that would stop Lucky Break, Shakir didn't know. He decided to hold off on notifying them for the time being. There were still a few days left. He wanted to use the time to see whether he himself could find Lucky Break. Certainly, this was an issue of national interest and monumental importance. But now it was also personal. He wanted to find Lucky Break and avenge the murder of his sister. If Shakir caught him, he would torture him—an idea so out of character that Shakir had been shocked when it first occurred to him—and then he'd put a bullet in his head.

Shakir stopped walking and looked around him. There were fewer people on rue Fuad at this time of night, but it was still quite crowded. Without sleeping the previous night—how could he?—he'd gotten out of bed at five thirty this morning, changed into his suit, and started walking the city streets, looking for Caucasians wearing a white suit, brown shoes, and a Panama fedora. He'd stopped at least two dozen men—more actually—but their passports had checked out. Now he was exhausted, hungry, and unshaven. His tie was loosened at the neck, and his suit was full of wrinkles, with sweat stains under his arms. He should go home, eat, shower, and go to bed.

But he didn't. He continued walking down the street. Maybe the next white suit he came across would be Lucky Break. If he went home now, he'd miss him. That was all he had to go by—a white suit, brown shoes, and a Panama fedora. He was here, somewhere! Maybe the next one, or the one after that ...

He walked for another block and then another one and another after that, passing stores, small shops, and cafés. *The arrogant bastard's got to be somewhere. Murderer. Aria's murderer. Don't stop.* He walked and walked and walked, looking for anyone wearing a white suit. He figured he had at least another thirty or forty hours before it was hopeless and he had to notify the security team. He wouldn't stop until then.

He hadn't eaten since yesterday and felt himself becoming weak. As he came to the next restaurant, he couldn't hold out any longer. He would stop for fifteen minutes—just fifteen minutes and no longer—to eat and then resume his search.

He went inside a Greek restaurant and paused briefly in the entrance. It wasn't crowded. He walked to the back and found a small table that was big enough for just one or two people and sat down. He nodded at the man at the next table. The man acknowledged him with a cheerful but curt greeting. Shakir noted the accent—American—and glanced at the brown sports jacket he was wearing. The man got up, placed some bills on the table, and left.

Shakir knuckled his eyes, sighed, and looked up at another man standing over him.

"Would you like to see the menu?" the waiter asked.

Chapter 29
CALM BEFORE THE STORM

Wednesday
3:00 p.m.

DAVID S. DEANS SAT CONTENTEDLY IN A CAFÉ, having his afternoon tea. To while away a few hours, he'd been to the British cinema to see a newly arrived film. He'd remembered reading favorable reviews of the film in the *New York Herald Tribune*. Films released abroad took only a week or so to arrive in Egypt. When he'd found out that *The Man Who Knew Too Much* was opening today, he couldn't resist.

This was the last day he'd have to move about freely, relax, and enjoy himself before chaos enveloped Egypt—and quite possibly the world. What better way was there than to sit for a few hours in an air-conditioned cinema and watch what the critics had said was a spectacular Hitchcock film? Deans couldn't think of one. He'd always been a fan of the director and considered him a compatriot, even though Hitchcock spent more time in America now than he did in England.

Deans sipped his hot tea and watched people walking back and forth. He wondered what these same people would be doing tomorrow at this time.

The film's acting and directing had been superb, he

thought, refocusing his mind. And the various location shots were credible. Some of the scenes, he'd read, had even been filmed in Morocco. Leave it to old Hitch to incorporate a sense of realism! Why use a soundstage in London when he could bring the whole team to North Africa for those shots? *Must have cost a few bob, nonetheless!* There was, in fact, only one thing about the film that he had disliked: the script.

The screenwriter obviously had no idea how to pull off a successful assassination. He'd made one massive blunder: he'd involved too many people in the plot. The most successful assassinations were done by one person—alone. Depending on the circumstances, however, that wasn't always possible. At times, an assassin had to work with another person. But he knew that the more people he involved in the plot, the less were his chances of succeeding. If he had more than three people, the assassination was sure to fail—as it had in the film. People talked too damn much. Hitchcock should have hired a few more knowledgeable people to do some rewrites. Deans himself would have been a good choice. The thought brought a smile to his face.

He sipped some more tea and wondered what Donatella was doing. How was she spending her last day? She had many plans herself, and he knew that she was looking forward to ... what was it? A new life? He snickered at that. So what was she doing right at this moment? Perhaps she was with her mother, packing her belongings in the temporary flat. Or perhaps they would leave everything there. That seemed reasonable enough if they were going to start all over. Traveling light would certainly make crossing over to Italy easier for them.

And then it suddenly crossed his mind—how could he have forgotten about the coin? Donatella wasn't about to go anywhere until their transaction was complete. Deans drank the last of the tea, put a few coins down on the table, and made his way back to the Hotel Cecil.

He had the money; now he wanted the gold coin.

———«●»———

6:30 p.m.

Alex Logan sat on a bench in Zaghloul Square across the street from his hotel, looking out onto the sea. He looked like a defeated man, a failure, and felt like one as well.

He'd gotten up early this morning and scoured the city for Deans. It had been an exercise in futility. In fact, he didn't even know why he was continuing the search. He was beginning to wonder whether he'd misjudged Deans. At this point, he was probably in hiding, taking no chances of being discovered, since tomorrow was the day Nasser would be giving his speech. He took little consolation in knowing that Morgan Stance had had little hope that Logan would succeed in finding Lucky Break. It had definitely been a long shot, and the attempt had failed.

At two o'clock this afternoon, he'd taken a taxi to police headquarters to talk with his cousin Shakir. Shakir had pulled his men off the search for Lucky Break and reassigned them to Nasser's security detail. They discussed the situation, even arguing at times about what to do next. In the end, Shakir had reluctantly agreed to give Logan another twenty-four hours to find the assassin. After that, he would notify Nasser's personal security, reporting that he'd just now discovered the plot to assassinate the president, and would urge them to convince Nasser to cancel his speech. That was the only thing that Shakir could do to protect Nasser, but Logan knew that it would only delay the assassination. Lucky Break would find another opportunity eventually.

From the station, Logan had gone back to Mansheya Square to have one last look. It was pointless, yes, but he couldn't think of anything else to do. He knew that he wouldn't find anything useful there. He was running on hope and not much more, and even that was dwindling. What he did find, however, was that the square had been cordoned off, preventing vehicles and pedestrians from entering. Workers were constructing a raised wooden platform, and a military band was practicing. Hundreds of people were looking out the windows from the surrounding buildings at the activities. The streets in the city center were crawling with uniformed security, who were mingling with the citizens, joking and laughing, some sharing cigarettes. It was a joyous atmosphere. That only made Logan more depressed because he knew what would happen following the first shots tomorrow, when there would be ten times as many people there. People were likely to stampede, and others would be trampled, resulting in injuries and deaths.

He lit his pipe and puffed. The smoke rose and then disappeared in front of him, caught by a gentle breeze. The sea was calm and beautiful. He was nearly ready to throw in the towel and phone Shakir. What could possibly happen in the next twenty-four hours to justify not warning the security forces now? Actually, it was more like eighteen hours. *I failed, my brother*, he imagined himself telling Shakir. *Convince them to cancel the speech.* He could take a late-night flight to London and grab a connecting flight to New York. He could be back in Georgetown in thirty hours, having prevented a nuclear confrontation between the Soviets and the West—if Nasser were convinced to cancel the speech. But there would be another doomsday looming in the not too distant future that he wouldn't be able to stop. The little satisfaction he might have had would be short-lived. Lucky Break would still be out there, somewhere. But the savage truth was this: Nasser would *never* cancel his speech.

Disgusted with himself, Logan knocked the pipe against his palm, clearing it of ash, and walked back to the hotel. Crossing the lobby to the elevators, he noticed Donatella entering the restaurant off to his left. She was a gorgeous woman. She was just as he remembered her from that day when he'd first checked into the hotel: tall with shoulder-length black hair, wearing a white dress with black high heels. He imagined the gold chain with a pendant that hung between her breasts. Maybe spending some time with her would improve his mood. After all, there was nothing for him to do now. He walked to the entrance of the restaurant and stopped. He watched her being seated toward the back. He walked up to her as she was glancing up from her table.

"Twice you mentioned coffee and brandy," he said in Arabic. "Is this a good time?"

Her face showed a mixture of surprise and spontaneous delight. "It's a perfect time, Mr. Frank Sullivan. Sit down and join me."

He took the chair opposite her. Those emerald eyes were what had mesmerized him on that first day. Now he was looking into them again. But if he were honest about it, he had to admit that her eyes might have mesmerized him, but it was her body that stirred him.

"I bet you don't remember my name," she said with a slight pout.

"What will I get if you're wrong?"

"I don't know. It depends on what you want." Her chin was raised higher than it should have been; she was as poised and self-assured as a lioness on the hunt.

According to both Shakir and Campbell, Donatella had been a high-class prostitute, so Logan had to be prepared for a prostitute's song-and-dance routine. She would flatter him and cajole him until she got him into her lair and into her bed. But Logan didn't care. He wanted a reprieve from Lucky Break, if only for a brief time, and what better respite than an evening with a beautiful woman.

"That depends on what you have," he countered.

She looked over his shoulder and saw the waiter coming with the menus. "Right now, what I have is an appetite."

After they gave their orders to the waiter and he left, Donatella lean in a little toward Logan, crossing her arms in front of her on the table. "I find you fascinating, Frank Sullivan. You told me you come to Alexandria frequently. You speak Arabic as well as I do, and I suspect you know the city as well as any taxi driver. You could even pass for Egyptian, yet your name is Sullivan. It's none of my business, but you must have many secrets."

"If what you mean by secrets is anything that you don't know about me, then I have a few ... Donatella."

She smiled at that.

"I was here during the war and fell in love with the city. I picked up the language fast. And I come back as often as my wallet allows me. As far as my skin color and name go, my father was born in Dublin, and my mother in Mexico City, which makes me first-generation American since they met each other in Washington. My looks came from my mother, and my name came from my father. Now the mystery is solved." He brushed his hands together, suggesting that was that.

The waiter returned to the table with bread and a dip— *aish baladi* and a bowl of *hummus bi tahina*. They were quiet for a few minutes, stealing glances at each other while they ate. Logan felt somewhat guilty about lying to her, but he didn't have a choice. He expected her to do the same to him. That was what spies and whores did: they lied.

"So you said that you stay here sometimes," he said. "Do you live in the city?"

"I live a little way east of the city. I stay here frequently because of my work."

He waited for her to continue, and when she didn't, he said, "Which is ..."

"I'm ... a ... translator." She stumbled over the words.

"Who do you work for?"

"Well, anyone who needs something translated," she said with a grin. "I speak, read, and write both Arabic and Italian."

"Your roots, then, are here?"

"My parents were born in Bologna. I was born here, so I grew up with both languages. But I can trace my family connections to Egypt in the last century. One of my relatives was on the medical staff in service to Muhammad Ali and his son, Ibrahim Pasha."

"Impressive."

The waiter arrived with bowls of taro soup, made from the leaves of jute and corchorus plants. They spooned the soup in silence and seemed relaxed and comfortable with each other. Logan was even comfortable in the net of lies they'd thrown around each other.

After ten minutes had gone by, the waiter returned and set a plate with skewered *kofta*, spiced meatballs, in front of Donatella and a plate of falafel, deep-fried balls of fava beans, in front of Logan. The silence continued until they were halfway through their meal.

"The city's been lively today," Logan said, chewing. "Lots of activity, especially around Mansheya Square." He put another falafel into his mouth and chewed some more.

"Oh, maybe you haven't heard. The president is going to give a speech at the square tomorrow. Alexandria is always like a festival whenever Nasser comes to town. He's very popular, you know."

"Yes, I've heard. Are you going?"

"Unfortunately, I have to work on a document for the Italian consulate that must be done by the end of the day. I've seen him before, though. He's a very exciting speaker to watch. You should go, Frank. It'll be something to tell your friends about back home." She forked the last piece of *kofta* into her mouth and pushed her plate aside.

"I'm sure there are going to be too many people there to suit me. I'd be claustrophobic. Maybe I'll watch it from here on the television. Do you know what his speech is about?"

"Something about the Suez Canal."

The waiter cleared the table, and a second waiter brought the coffee and *konafah*, a sweet made of a thick noodle-like pastry. They both put milk and sugar into their coffee and bit into the dessert.

After he swallowed and sipped his coffee, Logan said, "I heard the president's going to nationalize the canal, but I didn't know he was going to make the announcement from here. I'm sure it's going to ruffle a few international feathers."

"Oh, I stay out of politics. Governments do what they're going to do. Common people have no say."

In dictatorships, Logan thought. He didn't want to spoil the evening talking about politics, so he just nodded and took another bite of his dessert. After washing it down with coffee, he said, "Too bad I have to leave in a few days. Too bad you have to work tomorrow."

"Well," she said, "the night is still young, and I'm not doing anything."

"We're having our coffee, as you said we would, and I've got a bottle of brandy in my room. We could make a toast to our health and prosperity. What do you say?"

"I say I'd like that fine, Mr. Sullivan."

They talked for another ten minutes, finishing up their coffee and dessert. Logan then had the waiter add the check to his hotel bill. They left the restaurant and took the elevator to the fourth floor to his room.

————»«◉»«————

11:14 p.m.

Alex Logan and Donatella Marinetti lay back on the bed, exhausted, sweaty, and naked. Logan reached over to the nightstand and picked up his snifter and finished his brandy.

"It's a pity I have to return to the States so soon," he said, and he meant it. He swept the tips of his fingers across her forehead, brushing aside some strands of her hair, and then leaned over and kissed her gently on the lips. "It would be a pleasure to know you better."

"Don't leave then," she said, looking at him.

Logan looked into her eyes and saw sincerity and intense desire. He sensed panic in her voice. He nudged up closer to her and put an arm across her breasts. "That would be tempting, but I have commitments at home." Before he knew what he was saying, and before he could stop those insane words from escaping, he said, "Come with me."

Donatella shifted her body to face him. "How I wish that were possible, but I have an ailing mother to watch over. And ..." She looked down, her face shifting into a frown.

Logan kissed her forehead. With that, she suddenly jumped out of bed, startling Logan with her abruptness. "It's late, and I must get enough sleep so I can be alert tomorrow. Translations are demanding." She gathered up her clothes and shoes, took them with her to the bathroom on the other side of the room, and closed the door.

Logan rolled over on the bed to her side and grabbed her purse off the nightstand. He opened it and rummaged around. *Jesus, what the hell am I doing?* Old habits. He didn't see anything of importance; however, something gold was wedged in the corner, and he pulled it out. It was an American coin about the size of a silver dollar. On one side there was an eagle with the words "United States of America" and "Twenty Dollars" stamped above it, and on the other side Lady Liberty was holding a torch and an olive branch. He'd never seen a coin like this before. Souvenir? Good-luck piece? He put it back and closed the purse.

Donatella returned to the bedroom fully dressed, with her hair tied back, and walked over to the nightstand and picked up her purse. Logan wrapped a towel around himself and followed her to the door.

She turned around and gave him a long, deep kiss, her tongue finding his. "I won't say goodbye, Frank Sullivan. We will see each other again." With that, she opened the door and left, leaving Logan standing there by himself.

She'd been right when she'd said that they would have coffee and brandy together. Maybe she'd be right about this as well.

11:46 p.m.

Donatella put the key into the lock and entered Naguib's suite. Deans was dozing on an armchair in the living room. He stirred when he heard the door open. He was a light sleeper and had trained himself to be alert to the slightest sounds. In seconds, he was fully awake.

"Jesus, where have you been?" There was as much irritation in his voice as there was malice. "I haven't seen you all day."

"It's none of your business where I choose to spend my time," she said without so much as a glance in his direction.

"You have to be at your best tomorrow. You should have been in your bed hours ago, sleeping." He walked over to her and grabbed her by the shoulders, something he'd never done before.

For just a second, she was startled.

"We're not going to fail tomorrow because you—" He stopped, paused briefly, angled his head slightly, sniffed, and then said, "I smell sex on you."

Twisting herself out of his grasp, she said, "Get your hands off me." She walked over to the couch and sat down, sliding her feet out of her shoes. "I've smelled something from you for the last five years, but it hasn't prevented me from working with you." She looked at him askance. His voice was the same, but the man was different. She still wasn't used to Henry Nelson.

There was a lull in the exchange for a few minutes. Deans walked to the window, furious with her, and looked down at Alexandria while it slept. *Calm down*, he told himself. He couldn't risk alienating Donatella at this stage of the operation. It was a bitter pill for him to swallow, but he needed her tomorrow. Without her, he wouldn't succeed. It was much too late for him to change his plan. He turned around and walked to the couch and sat down near her.

"I apologize, Donatella. I don't know what got into me." The words were gentle and warm, but they left a bitterness in his mouth. "Perhaps it is just the stress of knowing that the day has finally come."

Donatella stared at a wall, mute.

When he realized that she wasn't going to say anything, he said, "How's your mother?"

"Fine. I have her in a hotel for now. Her apartment is free. The rent is paid to the end of the month, so the landlord will have no reason to come around." She paused for a long moment. "God, I can't wait to leave this country." She ran her fingers through her hair and then flung them out to the sides. She suddenly looked like a wild woman.

"Me too. I'll have your money ready when the assassination is done. You and your mother will live a good life in Bologna. Speaking of which, did you bring the coin?"

"Do you have the money?" She swept a hand across her head, smoothing her hair back.

Deans walked over to a desk, opened a drawer, took out a small package wrapped in newspaper, and returned to the couch. He dropped it on the table in front of them. "Count it if you want. The ten thousand is all there." After a few seconds, he added, "In British sterling notes."

She reached down and picked it up. She tore an edge back and looked inside. "Am I supposed to trust you?"

"I said you could count it, my dear. It's all there."

She gave him an unkind look and reached for her purse. She opened it and took the coin out. "Here. I hope it brings you health and wealth," she said curtly, barely containing her venom.

There was an edge to her voice that Deans didn't care for, but *c'est la vie*, he thought. Tomorrow would be another day, and with it would come a reckoning that would be heard around the world. History would be recorded tomorrow; while the powers of the Western world caved in to the demands of the Soviet devils, one man with wile, skill, and determination fought back against tyranny.

"Thank you, dear Donatella. That was very kind of you. Of course, I wish you the same."

Donatella put the package of bills into her purse, got up, and walked to the door of the bedroom. Over her shoulder, she said, "We should get some sleep. We both have a big day tomorrow."

"Indeed," Deans said. "Indeed, we do."

Chapter 30
WINDS BEFORE THE STORM

Thursday
9:04 a.m.

ALEXANDER LOGAN PUT THE RECEIVER DOWN on the cradle of the phone in his hotel room. He took a deep breath, attempting to head off panic. He closed his eyes and slowly counted to ten, and then he took another deep breath. With the exhalation, he felt a semblance of control again, but he sensed it was temporary. The room was starting to smell like a decaying corpse.

He'd just finished talking to his cousin. Whatever hope Logan might have had before this morning of preventing a catastrophe was now utterly smashed to pieces—like a ceramic flowerpot violently thrown onto a marble floor. Earlier this morning, Shakir had spoken to the head of Nasser's personal security detail, who was now in Alexandria, and had told him that he had reasonable intelligence to suggest there would be an assassination attempt on the president's life. When asked for details, Shakir hadn't given him much other than the name David S. Deans and the explanation that the would-be assassin was a British national working for the Secret Intelligence Service, but that the scoundrel had gone rogue. This information, of course, had been immediately passed on to Nasser himself. As Shakir had predicted, the president hadn't taken it seriously. There had been many assassination attempts on his life over the years—most of which had been instigated by Whitehall—and he'd survived them all. This was just another one. The speech and the timing were too important to be canceled. The event would go on as scheduled. Besides, in light of Nikita Khrushchev's warning to the West, Nasser felt that Britain wouldn't risk going to war with the Soviets. He was confident—even smug—about his safety.

Logan felt impotent. It would've been so damned simple for Nasser to cancel his speech. Instead, in roughly six hours, Nasser could be *dead*, spearheading an international crisis. At the very least, if the assassin failed and Nasser escaped, either wounded or unharmed, the West would still have the Reds to worry about. Would they go through with their threat? Either way, an assassination attempt would result in massive bedlam and hundreds of deaths of ordinary Egyptian citizens. Now Logan was forced to consider something he had never thought he'd have to: an exit strategy. He'd have to make plans to get the hell out of Egypt while he could.

Even if Lucky Break failed in his attempt, the borders, including the airports, would be locked down. Logan wouldn't be able to leave for days, perhaps weeks. If he wanted to avoid the chaos, he'd have to go to the airport now and take a flight out of the country; otherwise, he'd be stuck there for who knows how long. But it wasn't only the chaos he had to avoid. He was well aware of what the government would do. As a foreign national with an intelligence background (surely, Egyptian intelligence would eventually find that out), he would inevitably find himself being interrogated by the authorities. Torture was a real possibility. Shakir wouldn't be able to prevent that from happening. The likelihood of his being swept away with hundreds of other suspects and sent to one of the isolated prisons scattered throughout the country was real. Unlike in the United States, no lawyer would come to his rescue. Certainly, the CIA would pull back from him; hadn't Stance already told him as much? He knew enough of the Egyptian system to be concerned.

Logan didn't know whether it was because of ego or stubbornness, but he decided to stay. To leave now, he would have to admit defeat—something that he was unwilling to do even at this point. However, he didn't have a plan; he had no idea what he would do during the next six hours to find Lucky Break. All he knew was that he couldn't give up. Never in his life had he given up on anything he'd started. Considering his odds at succeeding, perhaps he was insane—or just plain stupid or terribly pigheaded.

He went to his bedside table and picked up the bottle of brandy from last night. There was still some in it. He gulped it down from the bottle and ran the back of his hand across his mouth. Unshaven, his face felt like sandpaper. He took his High Standard HDM semiautomatic pistol from the table, dropped the magazine to make certain it was fully loaded, shoved the magazine back in, and then slid the gun into his waistband. He put a second magazine in his jacket pocket and the silencer in another. He picked up the bottle again but realized it was empty. The brandy was gone. For a split second, he remembered last night with Donatella. God, she was beautiful. Had he decided to leave Egypt, he might have asked her again to go with him. He grabbed his hotel key from the desk, locked his room, and walked down the hallway.

Three minutes later, the elevator doors opened into the lobby. He stepped out, walked a half dozen steps, and stopped dead in his tracks. At the entrance of the hotel, he saw two people with their backs turned to him. He recognized both of them. He made his way to the right, behind the front desk and near the entrance to the restaurant. From that safe distance, he watched them. They were just standing there, talking to each other. After a minute or so, Donatella left the hotel, and Henry Nelson, the American he'd met at San Stefano last Monday, turned and walked toward the elevator. Logan couldn't for the life of him figure out how the two might know each other. Maybe Donatella was plying her trade here at the hotel while Kamal Naguib was busy with Nasser's security, and Nelson was a customer. The elevator doors opened, and Nelson stepped inside. Logan dashed toward the elevator. As the doors began closing, Nelson saw him and stuck his hand between the doors, making them slide open again.

"Almost missed the lift, eh?" Nelson paused a few seconds and then said, "Aren't you Sullivan?"

"Yes, Frank Sullivan. You're staying here. What a coincidence."

"Just until this evening. Then I'm heading home. Business calls, you know?"

The elevator doors closed again.

"Four, please," Logan said to the operator.

The elevator started to ascend.

Lift? Logan thought. And then it hit him like a ton of bricks. When the two had met that afternoon at the casino, Logan had been sleep-deprived, and he had subsequently forgotten much of what transpired. Now, with a clear head, he found it all coming back to him. He remembered the American using some British phrases—"cheeky" and "right old nutter"—but he'd been so tired at the time that he hadn't given it further thought.

"Did you end up winning anything?" Logan asked him.

The elevator passed the second floor.

"Broke even, but I had a great time. It's a wonderful place to unwind. Must remember it if I come here again. You look better today. I thought you were a bit under the weather when we met."

And then the third floor.

"I was just a little tired."

The elevator stopped on the fourth floor, and the doors pulled back.

Logan stuck his hand out. "It was good to have met you. Good luck."

"Right," Nelson said, shaking his hand. "Likewise, I'm sure. Perhaps we'll see each other again."

"Yes, perhaps." Logan got out of the elevator, looked over his shoulder, and said, "Goodbye."

The doors closed. Logan turned around and watched the arrow overhead as the elevator continued to five, the top floor of the hotel. Logan pressed the button and waited for the elevator to return. He then took it to the lobby, got out, and went to a desk near the back and sat down. There were envelopes and stationery atop the desk for guests. He took a sheet of paper, folded it into thirds, and then slid it into an envelope and ran his tongue across the flap. He wrote Kamal Naguib's name on the envelope and walked to the front desk, where he told the clerk he had a letter for the minister. The clerk took it, turned around, and put it into the mail slot for room 504. Logan made note of the number.

The clerk turned around again to face him. "Is there anything else I can do for you, sir?"

"Yes, there is one thing. I believe a friend of mine is staying here. We haven't seen each other in years. He's American as well. His name is Henry Nelson."

"Certainly. I'll check for you." The clerk took a few steps to his left and paged through the guest registry. "When did he arrive, sir?"

"I'm not sure. Maybe a week or so ago."

The clerk continued to search, running a finger down first

one page and then another and three more after that. "I don't see his name. I checked for the last several months."

"Maybe I'm mistaken then."

"He could be staying at the Majestic hotel." He pointed toward the entrance. "It's close by. You go down rue de la Gare de Remleh—"

"Yes, I know where it is," he said. "Thank you."

Logan went back to the elevator and pushed the button. When he arrived on the fourth floor, he walked to the end of the hallway, opened a door, and climbed the stairs to the fifth-floor landing. He opened another door and gingerly walked down the hallway, not knowing exactly what he was looking for. He stopped at a door that was recessed off the hallway in an alcove. He tried the knob and opened it—a utility closet. He walked into it and pulled the door almost closed, leaving it just slightly open. From there, he had a good view of room 504.

Something was terribly wrong. Could Henry Nelson possibly be Lucky Break? If so, why was he staying in Kamal Naguib's suite? Could the two of them—Lucky Break and Naguib—have planned the assassination together? If so, it certainly made sense, given MI6's penchant for using Egyptians in the past.

On the other hand, maybe Henry Nelson wasn't in the suite at all. Maybe he was in one of the other rooms, registered under a different name. With less than six hours to go, maybe he was going over the final stages of the assassination. And how did Donatella fit into all of this? Logan had to find out, so he decided to wait for Nelson to come out of one of the rooms. The only thing he knew for certain was that Nelson was somewhere on the fifth floor.

———◉———

11:24 a.m.

Logan looked at his watch. Time was ticking away. It was a matter of only a few more hours before Nasser would be driven down rue Fuad and into Mansheya Square. He couldn't wait any longer for Nelson to come out of whichever room he was in. He would have to try the suite. Naguib himself would be with Nasser, so either the suite would be empty, or he'd find Nelson there. If it was empty, he wasn't quite certain what he'd do then. He'd counted five other rooms on the fifth floor. He'd think about that later.

Logan took out his wallet and found his two tools that went with him everywhere. Old habits died hard. He walked to room 504, knelt down, and began working the lock. Using a simple pick and small tension wrench, he inserted the wrench into the lower portion of the keyhole. He applied torque to the cylinder, first clockwise and then counterclockwise to determine which way the cylinder turned in order to open it. It was to the left, and he held the wrench in place. Next, he inserted the pick in the upper portion of the keyhole and felt for the pins. He started pushing the set of five pins up until he heard them seat themselves in place. He used the wrench to turn the cylinder. The lock was disabled.

He had been careful to be quiet, but there was no guarantee that Nelson hadn't heard him—if, in fact, he was there at all. Logan proceeded with the expectation that when he opened the door, Lucky Break was going to be there, pointing a gun at him. Crouching, he pulled his pistol from his waist, attached the silencer, chambered a round, pushed the safety off, and then placed his left hand on the doorknob. He turned the knob slowly and quietly, at the same time using his right elbow to gently nudge the door open while holding the pistol firmly in his right hand. As he eased the door inward, he looked over the top of his gun and saw Nelson with his back to him, pouring something into a glass. Logan rose, and in slow motion, he eased himself into the room. When he was fully inside, he slammed the door shut. Nelson turned around quickly, with one hand going to the inside of his jacket.

"Don't try it," Logan said. If this was Lucky Break, then it was critical that Logan not make any missteps. One error of judgment could cost him his life. Lucky Break was a dangerous animal.

"Frank Sullivan," Nelson said, relieved. "Jesus, you scared the shit out of me. Why are you here? What's with the gun?" The hand that had been going toward the inside of his jacket now hung free at his side.

"Put your hands high above you," Logan ordered. When Nelson didn't immediately comply, Logan shouted, "Now!"

Nelson raised his hands.

"Slowly, very slowly, with your right hand reach into your jacket and take out whatever you have there."

"What's this all about?" His hands remained up, but he didn't do what Logan had told him.

Logan fired a round between Nelson's head and his upraised left arm. It buried itself in the wall behind him.

"Are you fucking *mad*?" Nelson cried out, clearly shaken.

"If you try anything cute, the next bullet will hit something you won't much like. Now take out whatever you have inside your jacket. And be smart about it."

Nelson's right hand went to the inside of his jacket and pulled out the dagger.

"Throw it across the room."

He did so. It landed by the windows, near the drapes.

"Walk over there," Logan said, waving his gun at a wall and keeping a safe distance away, "and stop when you're three feet from it." He waited until Nelson was there. "Now lean into the wall with your hands and legs spread. If you so much as move an inch, I'll put a nice little three-round grouping in the center of your back."

Logan crossed the room and picked up the dagger, never taking his eyes off of Nelson. He felt the razor-sharp edges. His thoughts went to Aria and Peter Cook, but only for a moment. He had to focus his mind as he'd never focused it before. He used the dagger to cut the cords of the drapes, all the time facing Nelson and keeping the pistol pointed in his direction. When he finished, he went back to Nelson.

"Turn around and sit on the floor." He threw one of the cords to him. "Take your shoes and socks off and tie your ankles tight. I want to see an indentation in your skin, and I want to see tight knots. You may get out of this yet, if you behave yourself." Logan had to give him a modicum of hope; a desperate man with nothing to lose would always act like a desperate man with nothing to lose.

Logan closed the gap between them but remained a healthy distance away. If Nelson was Deans, the trained MI6 agent, as Logan thought he was, he'd know all the tricks. Logan had a few of his own, but he couldn't underestimate his opponent. He made a slipknot with one of the cords. "Put your hands behind your back."

Nelson obeyed, and Logan went around him and looped the cord around one wrist and tightened it. "Put your hands together with your fingers interlaced and make a tight fist. If I see you let up on the pressure, it'll be the last thing you ever do." Logan wound the cord around both wrists, pulling it tighter and tighter as he did. Nelson didn't resist. Logan looped the end between his wrists and then tied it in several tight knots.

Logan brought a chair over to him and sat down, facing Nelson. "Now we can have our little chat."

"Would you mind telling me what this is all about?" Nelson

asked, looking up at him helplessly. "You're scaring the hell out of me."

"Let's start with that dagger of yours. Since when does a businessman from Minneapolis carry one?"

"I have it for protection. I didn't know what to expect here in Egypt."

"This is a professional dagger—military—World War II vintage. You wouldn't find one in the local hardware store."

"It was a war souvenir. I served in the army."

"Which unit—quick!"

Nelson hesitated and then said, "First Infantry Division. The Big Red One. Italy."

Too long ... bullshit! Logan thought about pursuing this but decided against it. Lucky Break might have a cover story, and Logan didn't have the time to verify it. He had to be absolutely certain Nelson was Lucky Break. He didn't want to kill an innocent man. He continued with questions. "What are you doing in Kamal Naguib's suite?"

There was a long moment of silence, broken only by the next question.

"Have you ever lived in England?" Logan asked, remembering the words Nelson had used—*lift, cheeky, right old nutter.*

Nelson looked at him but didn't say anything.

"How do you know Donatella Marinetti?"

Again, silence, silence, silence, and more silence.

Logan was considering running his hand over Nelson's face and pulling at his hair to see whether he was wearing a disguise when he noticed something on his chin. He stood from the chair and walked closer to him for a better look. He peered down and saw a moon-shaped scar on the man's chin. He pulled out the picture of David S. Deans that he'd gotten from Campbell and held it up to the man's face, his eyes darting back and forth. The scars were identical. Logan had his man.

He walked around the room, trying to decide what to do next. On the end table by the couch, he noticed a gold coin. He picked it up. It looked like the one he'd seen in Donatella's purse the night before. He flipped it into the air, caught it, and then put it in his pocket. He walked back to the chair and sat down.

"David S. Deans. Addison Davies. Henry Nelson. Spy, shopkeeper, and businessman. I'm afraid the jig's up, *old man*. I'll tell you exactly who I am. My name is Alexander Logan. I work for the CIA. My job was to come to Alexandria, hunt you down, and kill you."

Deans stared at him but said nothing.

"You were going to assassinate Nasser soon, but I guess you're all tied up now." Logan couldn't help himself. The words just slipped out. He was going to laugh in Deans's face but decided not to. There was nothing funny about Lucky Break or the attempted assassination or the murders of his cousin and the British agent. "I'm going to give you a chance to save your hide, but only one. I don't know why I am, after all the shit you've done, but you could be in a plane heading out of the country in a few hours. I'd tell the Agency back home that I couldn't find you." He paused a moment to let that sink in. "But I want something in return for my good deed. I know how people like you work. For a job like this, you always have a backup plan in case the first one peters out. I want you to tell me what that plan is. Once I can verify it, I'll come back and untie you, and you'll be free to leave. Now's the time to do your talking because, David, your time is running out."

"I suppose it would be fruitless of me to ask you for a guarantee," Deans said dryly.

"Fruitless? I'd imagine it would be. You know how this works. As one spy to another, you know there are no guarantees. I'm afraid you'll have to trust me. You played your last card and lost. Your options are gone. The only guarantee I'll give you is that if you don't tell me your plan B, I'm going to put a bullet between your eyes."

"There's no plan." His eyes flickered, as if he were embarrassed.

"I can't very well verify that, now can I?"

"There's no plan B. There was only one plan from the beginning. Someone else is going to shoot Nasser. That was always the plan. I did the engineering."

"Who's that someone else?"

"Her name is Donatella Marinetti. You don't know her."

Logan was stunned, but he didn't let Lucky Break see it. His heart was beating so hard that he wondered whether Deans could hear it. It felt like the walls of the suite were shaking. "Where is she?"

"In her mother's flat at 326 rue Fuad. Fifth floor, number 51. She'll fire down on Nasser as he drives toward Mansheya Square."

"Is Kamal Naguib involved in this?"

"I used Donatella to get intelligence from him, but he knows nothing about this."

"And you passed the intelligence she got on to MI6 in London?"

"Yes."

Logan looked at his watch. It was after two o'clock. Nasser was to deliver his speech a little after three. Logan hoped that the motorcade would be delayed en route before reaching the flat; nothing in Egypt happened on time.

"Lie on your side," Logan ordered.

Lucky Break complied. Logan put Deans's hands between his legs and used cords to tie them to his ankles, Deans grunting as he did. He checked and double-checked the knots. It would be painful for Lucky Break to move even an inch.

Once he had decided that Lucky Break couldn't work himself free, he said, "You don't have any other little surprises for me, do you?"

"No, but you need to hurry. Donatella's a crack shot. I taught her myself. She *will* kill him if you don't get to her first."

Logan went into the kitchen and found some rags. He went back to Lucky Break and shoved one of them into his mouth and tied the other one around his head, over the gag. He then dragged him into the bedroom and closed the door.

Logan was glad he'd given Lucky Break a way out. Deans obviously wanted to stay alive. He was no madman bent of self-destruction. He was simply a madman who didn't want to die.

Logan locked the suite, raced down the stairs, flew out the front doors, grabbed a taxi in front of the hotel, and started toward rue Fuad, hoping to get there before President Nasser passed by number 326 in an open-air Cadillac.

Chapter 31
THE STORM

2:04 p.m.

DONATELLA AND AN OLD MAN PUSHED THEIR way through hordes of spectators swarming both sides of rue Fuad. She'd hired the old man near the catacombs to carry a rolled-up rug—about six feet long—to her mother's flat. She would have carried it herself, but she needed to preserve her energy. She'd gotten sufficient sleep last night; now she had to maintain the strength, vitality, and sustained mental acuity that would be necessary for her to accomplish her one last task.

The old man was homeless and slept in alleyways, but he was reasonably fit; she'd offered him a five-pound sterling note to carry the rug, and he had enthusiastically accepted. This meant he wouldn't have to beg for food for the next week. They'd taken a taxi until the crowds thickened, and they could go no further. The old man was now walking with difficulty as they approached the apartment building. His shoulder clearly ached, and his legs were unsteady under the weight. Thank goodness, they were there.

Outside the door, Donatella pointed. "Put it there—upright. I'll take it upstairs." She hadn't the heart to ask him to carry it all the way to the fifth floor. She paid him the money, giving him an extra pound. He lowered his head as far as he was able out of gratitude and then turned, shuffled a few feet, and was absorbed by the crowd. She bent her knees slightly, resting the rug on a shoulder, and then hefted it up.

Once inside the building, she saw a man. He was standing at the end of the long hallway, in the shadows behind the cubbyhole under the stairs.

"It's you," she said in Arabic. "Carry this up for me. I don't want to strain my muscles."

He walked down the hallway at a measured pace and eased the rug onto a shoulder, and together they climbed the stairs, Donatella following behind. Neither spoke. Once on the fifth floor, he leaned the rug against the wall by the flat. "I'll see to it no one comes up here," he said, and then he descended the stairs.

She removed a key from a pocket sewn into her *milaya lef*, a black cotton wrap that many women in Alexandria commonly wore over their clothes. It would later help her blend into the crowds more efficiently. Donatella hated wearing it because it was a visible stigma of female servitude. Peasant Egyptian women wore them, not her. She wasn't a peasant, and she'd never considered herself Egyptian.

She stuck the key into the lock and opened the door. She could hear the crowds below. The last time she was here, she'd left the windows open. Closed, the flat would have been stifling. Quite frankly, she could have heard the din below even if the windows had been closed; the crowds were jacked up on the cult of Nasser, and the tumult—the shouting and screaming—was nearly deafening. She looked at her watch. In spite of her delay getting here, everything was on schedule. The flat seemed strange to her now, with her mother safely in another location in the city. Her mother had taken her personal things; all else remained as before. Donatella could see her mother sitting in the armchair, reading a book and drinking a dark cup of coffee. She shook her head. *Focus,* she told herself. She had a job to do. There was no time for anything else.

She threw her arms around the rug, lifted it, carried it to the center of the living room, and then eased it to the floor. She went to the door to close and lock it. Returning to the rug, she bent down and loosened the twine on either end. She rolled it out, exposing a long object wrapped tightly in burlap and tied with more twine. She undid the knots, and the burlap fell away. She picked up the British-made No. 4 MK1(T) sniper rifle that Deans had given her and held it in her hands.

It was a Lee-Enfield bolt-action, magazine-fed weapon with a telescopic sight, a steel butt plate, and a wooden cheek rest. Over the last few months, Donatella had become an expert with it, practicing almost daily in the dim lights of the paraffin lanterns, deep within the underground graveyard of the catacombs. She felt strong and confident as she held it in her hands. The rifle had become so much a part of her that she considered it an extension of herself. She knew every flaw, every nick in the wood; she knew its function with her eyes closed. More importantly, she could nail a stationary target with a three-round grouping in six and a half seconds. She was one with the weapon, so much so that its very presence excited her.

However, there was a problem: her target would not be stationary. She had never fired the rifle at a moving target. She had no experience—no practice—tracking a moving target and squeezing the trigger. But she wasn't fazed by this. Deans had taught her how to lead a moving target. All she had to do was aim just ahead of the target. How far ahead depended on the speed at which the target was moving. Nasser's vehicle would be pushing through hordes of well-wishers, so it would be moving slowly and most assuredly stopping every so often. It would be creeping along the street.

If the vehicle stopped near the apartment building, that would be even better. But Donatella couldn't count on that, so she prepared herself mentally for a kill shot while the car was slowly moving by her. During the last week of practicing in the catacombs, her three-round groupings had looked as if she'd fired just one round. All she had to do was aim ahead of the target—ever so slightly—and fire three rounds in six or seven seconds, and one of them would surely find its mark. Just one bullet in Nasser's head was all she needed, and her job would be finished.

She walked over to the window she'd selected days ago— her very own sniper's nest—and looked down upon the throngs of people eagerly awaiting the president of Egypt. She imagined what would happen down there once they realized that their beloved Nasser had been mortally wounded. Some of the people, those closest to him, would rush to him, hoping in vain to save his life. Others would scatter in all directions, hoping to avoid an errant round. Nasser's security force would spread out, looking in all directions for the shooter. Donatella suspected they'd even look up at this selfsame window. But by then it wouldn't matter because Nasser would be dead, and she would be running down the back stairs and out of the building, and she too would find the crowds and, like the old man, be absorbed by them. Who would suspect that a woman, wrapped in a black *milaya lef* as so many other women were, was the assassin?

She leaned out the window and looked down rue Fuad. She had no fear of being seen at this point because there were hundreds—perhaps thousands—of people doing the same thing at that very moment in her building and other buildings running parallel to the street. There was no sign of the motorcade. She had time yet to prepare herself mentally for the task at hand; however, her mind wasn't cooperating. Thoughts about her future tugged at her. She'd waited a very long time for this moment. Soon, perhaps today if she was lucky, but certainly in a few days—or if she was unlucky, even a week—she and her mother would be carving out a new life for themselves in Bologna. She had more than enough money to ensure that. If the stars were aligned right tonight, she might even hire a large boat to cross over to Greece. They could then fly to Italy from there. Or if that turned out to be impossible, they could wait until the borders were open and then simply fly directly to Rome and then on to Bologna.

She'd considered many times what she would do there. She had many options. At the top of her list was the idea of opening a small boutique specializing in fashionable clothing. She would love that. It was such a contrast to what her life had been here in Alexandria. She was physically moved at the thought of having a normal life, maybe for the first time. Perhaps she'd even meet a decent man to share all that. After all, she was still young, and bearing children wasn't out of the question.

Inexplicably, her mind went to the man she'd shared a bed with last night—this Frank Sullivan. When she'd first seen him at the hotel that day when the elevator doors had drawn back, she'd been attracted to him in a way she couldn't explain. His eyes were the first thing she'd noticed. They'd been full of mystery and passion. They'd had a mesmerizing effect on her unlike anything she'd ever experienced before. For a short time, she'd been transfixed; his eyes had held her attention to the exclusion of everything else. And then last night, they'd had a similar effect on her. Perhaps the universe had been telling her something. But now that was water under the bridge. Or was it? For a few moments, she fantasized about being in Bologna and hiring a private investigator—yes, she would be able to afford one then—who would tract down this

Frank Sullivan. She would invite him to Italy and eventually into her life. After all, he spoke Italian. She had discovered that while they were making love last night.

Yes, she thought, *I could love this Frank Sullivan. Perhaps I already do.*

———————«◉»———————

Alexander Logan got out of the taxi because the roads were too thick with people for it to continue, and he ran, pumping his arms as he went. When the crowds became too thick for that, he walked, pushing and shoving people out of his way. As he arrived on rue Fuad from a narrow cross street, he looked to his left. The spectators were cheering and jumping up and down, waving their arms fanatically in the air. They seemed to be almost hypnotized—in some sort of trance. Their eyes were glassy, and spittle was flying from their mouths. The sight was horrible. He'd seen something like this twice before: once on a trip to West Africa, where he had secretively witnessed a ceremony that involved human sacrifice, and once at the Democratic National Convention at Convention Hall in Philadelphia in the summer of 1948.

Logan could see that the motorcade was being led by a half dozen police on motorcycles, followed by the lead car, an open-top vehicle with uniformed security officers standing upright, scanning the crowds. Nasser's Cadillac limousine would be behind that, although at this point, Logan couldn't see it. From the reaction of the crowd, however, he was sure Nasser was there, standing up and waving to his people. Behind Nasser's car would be another six to eight cars, mostly security and dignitaries.

He turned right and pressed ahead on rue Fuad through the throngs. The apartment building should be a block or two away, but it seemed as if it would take him forever to get there.

He looked over his shoulder and saw the motorcade ease to a stop. Encouraged by this, Logan pushed harder, clawing his way through the dense forest jungle of humans. The people along the street were so engrossed in the electrifying atmosphere that they were unaffected by his pushing and shoving as he cleared a path through them. He looked back again and saw that the motorcade was now moving slowly forward, parting Nasser's followers as Moses parted the Red Sea. Logan put his head down and leaned forward as if he were doing the breast stroke, trying to separate shoulder-to-shoulder people who barely noticed him. He passed a pole—a streetlight—where men were standing upright on each other's shoulders, all the way to the top. He was so focused on getting through the crowds that he'd gone by the apartment building, number 326, without realizing it. He shoved his way back to the entrance. He was able to open the door only enough to squeeze himself through sideways because of so many people standing in front of it. Once inside, he was starting toward the stairs to his right when he heard his named called.

"Logan, over here." The voice was muffled.

Logan stopped and looked down the hallway. Halfway down, at the back of the stairs, stood John Campbell. He was pointing a semiautomatic pistol at Logan.

"Going somewhere?" Campbell asked.

The first thing that came to Logan's mind was that Campbell was Deans's one last surprise for him. Deans had led him into a deadly trap. His doubts about Campbell were now confirmed. The second thing that came to his mind was that Gamal Abdul Nasser was heading directly into the kill zone.

"You and Lucky Break," Logan said, out of breath. "The original Dynamic Duo." He should have been surprised to see Campbell, but he wasn't.

"Oh, you're mistaken. There's a third, and she's a crack shot."

Time was ticking away, and Logan was acutely aware of that. His pistol was at his left side, in his belt. The stairs were to his right—three feet away. The stairs would protect him temporarily. The trick was to get there so that he could get his pistol out. The shouting and cheering outside were getting louder, which could only mean that the president's limousine was getting closer to the kill zone, directly in front of the apartment building.

"Unfortunately, you won't be alive to witness her abilities," Campbell said. "But take my word for it. She's the best th—"

Before he could get the last words out, Logan dove for the stairs. Campbell fired off a round. Logan landed on his side, the edge of a stair digging into his ribcage, and had the wind knocked out of him. His right hand went to his pistol with difficulty, and he immediately switched it to his left hand. Crouching low and in intense pain, he swung the pistol around the banister and blindly fired four fast rounds, spreading them around the hallway, stopping only when he heard Campbell's body hitting the wooden floor. Suddenly, he felt pain in his left arm. He looked down and saw that he was bleeding. Campbell had nailed him. Deciding not to check on Campbell, he raced up the stairs to the fifth floor, hoping his adrenaline would keep at bay the real pain that he knew was coming. He looked for the number of the flat, found it, and tried the doorknob. It was locked. The doorjamb didn't look sturdy; in fact, there was some dry rot around it. He kicked the door just below the doorknob, and it flew inward. Donatella, sitting at the window with the barrel of the sniper rifle just a few inches beyond the frame, snapped her head around toward the door.

Logan stood with his feet apart, holding his pistol in his right hand, the left bracing it. They locked eyes. He watched her blink several times, as if she were trying to blink him away.

Below, the cheering was intensifying. Nasser's limousine was approaching the kill zone.

"Please, don't!" Logan yelled. He had to shout to make himself heard. "Donatella, please drop the rifle!"

She didn't drop it. Instead, she swung her head around and fixed an eye on the scope, the side of her face on the cheek rest. Steady! Alert! Fixed! Her finger was on the trigger guard. Logan could clearly see it.

The cheering became louder. Then the crowd began chanting, "Nasser! Nasser!" The president was in the kill zone below. Donatella tilted the rifle downward, adjusting the angle, her eye to the scope. Nasser must be in the crosshairs.

"Don't, Donatella! Don't!" Logan shouted.

Her finger slid down to the trigger.

Logan fired one round into the back of her head, and it was over.

But the chanting continued. "Nasser! Nasser! Nasser!"

Chapter 32
END OF THE STORM

4:43 p.m.

"QUE SERA, SERA, WHATEVER WILL BE, WILL BE ..."

This time Logan was singing the words, not just humming the tune. He sat on the couch with Deans in front of him on a chair—his wrists bound behind him, a cord wrapped around his ankles and the front legs of the chair. Logan made eye contact with Dean and held it.

"You said you'd release me if I told you the truth," Deans stated matter-of-factly, dropping the phony American accent. He paused to swallow some phlegm that had built up in his throat. "And I did."

Logan continued to stare at him and wondered what in this world had produced this beast.

After a minute or so, Deans asked, "Did you stop her?"

Logan continued to sing, but the tempo was half as fast as it should have been. It sounded like a funeral dirge. "The future's not ours to see. Que sera, sera—what will be, will be ..." Logan saw Deans's eyes drop to his left arm. A rag was wrapped around it, above the elbow. Blood had seeped through it, forming a deep red spot about the size of a silver dollar.

"You're wounded," Deans said. "Was it the security forces?"

"The future's not ours to see. Que sera, sera—what will be, will be ..."

"Stop singing that bloody song and say something!" Deans said. "I kept my word. Now cut these damn cords, and let me go." He ground out the words "damn cords," showing a neat row of stained front teeth.

Logan shifted his body on the couch. The gunshot wound was throbbing. He'd been trying to mentally block out the pain. He had succeeded for the most part, but it still hurt—stung, burned like hell. The bullet had ripped through some flesh just above the elbow. An eighth-inch closer, it might have shattered the humerus. Still, he needed to see a doctor soon. He was concerned about infection. He knew of an American here in the city who treated tourists and dubious characters. He'd keep his mouth shut.

Logan's pistol lay across his lap with the silencer attached. He picked it up and put it on the end table beside him. He then held his left arm with his hand. "Just before I came here to Alexandria, I saw a film—a new release. It probably won't be showing here for another few weeks. It was called *The Man Who Knew Too Much*." He looked at Deans thoughtfully, cocking his head slightly, and then added, "Jimmy Stewart and Doris Day had the lead roles." He spoke slowly, as if he were drugged, as if Deans weren't there at all.

"I saw the film yesterday," Deans said impatiently. "I asked you whether you stopped her!"

"It was about an assassination plot that the main characters stumbled upon," Logan continued, acting as if he hadn't heard Deans.

"Good God, man, I don't give a sod about some bloody film. You said you'd release me. I kept my word. Now keep yours!"

Logan's mouth was dry. Besides quenching his thirst, maybe some alcohol would take the edge off the pain. He rose from the couch and walked over to where Deans had been pouring a drink for himself earlier when Logan first entered the suite. The drink was still there. He looked at the bottle beside it. It was brandy, good quality. *This'll do*, he thought. He picked up the snifter, smelled it, and then put it to his lips. *Excellent.* He walked back to the couch and sat down. "Since you don't give a *sod* about the film, I'll cut to the end. They got the bad guy—the would-be assassin." He held the drink up to Deans. "Cheers."

"You were never going to turn me loose, were you?"

Logan sipped the brandy. He'd learned during the war never to answer a question put to him by the person he was interrogating. If he did, the control would shift. He wasn't, however, interrogating Deans, not really. Then what exactly was he doing? For the life of him, he couldn't answer that question. After a moment, he locked eyes with Deans again. "I pleaded with her to stop."

"Who?"

"Twice, maybe three times, I pleaded with her to stop, but she wouldn't put the rifle down."

"Donatella? That's not my fault."

"You must have had a powerful sway over her. What did you promise her?"

"Money, of course. Money provided her and her mother a way out of Egypt." After a long moment, he added, "She always had a mind of her own. You can't blame me for that."

"She simply turned her head from me and looked through the scope. That was what she was doing when I kicked in the door to the flat—looking through the scope down at Nasser. She must have thought that I wouldn't try to stop her, especially after last night."

"Then she *is* dead?"

"I was going to shoot her in the leg, but she still could've pulled the trigger. And I didn't want to risk shooting the rifle out of her hands because a bullet could've escaped. She had her finger on the trigger. I had no choice but to shoot her in the back of the head. The rifle fell to the floor at the same time she did."

Deans gazed at the floor and then back at Logan. He said nothing.

"Did you know that I slept with her last night?"

Still nothing.

"She was lovely—beyond words. It wasn't just the physical part. There was a certain attraction, a certain ..." For a moment, Logan started to drift away in thought.

Deans still said nothing.

"You know, I had this silly notion of asking her to return to the States with me. I felt that we had connected in extraordinary ways. I think she felt that too. Maybe that was why she thought I wouldn't try to stop her."

"Listen, she's gone, and there's nothing either you or I can do about that. But I'm here, and I told you where to find her. Nasser is alive because of that. I guarantee you, she was an excellent shot—one of the best snipers I've seen. I trained her myself. Nasser is alive because of me! Now stick to your part of our bargain and untie me!"

"Campbell was the one who shot me. Actually, he could have killed me if he would have shot me right away instead of talking. I'd be dead right now. You knew he was going to be there. You led me into a trap. With me dead, Donatella would have been free to ..." The words came out slowly, like the song—like a funeral dirge.

"No, I didn't. I had no idea." There was a tinge of panic in his voice. "You've got to believe me."

"Why do I have to do that? You're a drowning man, and I've got the life buoy. You'd say anything to get me to throw it to you."

"Listen, if this is about Donatella, then I can give you

some facts about her that you're unaware of. She was a lying, cheating, manipulative little whore, who would say and do anything to get what she wanted. I've known her for five years. You've known her for what—a few days, a week? I tell you, if you would have taken her with you to America, she would have made your life miserable. Eventually, she would have dumped you for some rich bloke. I saved you from all that."

Logan began to flush with anger. He took another sip of the brandy and set the snifter down on the end table beside his pistol. He sighed, deeply. "Actually, this was all about a war with the Soviet Union, which I assume was your main goal. Had you succeeded, that would have caused a global catastrophe. The Soviets had threatened to play their doomsday card, and you were prepared to set a fire under them. I'm sure you never considered that there wouldn't be any winners. Doomsday for the Reds; doomsday for England, France, and America; doomsday for the world."

"But you see, that didn't happen." There was a certain, undeniable panic in Deans's voice now, as if he were about to swallow his last mouthful of water before going down for good into a watery grave. "We both saved the world from that. Without me telling you where to find Donatella, we'd have a world war on our hands. Now ... untie these goddamn cords!"

"But you're right; this is also about Donatella. You brought her into this mess. I pulled the trigger, but it was you who killed her." Calmly and slowly, Logan reached for his pistol beside him on the table, swung it around to Deans, and fired three rounds into his chest. He set the pistol down again and picked up the snifter. He knocked the rest back with one gulp. He looked at Deans. His chin was touching his chest; his white shirt was turning red below it; his eyes were staring at his lap. "And doomsday for you."

Logan sat there for the next thirty minutes without

moving, without thinking, as if he were meditating into a void.

Suddenly, he got up, unscrewed the silencer from his pistol, put it in his jacket pocket, and then slipped the pistol into his pants in the small of his back. He reached into a pocket in his pants and pulled out the gold coin. He looked at it for just a moment. It was all he had left of Donatella. He returned it to his pocket.

He left the suite and then took the stairs down to the fourth floor. He had a suitcase to pack, a doctor to see, and a flight to catch.

Epilogue
A LEOPARD CANNOT CHANGE ITS SPOTS

Five years later

LATE ON JUNE 11, 1961, KLM FLIGHT 823 TOOK OFF
from Amsterdam on a scheduled milk run to Kuala Lumpur,
with stopovers in Munich, Rome, Cairo, and Karachi. Twenty-
nine passengers and a crew of seven were aboard the aircraft
on the third leg of the flight, between Rome and Cairo. At 4:11
a.m. on June 12, Cairo time, the Lockheed L-188 Electra was
approaching runway 34 at Cairo International Airport when
the bottom of the aircraft scraped high ground two and a half
miles south of the airport. The aircraft split in two on impact,
with both sections catching fire. Seventeen passengers and
three crew members were killed. After a lengthy investigation,
Egyptian authorities attributed the crash to pilot error.

=≡◄(◐)►=

Alexandria, Egypt

Ibrahim Mustafa el-Baghdadi sat in a small café off of rue
Fuad. Like most small cafés at this time of day, it was busy.

Pleasant Arabic music was playing, and the other men there were chatting among themselves—some even arguing over last night's soccer game. Several were engaged in a serious card game, and several more were relaxing while smoking a shisha.

Mustafa, which was the name el-Baghdadi preferred using, wore a dark red taqiyah and a white galabia. He sipped some tea and then ran his palm across his bearded face. He was exhausted. He'd been searching for a particular man for months without success. He'd chased him around Cairo, a city he didn't know well. Nevertheless, he had finally tracked him down in Sharia el-Muski, the old Islamic quarter of the city, when the man had disappeared once again. Mustafa had become disillusioned and was about to give up when he received a message that the man was now in Alexandria. Furthermore, the message had provided him with an address. That was fortunate; Mustafa knew Alexandria like the back of his hand. But after a bus ride through the hot desert, he needed to rest first and regain his strength. Tomorrow would be soon enough. He took a bite of bread—*aish baladi*—and then sipped some more tea. If the man was indeed here, as the message had said, let him enjoy his last day on earth.

———●(●)●———

Mustafa rose from his bed the next day. He poured some water from a pitcher into a ceramic basin and washed his face, head, arms, and feet. He then unrolled his prayer rug, positioning it so that he would face Qibla, the direction of the Kaaba Muazzama, a structure at the center of Islam's most sacred mosque, Al-Masjid al-Haram, in Mecca. He was now ready to perform salah. Prayer was communicating with Allah. It purified and cleansed his mind and served to bring peace to his life. Prayer was his way of thanking Allah and reminded him that Allah was watching over his life, giving him the courage to face adversity.

He stood erect, placing his thumbs to his earlobes, his palms facing outward. "Allahu Akbar," he said softly, meaning "Allah is great." He then placed his hands below his navel, his right hand over his left, his wrists overlapping. After reciting surah Al-Fatiha as well as a portion of another surah, he bowed, placing his hands on his knees. "Allahu Akbar, Subhana Rabbiyal al-Adheem" (All praises to Allah, the great).

He then rose, while saying, "Sam'i Allahu liman hamidah" (Allah listens to those who praise Him). Dropping to his knees, he touched his forehead and palms to the prayer rug, reciting, "Subhan rabbi al Ala" (Glory be to my Lord, the most high) three times. It took him another five minutes to complete his morning prayers. He'd had a difficult time focusing his mind. His thoughts had been elsewhere—on the man he would assassinate today.

Mustafa's rented flat was small and located somewhere in Alexandria. He changed locations so often that he had difficulty remembering where he was. But now he was finally back in Alexandria, and with a good night's sleep and his morning prayers behind him, he felt refreshed. He reached under his mattress for a folded piece of paper and took it out. He was supposed to have memorized the message and destroyed it, but his fatigue had been so great yesterday, even before he'd left Cairo, that he'd forgotten. *Idiot*, he thought. If the authorities discovered it, he'd most certainly go to prison. Or worse.

He sat down on the bed, which was basically all that was in the room—that and a wooden plank with a pitcher and washbasin and, of course, the prayer rug—and looked at the typewritten message. He needed to commit it to memory before destroying it. It was a half-sheet of paper, the wording succinct and in English:

Shawki el-Din Hussein

Address: 45 rue des Fatimites (family home of parents), Alexandria

Arrival (confirmed): August 28

Eliminate

Mustafa looked up toward the one window in his room. It was dirty and cloudy, and he could barely see through it. The sun beyond it was a hazy painting by a surrealist, framed by the edges of the window. He looked back at the message. The man's name had been seared into his brain, so there was no need to memorize it. He knew where rue des Fatimites was, although he was unfamiliar with the neighborhood. All he had to remember was the precise address—the number 45. He knew what he was going to do when he got there. He wadded up the paper, put it in his mouth, chewed it several times, and then swallowed it.

It was now August 30. Mustafa had never met the man; nevertheless, he harbored great hatred for him. He reflected on the KLM flight that had gone down several months before and the report the Egyptian government had released. The investigation had been a complete sham—and the follow-up report had been written to appease the International Civil Aviation Organization, its Middle East regional office located in Cairo. It had been easy and convenient to blame the pilot. After all, he was dead and couldn't defend himself. The same with the copilot and the flight engineer—dead. But Mustafa knew what had happened on that fateful day.

El-Din Hussein, a member of President Nasser's government, had used a drug-induced underling, instructing him to shoot the flight crew in the cockpit on approach to the runway. The operation had been sanctioned by the Egyptian government, which meant that Gamal Abdel Nasser either had known about it before it happened or had given the order. What hadn't been reported to the public was that among the passengers who'd been killed, there were high-ranking American dignities, including several CIA officials and one Georgetown University professor who'd been going to Egypt on vacation. Mustafa had been close friends with the professor. The CIA wouldn't go after Nasser himself— although they certainly had the means and the motivation to do so—but they could go after the man who'd orchestrated the nuts and bolts of the operation: Shawki el-Din Hussein. Mustafa had turned a routine operation into an act of revenge. He would never set things right again—his friend was dead— but he could impose a terrible retribution.

He took a tram as far as the line went and then hired a taxi to take him to the outskirts of the city. He had the driver stop two blocks from the house. He walked the rest of the way on rue des Fatimites until the house was in sight. It was smaller than a mansion but bigger than most of the surrounding houses, and it was in a wealthy neighborhood. El-Din Hussein's father had to be either a high-ranking government official or a successful businessman to be able to own such a house. A wrought iron fence wrapped around a portion of it, with a spacious garden in the back. *El-Din Hussein must be visiting his parents*, Mustafa thought.

Directly across the street, on a corner, was a small upscale restaurant with tables outside and a clear view of the house. Mustafa walked to the restaurant, sat down at one of the outdoor tables, and ordered a coffee. He mostly drank tea, but in the mornings, it was always strong black coffee with lots of sugar. After the waiter brought his coffee, he glanced at the house while putting the cup to his lips. No one was outside. He had to decide where he would kill this man. He wouldn't do it inside the house. His parents, as far as Mustafa knew, had nothing to do with bringing the aircraft down. They were innocent, and he had no clear idea how the situation might play out once he was inside the house. There would be too many variables beyond his control. If he found his man armed, it could lead to a shootout. A stray bullet could find one of the parents. For all he knew, el-Din Hussein was capable of using his parents as a shield. Killing him inside the house with his parents there, and perhaps the servants, was out of the question.

Instead, he would wait until his man left the house and would then follow him. He hoped el-Din Hussein would leave on foot. Maybe he would go for a stroll. Yes, that would be best. If he took a car—there wasn't one on the property—it would complicate matters. In that case, Mustafa would have to wait until he came home again and kill him outside the house. At any rate, however it was to be done, he would wait until nightfall. Killing someone in broad daylight wasn't out of the question if you didn't care whether you were captured. But Mustafa wasn't about to be captured.

After an hour went by, and he'd had two cups of coffee, he got up and paid the waiter. While there wasn't any activity that he could see around the house (perhaps they were sleeping), he decided to walk around the neighborhood. The sun was out, there were no clouds to speak of, and there was a refreshing breeze blowing. It was a wonderful day. He hoped Shawki el-Din Hussein was enjoying it.

He walked up and down rue des Fatimites, and then he took to the side streets. The walk took him nearly two hours. He hadn't been leisurely whiling away his time, even though he certainly could have done so on a day like today. He'd been familiarizing himself with every nook and cranny of the neighborhood, every main road, every side street, every house, every building, every park, every garden, and every thicket, so that he would be able to disappear after he killed his man. He'd never leave that to chance. Once he was satisfied with his options, he returned to the restaurant and ordered a tea and a sweet cake—*basbousa*—soaked in syrup and made with farina, rose water, lemon, and honey. He was famished, but he didn't want a full stomach yet—just a little something to head off the hunger. He would eat after el-Din Hussein was lying dead somewhere, bleeding into concrete or earth.

At dusk, when he was considering the possibility that no one was at home, several windows lit up in the house. Perhaps the servants were inside—certainly the family must have them— or perhaps they were *all* inside. He'd have to have patience and wait. Unfortunately, waiting was a part of the job he didn't much care for, but it was unavoidable. So that he wouldn't cause anyone in the restaurant to become suspicious—he'd been sitting there for the better part of the day already—he left and found a suitable place nearby that had an even better view. He had noticed the spot earlier on his walkabout. It was an empty lot with large trees and bushes bordering it on all sides. There were plenty of places to conceal himself, and the distance was just right for the weapon he would use. It was there Mustafa waited.

He tried not to think of his friend—the professor from Georgetown—but he found it difficult not to. His death and the manner in which he'd been murdered had sent Mustafa into a rage when he'd first learned of it. With the man who'd orchestrated his friend's death so near inside that house, Mustafa knew the rage could resurface now if he didn't control himself. He'd need the steady hand of a professional cold-blooded killer to aim his weapon.

Mustafa continued to wait. Suddenly, the side door on the second level of the house opened, and a woman descended the cement steps. She was carrying a large pan, and her clothes told Mustafa that she was a maid. When she reached the bottom, she tipped it to the side and poured water out onto the grass. Maybe the family had just finished a late supper and the maid was dumping out the dishwater. She turned and climbed the stairs just as a man stepped out. He was smoking a cigar. The maid passed him, bowing her head in deference, and went inside.

El-Din Hussein stretched his arms over his head and then blew smoke from his mouth. His face was unmistakable. He was wearing a white button-down shirt and dark trousers. It was a beautiful night—cooler than normal, with low humidity. Perhaps he had stepped out to enjoy it. He seemed to be in no rush to return.

Now was the time. Mustafa hoisted his galabia to the waist and pulled out a High Standard HDM semiautomatic, with a magazine of ten full metal–jacketed .22 LR rounds. From his pocket, he pulled out a silencer and screwed it onto the barrel of the pistol. He pulled back the receiver and eased a round into the chamber; and then he switched off the safety. Using a wide tree to hide behind, he had a clear shot. There was an overhanging light beside the door that illuminated his man. Perfect.

Mustafa used the tree to steady his grip and aimed his pistol. He took several deep breaths, holding the last one. He squeezed the trigger three times at a nice, steady pace. The bullets hit the man's chest, forcing Shawki el-Din Hussein backward into the door. He slid down, his teeth still locked onto the cigar.

Mustafa unscrewed the silencer and put it back in his

pocket and then slid the pistol into his pants at the small of his back. He walked down the side street at a measured pace and became one with the shadows.

———«☉»———

At this point, Mustafa was nearly starving, so he took a taxi to the Corniche and found a restaurant where he'd eaten many times before. He ordered his favorite dish: koshari, made with rice, black lentils, spaghetti, hummus, onions, and thick tomato sauce. While he ate, he thought about his friend, the professor who'd been murdered on the KLM flight. If Mustafa had had a close friend, it was he. Now that he'd killed his friend's murderer, he decided that it was time to go to Georgetown to comfort his friend's wife of four years and their three-year-old daughter. Of course, he'd first have to clear the trip with CIA headquarters in Washington's Foggy Bottom at the E Street complex, but that was just a formality. He'd accrued enough vacation time. He was thankful that his friend's wife and child hadn't been on that same flight with him. Annie and their daughter, Alexandra, were supposed to have met him in Cairo a week later. The plan had been for Mustafa to drive them all to Alexandria for a short vacation. They were more than just friends; they were like family to him.

After he finished his meal, he ordered tea. It was late, and he was mostly alone in the restaurant. He reached under his galabia into his pocket and took out a gold coin. He held it tightly in his fist for a moment and then turned it over and over in his fingers. He wondered what his life would be like now if Donatella were still alive. He didn't regret changing professions five years ago. He had remained resolute in his decision. Although he'd never tell this to anyone—and if someone accused him of this, he would vehemently deny it—he had missed the war and being a spy. This had come home to him after he killed Lucky Break.

He took a swallow of tea, set some piastres on the table for his meal and a generous tip, got up, and left the restaurant. It was a good night for a stroll down the Corniche. But his friend's murder still weighed heavily on him. Bob Albright had been like a brother to him. He and Annie had named their only daughter after Alex.

Mustafa leisurely walked down the Corniche, feeling the mist from the waves of the sea on his face. The moon was full, and there was a slight breeze that tousled his hair. He was as despondent as a man could be. The tune came back to him after all these years, but it was no longer the joyous one he'd known. Nevertheless, he hummed the melody anyway. "Que sera, sera—whatever will be, will be. The future's not ours to see. Que sera, sera ..."